A Gift Most Rare

TOM LEIHBACHER

EDITED BY MEG SCHUTTE

ISBN 978-1-0980-3281-4 (paperback)
ISBN 978-1-0980-4380-3 (hardcover)
ISBN 978-1-0980-3282-1 (digital)

Christian Faith Publishing, Inc.
832 Park Avenue
Meadville, PA 16335
www.christianfaithpublishing.com

Printed in the United States of America

A Gift Most Rare is the property of Tree Streets Entertainment

For as you have done it to one of the least of these, my brethren,
so also have you done it to me.

—Matthew 25:40

Hello and thanks for purchasing a copy of *A Gift Most Rare*. I hope you enjoy the book and that it might even help to enrich your holidays.

There are a few things you might like to know:

Although this is a fictional work, the story unfolds in a real place: my hometown of Briarcliff Manor, New York. Those of us who grew up there enjoyed many shared experiences; the memories of which helped seed the content for various chapters.

Most of the places mentioned in the story are still there today including the Briarcliff Congregational Church, Law Park, Todd School, and Sleepy Hollow Country Club. Others like The King's College and the Briarcliff Middle School have been redeveloped as residential properties.

A handful of the characters you'll meet are based on actual people like Coach Cadman, Mr. Weldon, Dr. Cook, and Reverend Higgins. Others in the cast like Parker Jones, Derrick Marks and Winthrop Smythe are imagined, so any passing resemblances are purely coincidental.

The main goal for this project was to write a God-honoring Christmas story. That's one reason why each chapter opens with a Bible verse, setting the tone for what's about to happen. It's also why the story focuses on caring for the lonely and the less fortunate, which the Bible emphasizes second only to the offer of grace in and through the Christmas event.

Another goal was to write a coming of age story and period piece going back in time to the weird but wonderful days of the early

1970s. For me, that meant anchoring the story in those unforgettable middle school days of discovery.

There are a few people I'd like to single out for heartfelt thanks, starting with my English teachers at Briarcliff High School. In particular, Mr. Kersting, who turned me on to literature and reading, and especially Mrs. Oraby, who told me often that she felt I had potential as a writer someday. Her encouragement stayed with me and helped fuel this effort.

Major thanks also to my fun and talented friend Meg Schutte (a fellow Briarcliff High School graduate), who combed through each sentence of the manuscript, making key edits and providing invaluable input and creative ideas.

I'm also greatly indebted to the kind and generous Shelly Poulton who patiently provided expert guidance from her days in the book publishing business.

Another great friend and accomplished writer, Jamie Malanowski, was always available to dispense advice and words of encouragement over cups of coffee—thank you, sir!

The same goes for Joe Gleason (also a Briarcliff High School graduate), who writes under the name of J. Boyce Gleason and who was very generous with objective thoughts and input.

Lastly, sincere thanks to my wife Rachel and the super-special friends and family who also read the manuscript and provided beneficial feedback. In particular, Bruce Bloom, who was a fantastic sounding board during our frequent evening walks with my rescue dog, Jack.

I pray this will be a fun, enjoyable reading experience for you. Peace and Christmas blessings to you all year long.

Tom

CONTENTS

Prologue...13

Chapter 1: Frozen Pond, Melted Heart 15

Chapter 2: Change In The Air 28

Chapter 3: Dreams And Visions...34

Chapter 4: Inklings, Instincts, And Intuitions............................39

Chapter 5: Coming Of Age...46

Chapter 6: Soldier Down 53

Chapter 7: Boys Will Be Boys..64

Chapter 8: New York Christmas Amble 71

Chapter 9: Tree Trimming 84

Chapter 10: Best-Laid Plans...96

Chapter 11: Je Ne Sais Quoi 102

Chapter 12: Parker And The Park 108

Chapter 13: Carols And Lights 118

Chapter 14: Boys About Town...125

Chapter 15: Christmas Villain 132

Chapter 16: When A Plan Comes Together 139

Chapter 17: The Way The (Bowling) Ball Bounces.....................143

Chapter 18: County Center Encounter.......................................149

Chapter 19: Holiday Field Trips...155

Chapter 20: Man About Town 159

Chapter 21: Skating Party..167

Chapter 22: Towering Mistake...171

Chapter 23: Out With The Old..175

Chapter 24: Library Lessons 183

Chapter 25: Mom Time..190

Chapter 26: Home Fires 197

Chapter 27: Trial By Fire 201

Chapter 28: In With The New...211

Chapter 29: Christmas Spirit Abounding...............................219

Chapter 30: Christmas Clues 226

Chapter 31: The Christmas Club..236

Chapter 32: Let It Be 241

Chapter 33: Goodbye, Sky..248

Epilogue..253

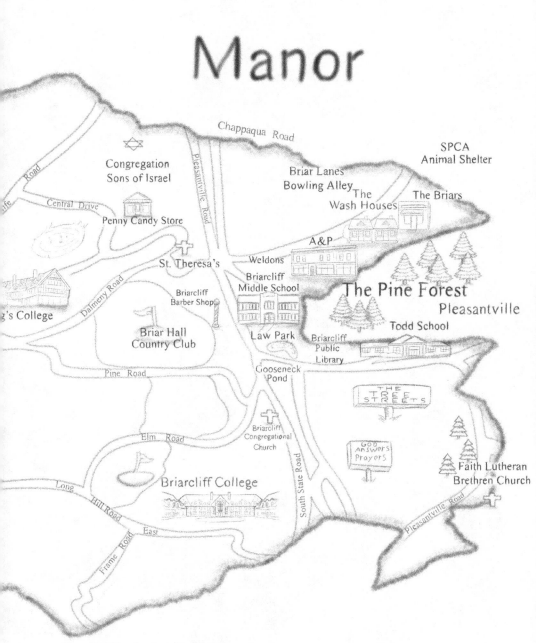

PROLOGUE

You are the God who works wonders; you have
made known your might among the peoples.
—Psalm 77:14

Whether we realize it or not, God's celestial intentions are always stirring in wondrous ways that answer prayers and change lives forever.

Such was the case one Thanksgiving Eve in Briarcliff Manor, a pocket-sized village in the pastoral midlands of Westchester County, New York. Heaven-fated happenings were afoot and holy phenomena were set in motion during the still hush of the overnight hours.

The stealth way in which an undetected snowstorm secreted through the great Hudson Valley was nothing short of baffling. To this day, no one has fully explained or adequately described the unusual event.

Flurries began to fly on cue soon after everyone had tucked in for a late November night's sleep. Completely unforeseen by local weather forecasters, the storm seemed to tiptoe in from out of the blue.

The Scarborough section of town stood like nature's rampart, rising up from the weathered edge of the Hudson River. It took the windswept brunt of the storm. Meanwhile, the valley area of the village consented to the lion's share of the whiteout.

Accumulations were mystifying. By the time the bells at St. Mary's Episcopal chimed one o'clock in the morning, a foot of the most pristine, sparkling snow had accumulated with more yet to fall.

The clandestine storm cast a charmed tranquility over Briarcliff's hills and dales. The air took delivery of a fresh, uplifting scent while powdery snow dusted the evergreens and coated the ground with smooth, unspoiled contours.

Caught completely off guard, people awoke to a holiday scene worthy of the best-ever by Currier & Ives. As preparations for Thanksgiving dinners began in one house after another, everyone was filled with the most curious sense of delight and fascination. Stammering sentence fragments dominated morning conversations between family and neighbors. People greeted each other like giddy school children, unable to fully complete their thoughts on the sanctified incident. Later, as locals gathered for traditional turkey dinners, people bantered on endlessly about the first snow coating of the season.

True enough, it had been colder than normal. In fact, Gooseneck Pond, over in Law Park, had already attracted hordes of skaters and hockey-playing teenagers. Still, no one could ever remember being kept from backyard football games on Thanksgiving Day because of thigh-deep snow.

With the early arrival of this seasonal delight, fireplaces began to glow. Houses that had been craving their families long-lost to outdoor activities, began to come alive with warmhearted goings-on.

Much to its chagrin, the local weather service was completely bewildered by the wintry blast. Some felt the sudden whiteout came as a result of an abrupt change in the wind out of the north. Others saw it as connected to some odd occurrence of the lunar cycle. Most were content to chalk it up to the whims and quirks of winter's prelude.

Even so, a few perceptive people recognized something special was in the air. They sensed God's invisible hand reaching down to stage-manage the beginnings of a simple blessing across their quaint village.

Although the unusual origins of the "Blizzard of '72" could be debated, no one ever disagreed that it seemed to shepherd in a string of events that resulted in an inspired change in the hearts and minds of Briarcliff Manor residents.

These were not just external changes. They were heartfelt and forever altered the ways in which those who dwelled there honored the Christmas event each year.

Chapter 1

Frozen Pond, Melted Heart

Bear one another's burdens, and so fulfill the law of Christ.
—Galatians 6:2

Law Park was a beehive of seasonal activity that memorable Thanksgiving weekend in 1972. The air was crisp and bracing, the sky sapphire blue, and the newly whitened landscape seemed to make everything glisten. Friends and families greeted each other with that one-of-a-kind holiday spirit, as the smoky pong of burning logs mingled with the glint and shine of the mid-afternoon sun.

Set in the heart of the snug village of Briarcliff Manor, Law Park occupied a rustic bit of land at the junction of South State and Pleasantville Roads. Eponymously named for the town's founder, Mr. Walter William Law, the park seemed perfectly placed to warm the very soul of the community itself.

The village of Briarcliff hugged the enviable countryside along the eastern banks of the Hudson River. Tucked neatly between Tarrytown to the south and Ossining to the north, it was a handsome setting in central Westchester County, New York. Its unique geography provided far-reaching views across the widest stretch of the Hudson. On clear days, the sightlines opened up all the way north to West Point and across the inland valleys of Rockland County and Northern New Jersey. On clear evenings, the lights of the northern tip of Manhattan came into view. To the east was the Pocantico River, and beyond that, the aptly named town of Pleasantville.

Mr. Law came to America in the mid-1800s in search of work and a future. He started as a clerk in the offices of a carpet and flooring business in Yonkers, New York, and eventually worked his way up to president and owner. Along the way, he made a fortune.

When he first visited what later would become Briarcliff Manor, there were nearly four thousand acres available. He fell in love with the bucolic tract of open farmland and forested countryside—and purchased it all.

His intention was for it to be a place where he could retire with his family. While that was an appealing plan, he soon grew restless. Before long, he was dabbling in a range of hobbies that grew into lucrative businesses and world-renowned brands such as Briarcliff Farms Dairy, Briarcliff Table Water, and the Briarcliff Rose. He was especially known for developing the ultra-toney Briarcliff Lodge, a luxury resort, which became a popular east coast getaway for the rich and famous.

As his businesses grew, he hired more and more workers. They, in turn, needed places to live, so he built homes for them. Soon there were enough people on his payroll and living on his land that he was able to incorporate his property as a village. In 1902, that's exactly what he did.

Local townsfolk always said that Briarcliff had the special feel of an extended family. Perhaps it could be traced to the actual origin of the village itself.

Gooseneck Pond was the centerpiece of Law Park. It was excavated from underground springs so that local residents would have a place to swim on summer days and ice skate during winter months. It usually froze over around Thanksgiving and stayed that way until St. Patrick's Day. Some years, even longer. One side was reserved for families with young children just learning to skate. The other side was the domain of middle- and high-school-age boys who played endless hours of hockey with the rousing brand of passion the sport is known for. Taken all together, it seemed like everyone in Briarcliff took advantage of the simple pleasure of skating on a frozen pond.

A circular bit of stonework in the middle of the pond, created a natural demarcation between pleasure skaters and hockey players. It was also the coveted spot where sixth and seventh graders labored for their first kiss during Friday night skating parties.

Just off the west side of the pond, near the tennis courts, was a glen of pine trees with unique, orange-tinged bark. They were planted there by Christian missionaries to Japan, sponsored by Mr. Law. They knew he had a keen appreciation for trees so they brought these particular specimens back with them as a gift. These trees were particularly aromatic, and everyone always said it smelled like Christmas in that spot.

That natural dale was where the village recreation department kept a lively fire pit and served donuts, hot chocolate, and warm apple cider. The scent of kindling firewood and the seasonal tastes of the warm drinks made this a very popular place for skaters young and old. Children sat close to each other around the fire sipping and snacking while parents chatted about everything from the Space Race, to the Vietnam War, and an odd, escalating political scandal called Watergate. Briarcliff Bears varsity sports also supplied a steady supply of subject matter for conversation and debate.

From time to time, a spontaneous snowball fight would break out. Usually, it was boys trying to flirt with girls who had come to skate. Families also teamed up to make snowmen and snow forts. Still others would hike through the pine forest on the other side of the park beyond the ball fields. In every direction, it was a lively scene straight out of a rendering by Norman Rockwell.

Henry McBride, director of recreation in Briarcliff, was an avid hockey player himself. He personally tested the ice at Gooseneck Pond for safety. He also took great pride in keeping it cleaned off and ready for smooth gliding. Each year, he strung together a group of helpers that included local college students who were home on school break as well as a few upperclassmen from Briarcliff High School. They were glad to earn a small stipend in the midst of all the outdoor winter fun.

There was a well-oiled system of rotating responsibilities. Some staff hauled logs over to the fire pit, others stirred the huge drums of cider and hot chocolate as they warmed on the open fire. Some helped novice skaters to get up and go, while others refereed hockey games.

"Keep a close watch on Mrs. Carson!" Henry shouted. "She's determined to make it all the way around the pond without falling, and she's pretty banged up already. I don't want to have to call the ambulance!"

"She's keeping things lively," said Matt Gilroy, everyone's favorite local teenager. "Might be the only person who actually laughs when she falls! Don't worry, Henry, I got this!"

"My only concern is that she might skate into some of the ankle biters! Those little kids have a way of getting underfoot. Stay close behind her, Matty!"

Meanwhile, the Cliffton brothers were taking care of logs for the fire pit. "That's the umpteenth log I've lugged over from the pine forest, and it will be my last for today!" huffed Tommy Cliffton.

"Yeah? Well, splitting them was no bargain either," replied his brother, Robbie.

"Can it, you nit! Everyone knows you love to hit things."

"Keep it up and I'll be hitting you!"

"You have to catch me first, big boy!" Tommy teased as he faked running away.

In the midst of their razzing, Henry broke in with an urgent tone. "Guys, I need you over with the hockey players. Things are heating up."

The Cliffton brothers gladly laced up their skates and hustled over to what had become a hotly contested six-on-six contest of hockey staying power. The Clifftons were powerhouse upperclassmen athletes, so they had a lot of say-so with the younger boys, who currently were playing as though the Stanley Cup was on the line.

"Wow, what happened to the 'no contact' rule?" asked Tommy.

"Yeah, there's enough bruises and scrapes here to call the game!" added Robbie.

"Quit stick checking us," shouted Charlie Riverton, the good-hearted-to-the-core unofficial leader of his small pack of buddies.

"I will when you stop high sticking," yelled Derrick Marks, Charlie's blood brother and closest friend. They had opposite personalities and temperaments but were thick as thieves nonetheless.

"That wasn't a high stick. *This is!*" howled Charlie, skating toward Derrick with his stick positioned in a way that would send him straight to Dr. Rozinsky, the local dentist.

In the heat of a game, even close buddies might need to be separated, so the Cliffton brothers skated in and pulled the two apart. Right then, Henry blew his whistle to clear the ice for the 3:00 p.m. Adult Skate. The boys continued to reach for and poke their sticks at each other as the Clifftons hauled them off like puppies in a headlock.

"Okay, boys, let's have a time out," said Tommy as he and his brother deposited Charlie and Derrick, or DMarks as he was known, off to the side of the pond.

"Right on, brother," added Robbie. "You two need to mellow out! Keep this up and Henry's going to kick you off the ice for the rest of the day."

DMarks, a pro at putting his mouth in gear before his brain was engaged, replied with a sarcastic, "No, duh, Einstein!" In response, The Cliffton brothers delivered two swift punches to the outer part of DMarks's biceps for a perfectly administered pair of dead arms. He practically hyperventilated from the momentary muscle spasms.

Insolent and bad-mannered as he was, DMarks was not backing down. "That's all you guys got?" *Boom!* The Clifftons cocked their elbows and landed blows to DMarks's thighs for equally precise charlie horses. More pain. More spasms.

"Should we top things off with a few wrist burns, Marks?" asked Tommy.

"You guys are real tough when it's two against one," groused DMarks.

"Listen, ding-a-ling, our little sister could take you with a Ping-Pong paddle and a feather duster," teased Robbie. "Keep it up and you'll be getting the Briarcliff Bobsled treatment. Catch my drift?"

In those days, there was an age-related pecking order between the younger kids and teenagers. Sometimes, older boys would lay down the law and give an old-fashioned lesson if needed. A Briarcliff Bobsled was when an offender was dragged through the snow. Shirtless.

"This should be good. I wish I could sell tickets!" said Bruce "BB" Brown, another key member of this close circle of buddies.

"Hey, Marks, you going to take that?" egged on George Palmer, the last of these four musketeers.

"You guys are bogus. I double dog dare ya!" said DMarks to the Cliffton brothers.

Most of the time, the older boys never really did anything. And, truth be told, getting recognized in any way by well-known varsity athletes was a cool mark of distinction. So DMarks knew exactly what he was doing. Or so he thought.

"I'd say this dweeb needs a dose of humility. STET!" said Tommy.

"Roger that, brother." In an instant, the Clifftons took the law into their own hands. "Hey, Marks, give us some skin." Off came his sweatshirt, up over his head, leaving him completely shirtless and with a look on his face that suggested he had made a serious miscalculation.

"Yeah, catch you on the flip side!" In an instant, DMarks was on his back in a snowbank with his feet up in the air, as the Clifftons cut him down with his own hockey stick. Tommy grabbed the blade of his right skate like a door handle, and Robbie grabbed the other. From there, they dragged him up the hillside through the frosty snow. Charlie, BB, and George convulsed with laughter as a small crowd gathered to look on.

"Check you later, Marks!" yelled Charlie.

"Keep on truckin', Marks!" said George, leaning into the others and laughing so hard he cried.

"Don't forget to write!" shouted BB. Tommy Cliffton looked down to make sure the punishment wasn't too harsh. "Hey, Marks, who loves ya, baby?" he said.

As they got up to the War Memorial near the library, on the other side of the park, they dropped his skates and began dragging him by his arms.

"Hey, Marks, let's do the hokeypokey and turn yourself around!" suggested Robbie. With that, they flipped him so that he would return facedown. Back they went, past the town pool and over to the pond.

"You guys are dew droppers! Can't you go any faster!" DMarks tried to shout in defiance, but his voice was muffled by the snow. "You out of shape or something?"

The Clifftons just looked at each other and shook their heads. The kid talked a good game, but he backed it up. Finally, they made the loop and were back by the hockey side of the pond. The Clifftons dropped him off, handed him his sweatshirt, and then headed back to work by the fire pit.

"You're a piece of work, Marks," they said in unison. "Better wise up. Not all the older guys around here are as nice as we are," warned Robbie.

"Oh yeah? Well, next time make sure you guys eat your Wheaties!" Charlie, BB, and George just shook their heads at their friend.

"Hang it up, Marks!" said Charlie, as he handed him his hockey stick and gloves. "You're going to get the rest of us in trouble."

"Listen up, chump. I'm like a Timex. I can take a licking and keep on ticking. Besides, you don't have to be concerned about those guys. I had them one year as counselors at summer camp. They dunked me in the Pocantico River once, but they'd never let you get hurt. You've got to know your onions around here!"

"Yeah, well, that's good for you, but maybe the rest of us would rather be law-abiding citizens," said Charlie.

"Tell it to your Ken Doll, you geek. The name of the game is to test the boundaries!" said DMarks.

"Says you. It still doesn't mean you should rag on the older kids," George chimed in.

"It's like a sport! You get your game on and roll into action. Of course, if you're not up for it, you can always stay on the sidelines like a bunch of popcorn eaters!"

"Oh, shut up, Marks!" said BB.

"Speaking of food, I'm getting hungry. What's your mom cooking for dinner tonight?" DMarks asked Charlie.

"Steak and rice, want to come over?"

"Psych! I love your mother's steak and rice! Six o'clock?"

"Yeah. Sharp. And afterward, you can stay around and watch *The NBC Mystery Movie*. I think it's *Columbo* or maybe *McMillan and Wife* this week."

"Awesome! I'm in."

This was the way it was with middle school boys. One moment they were sparring with each other, the next they were acting like family—at all times, they were inseparable. Everyone in town was used to seeing the pack of four together.

Charlie was slightly tall for his age with a sinewy, athletic build that gave him great speed and agility for whatever sport he was playing. He kept his thick black hair neatly combed and fastidiously parted on the left side with generous portions of Brylcreem. His lean, angular face was set off by big, blue, compassionate eyes.

DMarks, on the other hand, was stocky with a low center of gravity. His reddish blond hair was wavy and a bit unruly, much like his personality. He had fire in his eyes all the time and a certain way of gritting his teeth, especially if in the middle of some athletic activity or an argument. Although his growth spurt was still in the offing, he had the look and shape of a future offensive linemen.

George was slightly taller than Charlie but so lanky that his clothes never seemed to fit right, hanging off his long limbs. His blond hair matched his sunny outlook and good-natured demeanor. It was a rare thing to hear him raise his voice or show any anger. During the summer months, when the sun bleached his locks totally white, his nickname was "Cotton."

With an average, well-proportioned build and long, dark hair that was forever falling in his face, BB rounded out the group.

Although he wasn't blessed with outstanding size, he was an incredibly skilled and crafty athlete. As a result, the older boys often picked him to play-up with them when they needed an extra body in the game. To his great credit, he never accepted the coveted invitation if it meant the rest of the guys would have an odd number without him.

As they waited for the Adult Skate to finish, Charlie happened to glance up the hillside toward the flagpole in the center of Law Park. There, he saw a sight that pierced him, awakening something vital in his heart.

"Guys, look up there at poor Mr. Olson. Have you noticed how lost and lonely he seems since his wife died?" Charlie knew Mr. Olson well. He cut his grass during the summertime and raked his leaves every autumn. "Is that a handkerchief? I think he's wiping away tears or something."

"If you spent your entire adult life with someone who died without warning, you'd feel lost too!" The group could always count on Derrick Marks to size things up in blunt terms.

"Wow. That was cold. Even by your standards. I realize everyone's allowed to act like a jerk once in a while, but you're really abusing the privilege," said BB.

"I can't even imagine how hard it must be. And it's so sad! I don't think they ever had children, so he's all alone now," said Charlie. "All alone."

"Yeah, and you know when it's really going to hurt? In about a month when Christmas comes around," added BB. "I wonder what he did for Thanksgiving."

"Oh, leave him be. He's a grown man. Fought on the ground in Europe during World War I. He'll figure it out," lectured Derrick.

"You're all heart, DMarks," replied Charlie. "We should go up and say hello to him. Maybe he might need help with snow shoveling or something."

"Are you crazy? We only have an hour of daylight left, and Adult Skate is just about over," said George.

Charlie didn't care, his focus had shifted from hockey to Mr. Olson. His genuinely good and caring heart couldn't just let go. Suddenly, a uniquely warm feeling washed over him. *Where did that come from?* he wondered. It reminded him of those times when he was small and his father would wrap him up in his arms until it felt like he had been swallowed whole. Usually those bear hugs provided encouragement and support. Without thinking about it any further, he got to his feet and hobbled up the hillside in his hockey skates.

"Oh, good night, John-Boy," said DMarks. "There goes Mr. Wonderful. If he doesn't get back in time to restart the game, I say we get Matty Gilroy to fill in for him."

Charlie loved hockey, but at that particular moment, he was carried away with a desire to do something, anything he could to ease Mr. Olson's pain. He slowed down once he got closer and just kind of glanced at Mr. Olson. The gentlemanly old man was just sitting there, all bundled up, quietly weeping, sad as raindrops on a gravestone.

"Mr. Olson? It's me, Charlie Riverton. I wanted to say hello." At first, Mr. Olson was startled as he rallied out of his deep thoughts and reflections. Then, he immediately warmed to Charlie's presence.

"Charlie, you're very kind to visit with me. How are you and your family?" His voice was tired and spiritless but sincere.

"We're all fine, sir. My dad still commutes to Manhattan each day from Scarborough Train Station and my mom still teaches kindergarten at Todd School. We've been talking a lot about you lately." As the words came out, Charlie realized it wasn't the best way of letting Mr. Olson know that he was in their thoughts. Still, he could tell Mr. Olson understood and appreciated the sentiment.

"Thank you, Charlie. Thank you very much. You know, I've noticed lately that it feels like I've been having company, even though no one has visited since Mrs. Olson passed away. It must be your family's kind thoughts and prayers making me feel that way."

"Is there anything you need help with, Mr. Olson? Need me to shovel snow for you? Run errands? Maybe clean up your yard?"

"That's very kind of you to ask, but I'm getting along fine. Besides, those little tasks give me something to do, which helps keep my mind off of things."

"Okay, I understand. But please be careful. There's a lot of black ice and stuff like that out there."

"Right. And the way my driveway slopes down to Pleasantville Road, it can be pretty slippery."

"It must be lonely without Mrs. Olson," Charlie said sincerely.

"She was the light of my life, Charlie. And we were never able to have children. So it feels pretty empty without her. I miss our daily walks up to town."

"I'm so sorry, Mr. Olson."

"Thank you, Charlie. I'm grateful to you. Hey, it looks like your friends are back out on the ice. You better go and rejoin them before they start the game without you.

"Actually, they can't start without me. I have the puck!" Charlie said with a smile as he reached in his pocket and held it up for Mr. Olson to see.

"Ha! You've always got the situation under control, Charlie."

It was a very warm encounter, and Charlie could tell Mr. Olson felt a bit rejuvenated by it. He hobbled back down to the pond. A short time later, Mr. Olson began to make his way across the park and over to his house. As he walked by the pond, he waved to Charlie and made the gesture of a slap shot with an imaginary hockey stick. Charlie mimed a return shot and gave him a big smile back.

About an hour later, moms and dads began to arrive at Law Park to pick up their children. Reluctantly, the boys began to leave the ice, never mind that the sun had long since set over the crest of Elm and Pine Roads and the hills of Briarcliff College.

Charlie slid carefully into the passenger seat of his mom's Volkswagen Beetle, skates, stick, and all. As Mrs. Riverton pulled out of the parking lot, Charlie glanced up at Mr. Olson's house across the street from the park entrance. The entire house was dark, except for one faint light in a room toward the back. It looked so cold and lonely that Charlie's heart sank and his concerns came right back again.

Charlie and the guys were used to seeing Mr. and Mrs. Olson walking formally, arm-in-arm, each day to Pete's Stationary. Once there, they would pick up a copy of the *Citizen Register* to read up on local news while sitting at the soda fountain for morning coffee. Mr. Olson was always in jacket and tie, while Mrs. Olson donned white gloves and a modest hat with half-veil. As Charlie's mom drove on, he glanced over his right shoulder at Mr. Olson's house with a growing knot in his stomach.

"You seem a little concerned about something, Charlie. Everything okay?" inquired his mom.

"Yeah, fine. Okay if Derrick comes over for dinner and TV?"

"Yes, of course. We have plenty of food."

"Mom, maybe we could invite Mr. Olson over for dinner too? He looked so lonely in the park today."

"Is that what's on your mind? It's a very sad time for Mr. Olson, but I think it might be best if we wait a little while for him to adjust to things. Maybe in a few weeks, okay?"

"I guess. But he seems to need company now."

"You're right, Charlie. But people usually need a little time to themselves after the loss of a loved one. I'm sure Mr. Olson will get back into the things of his life before long."

"I guess, but it really bothers me to see him all alone."

"Trust me, we all feel for Mr. Olson. But the longer you live, the more you realize that this kind of thing is a natural part of life. It's not easy, but then again, God doesn't promise we'll never experience challenges, hurts, or disappointments. What he does promise is that he'll never leave us or forsake us."

"That's such a hard lesson, Mom! Mr. Olson was sitting on a park bench crying. I mean, he was really hurting and he needs help now! What's God waiting for?"

"I know, son, I know. It's a tough one for sure. We won't always have answers to our questions or understand God's ways or timing.

But we also know that we won't face anything he hasn't already experienced or dealt with himself."

"I'm glad that God understands, but I wish he'd hurry up and fix things for Mr. Olson."

"Well, there are a lot of people who have been praying for Mr. Olson. When we pray hard, God answers. I'll bet he's working out a plan right now."

Charlie just listened as his mom talked.

"In fact, Charlie, God likes to work through the lives of ordinary people all the time. Just you watch!"

For some reason, that last comment hit home with Charlie. Instead of saying anything back, he just looked out the window and whispered a silent prayer.

Chapter 2
Change In The Air

Do not neglect to show hospitality to strangers, for thereby some have entertained angels unawares.
—Hebrews 13.2

The Thanksgiving Eve snowfall seemed to leave a special heaven-sent spirit in its wake. All around Briarcliff, there was a charmed sense of something magical in the air. It defied narrative explanation, yet everyone felt it—children and adults alike. It was more than the customary holiday good cheer.

The weather was doing its part—rich, sunshine-filled skies, a few fit-to-burst passing clouds, and 29 chilly degrees with no wind. Because temperatures were well below normal, Gooseneck Pond was extra busy. As a result, the Recreation Department hired an additional person to supervise the increased workload.

Enter Skylar Northbridge, newly arrived in Briarcliff during the pre-dawn hours on Thanksgiving morning. After a brief phone interview the week prior, Henry hired him to start as soon as possible. He came strongly recommended by Dr. Cook, who was president of The King's College up on Lodge Road. King's was a great neighbor to the Briarcliff community and the student body provided a healthy supply of babysitters for village families, so Dr. Cook's recommendation came with a lot of standing. During his phone conversation, Henry felt like he detected a uniquely considerate and capable demeanor in his new hire. He couldn't quite define it, but it left him with a very good feeling.

On his first day, Skylar arrived at Gooseneck Pond a couple hours before it was scheduled to open. By the time the other staff members got there, he had already brushed off the ice, hauled and stacked extra logs for the fire pit, and shoveled a few massive snowbanks to make room for extra parking. Henry could hardly believe his eyes when he showed up for work. He had asked the Public Works Department to use their heavy equipment to plow those mountains of snow, but they told him it would have to wait until some of it began to melt.

To be sure, Skylar was not your average person. Strongly built, he stood about six-foot, five inches, had thick, longish, sandy blond hair, and a full, well-groomed beard. With his broad shoulders, muscular arms, rugged good looks, and megawatt smile, it seemed like he came straight from a Hollywood movie lot.

He also had a warm countenance and kind-hearted way about him. His welcoming personality seemed to reach out and bear hug everyone he met. When in conversation, people got the sense that they knew him from somewhere. His ability to make others feel like kith and kin was uncanny. Then there was his expansive awareness of Briarcliff's history and present-day goings-on. For these reasons and more, it wasn't long before a curious allure developed among local residents about this new person in town.

Mayor Kennard stopped by the park to make sure everything was up and running. He gave Henry a warm greeting.

"Hey, hail fellow! I'm impressed with your team! That was quite a storm we got Wednesday night. Looks like you didn't miss a beat!"

"Actually, Mr. Mayor, the staff hasn't arrived yet," Henry filled him in. "See the guy over there working by the fire pit? His name is Skylar Northbridge, and basically, he did all the prep and setup work on his own."

"Well, give him a raise!" bellowed the mayor.

"I know! I still can't figure out how he did it."

At the same time, Charlie and his buddies were making their way to Law Park, skates dangling from hockey sticks slung over their shoulders. When they got there, Skylar was down on one knee tending to the fire pit but was still able to give them an enthusiastic greeting.

"Hi, guys! Looks like you're my first customers today. You know what that means? Free Cokes! Help yourselves." He nodded toward the snowbank to his left. The boys looked at each other with surprise, then delight as they gladly took advantage of the offer by yanking the four bottles of Coke from the natural outdoor icebox. He tossed them a bottle opener, and they drank up on the spot. There was nothing like the taste and feel of ice-cold Coke in those curved glass bottles.

After squaring up the logs so that they'd get enough oxygen to stay burning, he stood up to shake hands, towering over the boys. They were amazed at how tall and powerful-looking he was. Their jaws dropped and their heads pitched to 45-degree angles as they each tried to look him in the eye while placing their right hand in his. His handshake was amazingly strong and masculine. As he moved from one to another, he bent over to make direct eye contact.

Skylar's smile put the boys at ease, glowing with friendliness and hospitality. He was dressed in a red flannel shirt, tucked into a pair of Levi's that were rolled up neatly with two-inch cuffs; thick red suspenders held everything in place; and a pair of tan laced-up storm chaser work boots to keep his feet warm and dry. He also sported a long gray scarf, knotted neatly around his neck and tossed backward over his massive shoulders. The sleeves of his flannel shirt were turned up to his elbows, exposing a textured long-sleeved T-shirt underneath.

He didn't wear a wristwatch or any other kind of jewelry, except for a unique pendant that swayed and swung down to about the top of his chest plate. It was a cross with a crown of thorns and it glowed with an uncommon golden luster. Charlie noticed it right away dancing off Sky's chest as he moved around poking logs and stacking firewood.

"I'm Skylar, Sky for short." And just like that, Charlie felt an unusually positive feeling about him, as though they were long-time friends.

"Thanks, Mr. Sky! Cokes are our favorite."

"No, no. Just Sky. I was hired for the season to help keep things running here at the pond."

"Cool. Where are you from?" asked Charlie.

"Oh, I'm from up north," hesitated Sky. "Tell me, what grade are you guys in?"

"Sixth grade," replied BB. "That's our middle school, right over there next to the varsity baseball field."

"Ah, yes," replied Sky. "The Alamo."

"Right, The Alamo. Wait, how did you know it had a nickname?"

Sky caught himself, then gestured toward the building. "Oh, well, it kind of looks like the Alamo, so that's what came to mind."

"Cool," replied BB. "Hey, aren't you cold? All you're wearing is that flannel shirt."

"Nah, between hauling logs and this fire, I'm fine. Besides, I prefer cold over hot. Hey, Charlie, you attend church at Briarcliff Congregational, right?" asked Sky.

"Yeah, right over there on the corner of South State and Elm."

"Looks like a beautiful church. And I hear the minister is a pretty lively guy."

"Reverend Higgins? He's awesome! Sometimes, he even comes out and plays hockey with us," Charlie agreed as he mimed hitting a puck.

DMarks was listening impatiently to the exchange. "Hey! Is it soup yet? The Ice is calling our names!"

Sky smiled and took the interruption in stride as though he knew exactly what to expect from Derrick. "I think I'd like to come for Sunday worship."

"Cool! The service is at 10:00."

"Okay, Charlie, I'll put on my Sunday shoes, and see you at church," said Sky.

"C'mon, guys, let's lace up. And no spitting on the ice!" said BB.

"What's wrong with spitting?" asked DMarks.

"Nobody wants to slide through your spit, Marks!" replied BB.

"Well then, stay up on your skates, you spaz," said DMarks. In defiance, he coughed up some chaw like a humpbacked cat and let it fly.

The guys just shook their heads. DMarks was hardwired to stir the pot. As they took to the ice to warm up and take practice shots, the boys were thinking about their encounter with Sky.

"Yo. Charlie. How'd he know your name?" asked BB.

"Yeah, and he knew where you attended church too!" said George. The boys kept talking as they skated around the pond.

"Did you see the size of his arms?" asked BB. "He must have been a professional athlete or something. I bet he could hit a slap shot from here to White Plains!"

"Yeah," said BB. "Cool beard too. I'm going to have one just like that someday."

"That is, if you ever outgrow that peach fuzz!" teased DMarks, skating away laughing.

"You're such a jerk!" yelled BB.

"Was it curious to you guys that he had free Cokes for us?" asked Charlie. "It was like he knew our favorite thing to drink."

"I did notice that," said George. "And he kind of had them off to the side…as though we were the only ones that were going to get them."

"Yeah, and he only had four," said BB. "Coincidence?"

"The guy does his homework!" said George.

"Oh, brother," sighed DMarks. "You guys want to go sing around the campfire with him or do you want to play hockey?"

"You aren't curious about any of this?" asked Charlie.

"Sure, but you're acting like he's some kind of gift from God! Just remember, he works for us!" said DMarks.

"Why do you always have to be such a pain, Marks? Seriously. I'd really like to know!" asked Charlie.

"It's what I do. Now pass the puck, Girl Scout," replied DMarks.

"You want the puck? I'll pass the puck. Open your mouth nice and wide!" replied Charlie. With that, Charlie pulled the puck back with his stick, then thrust forward with a flick of his wrist. The puck was flying straight at DMarks, head-high, which forced him to duck, spin around, and face-plant right into a snowbank. The boys split with laughter. Even Sky was smiling, shaking his head, and quietly laughing. *Boys will be boys,* he thought.

"That was awesome!" BB said to Charlie. "Give me some skin!"

"Very funny!" said DMarks. "Headhunters. That's what you guys are! I thought we weren't supposed to lift the puck above our knees."

"Sorry, Marks. That one got away from me!" said Charlie.

"Yeah, well, it's a good thing your aim stinks because you would have been paying my dentist bills! That's a hockey puck, not a Wham-O Frisbee, you moron!"

"Don't worry, Marks, I would have taken up a collection around town to pay for your dentist bills," said George.

"Yeah, people would have lined up to contribute. We'd have left over change!" added BB.

"You guys are a riot. A regular riot. You should be on the *Flip Wilson Show*!" After a few more minutes of warming up, with banter flying as fast as the puck, they began playing hockey in earnest, game after nonstop game. It seemed like they could skate forever, or at least until their ankles caved in, whichever came first.

Eventually, the sun began to set and people started to head home. The boys made it a point to shake hands again with Sky before they left. They wanted to experience his bear-paw-sized hand again.

"I wish I could bottle your energy!" said Sky.

"Thanks, Sky. It's really nice to meet you," said Charlie, really meaning it.

"Why, thank you, Charlie. I promise, that feeling is very mutual."

There, in the remains of the day, Sky began to put the park to bed, extinguishing the fire and stacking the cider and hot chocolate vats. Once done, he looked up, gave thanks, and hung out the "No Skating" sign.

CHAPTER 3
DREAMS AND VISIONS

*I saw a dream that made me afraid. As I lay in
bed, the visions of the dream alarmed me.*
—Daniel 4:5

The Rivertons lived in a comfortable, middle-class home. Charlie's mom anchored it all. She found great meaning in all she did to take care of the home front. Not only did she work five days a week, she also took care of day-to-day household things and even managed to prepare a balanced dinner each night, which was served promptly at six o'clock pm.

During supper, everyone talked about the day that was. Charlie's dad always wanted to know about the good and the not-so-good. The answers provided content for family prayer once everyone was done eating. By six forty-five, they were usually doing the dishes, cleaning up the kitchen, and taking out the garbage. By seven, Charlie was up in his room, hitting the books. He was a solid student who did well with most subjects; social studies and English in particular. To the complete exasperation of his friends, he didn't mind homework.

Soon enough, he'd be back downstairs to watch TV with his parents who, invariably, sat next to each other reading the *Citizen Register* and other newspapers to stay current with what was happening. If there wasn't a Knicks or Rangers game to watch, they'd turn the dial to the three network channels for the latest episodes of programs like *The Carol Burnett Show*, *The Mary Tyler Moore Show*, *Emergency*, and *The Bob Newhart Show*.

Charlie had a self-imposed bedtime of ten thirty, so after the teaser for the next week's episode ran, he got up and gave his mom and dad their nightly hug good night. Then he headed down the center hallway and up the stairs to wash his face, brush his teeth, and change into his pajamas. That night, he was uncharacteristically restless, tossing and turning for the better part of an hour before finally dozing off.

The next thing he knew, he was wandering around Briarcliff all by himself. Usually that would be a happy place to be, but not this time. Cheerless as a gravesite, everything was colorless and gray. Even the overcast sky seemed hostile. Moreover, it seemed that the only people he encountered were friends and acquaintances who were struggling with loneliness, sorrow, and heartache for one reason or another. It was as bleak a town as he had ever seen.

First, he crossed paths with Mr. Olson who, of course, was coping with the recent loss of his wife and trying to find the will to carry on without her. He was lifeless and expressionless, like he was sleepwalking his way through the day.

He also encountered Mr. and Mrs. Murcer walking silently around the Tree Streets neighborhood, so called because most of the streets were named Oak, Maple, Larch, Ash, and the like. Their faces were vacant; their eyes unresponsive. They were coping with the crushing news that their son would not be coming home from Vietnam alive. They just kept circling the neighborhood as though by walking without stopping they could somehow change the reality they were facing.

Charlie then happened upon the Jackson family sitting in a booth at the Greasy Spoon. They were living separate lives after a tragic house fire burned their home to the ground. The family survived, but Duke, their cherished German shepherd, did not. For the time being, Mrs. Jackson and the girls were sleeping on couches at her sister's house in nearby Millwood, while Mr. Jackson and their son were bunking at his mother's apartment in Ossining. The blank looks on their faces spoke of the numbness and devastation they were experiencing.

Next, he saw a despondent Mr. Ryder coming out of Pete's Stationery. His wife recently left him to be with a local golf pro with whom she had become romantically involved. He was disheveled, exhausted-looking, and needed some way to pull himself together. He clenched a bottle in a brown paper bag, periodically lifting it to his mouth as he plodded along.

In each case, Charlie sought to provide encouragement. But no matter what he did or said, it was as though he was completely invisible and could not be heard. He was right there talking out loud, but they just looked right through him. He tried everything to get their attention. He raised his voice, but they were deaf as trees. He jumped up and down in front of them, but their facial expressions remained blank and distant. He reached out to try to tap them on the shoulder, but his hand just passed right through them as if they were ghosts. They just kept wandering along, dejected and completely oblivious to Charlie.

The more people he came across, the more alarmed he became. He began to panic. What was this bewildering world and how did he get there? Fear set in. It was raw and petrifying. He couldn't make sense of what was happening. Finally, he ran for the familiar confines of Law Park, looked heavenward, and cried out to God.

In that split second, he heaved forward to a sitting position in bed just in time to catch himself from screaming out loud for real. His pajama top was soaked with sweat, and his chest was heaving as he breathed deeply. The blankets were tossed aside, and his pillow was on the floor. His mind raced as he tried to make sense of this surreal and unnerving dream.

As he thought about it, the dream seemed textured to provide him with a special message of some kind. Now wide awake, he suddenly heard a voice as though it was coming from someone right next to him there in his bedroom. At first, he was startled, but the pleasant, encouraging, and positive tone made him feel calm and at ease: *Don't be troubled, Charlie. You were born with the gift of compassion, and your caring heart will make all the difference this year at Christmas.*

The voice was clear as could be. Charlie even thought that it sounded vaguely familiar. "Who are you?" Charlie whispered, but there was no one there to answer. "What does this mean?" he asked. Again, there was no reply. He quickly got out of bed and turned on a light. He rubbed his eyes as they adapted to the brightness, then he scanned the room closely. Everything was exactly as it normally was.

After looking around, he tiptoed down the hall to his parents' bedroom. He thought perhaps one of them might have looked in on him thinking he was having a nightmare, but they were sound asleep. Besides, the voice he heard did not belong to either of them. He headed back to his room. Just as he walked through the doorway, he happened to glance down and noticed a single white feather lying on the carpet. Did it somehow come out of his pillow? He picked it up to take a closer look and decided it was way too big to have been used for goose down. As he examined it further, a terrific sense of peace came over him.

After standing there awhile thinking things through, he realized it was three in the morning and needed to get back to sleep. He placed the feather on his dresser, changed his pajama top, picked up his pillow, and slid back under his comforter. Lying there, looking up at the ceiling of his bedroom, he was curious and intrigued to say the least. It was all so real, yet only a dream. *But what about the voice? And what about the feather? And what about making a difference at Christmas?* These thoughts and questions rolled through his mind as he gradually fell back asleep.

Before Charlie knew it, his alarm clock went off. Somehow, he awoke feeling deeply refreshed even after all the commotion he had experienced. He once again scanned the room as he rolled out of bed. Was his experience just some kind of dream within a dream? *It had to be,* he thought. Then he noticed the feather lying on his dresser. He picked it up and inspected it all over again. There was something exceptional about this feather, and yet it wasn't anything obvious. He put it back down, then grabbed a quick shower and got dressed. On his way downstairs, he put the feather in his book bag.

There had to be more to this, and he was going to figure it out. At breakfast, he asked his mom if she heard or saw anything unusual last night.

"Last night? Slept like a baby," she said.

"So you and Dad weren't up having a conversation or anything at around 3:00 a.m.?"

"No, dear. We both slept through the night. Why do you ask?"

"Oh, no particular reason. I had a dream and thought I heard voices. By the way, Mom, were you maybe using a feather duster in my room yesterday?"

"A feather duster? Don't even own one," she answered. "That's kind of a strange question, Charlie, what made you think I had?"

"I found a pretty large feather in the doorway of my room and wondered where it could have come from."

"A feather? In your bedroom? No clue on that one, buddy."

"Well, I guess it's a mystery for now," said Charlie. He stuffed what was left of his Pop-tart into his mouth and washed it down with a gulp of Tang. "Thanks for breakfast, Mom. Love you!" He headed out the front door to walk to school.

"Have a good day, Charlie. And zip up that jacket, I don't want you to catch a cold with Christmas just around the corner!"

"I will, Mom. See ya tonight!"

That voice, that dream, that feather, that message—what was the connection and what did it all mean? Charlie was in deep thought as he left his house, but his friends were waiting for him at the end of the driveway. Soon he was caught up in their typical chatter on the walk to school. He'd have to put more thought toward this later.

Chapter 4

Inklings, Instincts, And Intuitions

*For I was hungry and you gave me food, I was thirsty and you
gave me drink, I was a stranger and you welcomed me.*
—Matthew 25:35

There's something uniquely uplifting about sunny, crisp Sunday mornings. With seasonal weather prevailing, the Rivertons bundled up and headed out to their car at nine forty-five sharp for morning worship at Briarcliff Congregational Church. Charlie's dad was a trustee there, and his mom ran the popular children's Sunday school.

The year prior, Charlie made his Confirmation, so now he stayed in the sanctuary for the entire worship service. Sometimes, he missed heading across the street to the Parish Hall after the Junior Sermon. He always loved Sunday school; plus, he got to spend time with friends from other towns who he didn't see during the week.

Charlie enjoyed attending church, so getting up on a day when he could otherwise stay in bed was never an issue for him. Besides, his two rescue dogs, Barnes and Noble, had to be fed and walked first thing, for which he took full responsibility.

Briarcliff Congregational Church was a special house of worship with its Norman tower, pipe organ, and world-renowned Tiffany stained glass windows. He enjoyed singing the traditional hymns and listening to readings from the King James Bible as well.

Reverend Higgins was an older but extremely lively presence in the pulpit who loved to celebrate his Scottish lineage complete with an authentic Scottish shepherd's mustache. This was the fifth parish he had served and, most likely, would be his last. He stood about six-feet tall and was known for his booming voice and a flair for the dramatic. Once in a while, he'd even toss in a Scottish accent to drive home a sermon point. He always said it was his job to put God's Word in shoe leather so that people could take it home with them once he ran out of steam preaching.

Mature beyond his years, none of the Reverend's preaching was lost on Charlie. That particular Sunday, the sermon theme from Matthew 25:40 was especially relevant: *"Truly I tell you, whatever you did for one of the least of these brothers and sisters of mine, you did for me."*

On hearing that verse, Charlie's mind went straight to the snapshot of Mr. Olson weeping on that bench in Law Park. The memory intensified as the image burned into his mind's eye. The more he mulled it over, the more he pined for a way to help make a difference for Mr. Olson and others like him.

After the sermon was over and the offering plate was passed, it came time for the closing hymn, which Reverend Higgins always selected in order to put an exclamation mark on the sermon. That week, he chose "We Bear the Strain of Earthly Care." *How appropriate*, Charlie thought. It was as though the opening verse was speaking directly to him: *"We bear the strains of earthly care but bear them not alone. Beside us walks our brother Christ and makes our task His own."*

After the service, Reverend Higgins enthusiastically greeted everyone as they exited the sanctuary. Charlie thanked him and commented on that choice of a hymn.

"Curious that you would inquire about that, Charlie. I haven't included that hymn at a church service in forty years!"

"It sure has a timely message, sir."

"Yes. Yes, it does. And especially at this time of year."

"Right, yes. But I don't think it should be just Jesus who looks after those in need. I think he would want each of us to get involved too."

"By Godfrey, you might have just given me the theme of my next sermon!" boomed Reverend Higgins. He patted Charlie on his back and shook hands with his dad as they made their way through the receiving line. From there, they buttoned up their overcoats and headed through the vestibule of the sanctuary, then across South State Road and over to the Parish Hall for the post-worship coffee hour.

A genuinely warm time of fellowship, coffee hour gave everyone an opportunity to say hello and catch up with each other. After shaking hands with the last parishioner, Reverend Higgins walked briskly across the street, burst into the Parish Hall and shouted, "I need a cup of coffee—black as a landlady's heart!"

"Here you go, Reverend. Good to the last drop!" Bob Beicke said, just like every Sunday, as he reached out with a warm smile and a fresh cup. "Is that black enough for you?" Bob egged him on.

"Not bad, but next week pour me some high test unleaded!" Reverend Higgins loudly responded, giving his cup a healthy sniff. The Parish Hall was a separate building across the street from the sanctuary. It was a sturdy, functional structure that had a two-story wing for Sunday school classrooms and a large common area that could be used for church meetings and all sorts of other purposes. Sunday school classes were just letting out as Charlie and his dad walked in. Children were everywhere, bursting with youthful exuberance. Charlie's mom had helped straighten up a few of the classrooms and was coming down the stairs with an armful of teachers' supplies.

That Sunday, Reverend Higgins made it a point to chat with Charlie's parents. Clutching his lapels, like when he was emphasizing a sermon point while preaching, he told them, "I'm so very impressed with Charlie. Polite, intelligent young man. Plus, he keeps me honest! Asks me questions. Seems to absorb every word I say." Then he paused, raising an eyebrow. "Actually, that might not be such a good thing!"

"Charlie thinks the world of you! Thank you for the ways you make him feel so important," said Charlie's dad.

"He has such a good heart! It's not often we see someone his age desiring to live a life that's pleasing to God. Come to think of it, I think there's a sermon in that too! The lessons we older kids can learn from our children!"

"Wish we could take credit, but he's just naturally that way," said Charlie's mom. "By the way, he's been expressing concern lately for Ole' Mr. Olson."

"Oh yes, I think we're all concerned for him. I've been calling on him as much as possible," offered Reverend Higgins. "In fact, I was just there last night. Went over to The Half Moon in Ossining to pick up a pizza. He and I split it. Four slices for me, two for him!"

"The next time you visit The Half Moon, feel free to pick up a large pie for us!" chimed in Mr. Riverton.

"I'm afraid our friend Mr. Olson is really lost without his wife. Can't seem to get his bearings. Wish I could say that he's up and down. But really, he's just down," the reverend continued. "After we finished the pizza, I stayed around to watch *TV*. Then, before I knew it, he was dozing off in his chair."

"Mrs. Olson was his other half for sixty years and more," said Charlie's dad. "They were so dedicated to each other and to their daily routines. How do you carry on after that?"

"I was reading the other day about how people can die of a broken heart," added Charlie's mom. "I totally believe it! The emotional stress must be so overwhelming!"

"And I've heard of couples who were together for long periods that died within days of each other from the burden of the loss," said Charlie's dad.

"The short answer to the question you raised is that you carry on by the grace of God, who knows all about our sufferings and has promised to be faithful to our prayers. There's a plan here somewhere, I can sense it. God's going to bring it to the surface when the timing is right," said Reverend Higgins.

"I love hearing that!" Charlie's mom reached over and hugged her husband.

"By the way, it's impressive that Charlie's been so sensitive to Mr. Olson's trials. Being mindful of those who are lonely and in need aligns with the most prominent lessons in the entire Bible, both Old Testament and New. And for the record, no one embodied that outlook better than Jesus himself!"

"Thank you, Reverend Higgins. Charlie is a wonderful kid for sure! We couldn't be any more proud of him," said Charlie's mom. "Something tells me he's going to do something that will leave us all shaking our heads but in a good way!"

The conversation was cut short by the siren of Engine 94 out on South State Road in front of the Parish Hall. Each year, on the first Sunday in December, the Volunteer Fire Department kept a tradition called The Santa Express. One of the members would dress up in a Santa Claus suit and position himself on top of the truck. Then, with sirens ringing out, they'd drive around town and toss lollipops to eager children in each neighborhood and at the houses of worship.

Charlie ran outside with the rest of the kids to the open lawn area known as God's half-acre. After filling his pockets, he picked up whatever was left on the ground and brought it over to the table in the foyer of the sanctuary where they kept the Penny Pot. He knew that some of the parishioners had a sweet tooth and figured they'd help themselves going to and from worship services while depositing their pennies, which were collected and donated to local causes.

As he walked back to the Parish Hall, he began to smile. The Christmas season was officially open, and the next several weeks would be filled with fun and wonder and gladness and joy. Peace on earth and goodwill to all was on the ascent. Many families had already dressed up their houses with Christmas lights, wreaths, and candles in the windows.

Soon enough, the commotion from The Santa Express died down and Charlie found his parents. People were still visiting with each other, talking about the sermon message and family plans for the holidays. Everyone seemed to have something lined up for Christmas Day. Some were hosting while others were traveling; but no one was without a place to go.

Suzie Berkshire, the popular and effervescent local realtor, was helping to clean up as coffee hour wound down. She stopped to say hello to the Rivertons, mentioning how concerned she too was about Mr. Olson.

"Oh, have you been visiting with him lately?" inquired Charlie's mom.

"Well, yes, a few times. He's thinking about putting his house on the market. I'm not sure if he'll actually go through with it, but he's leaning in that direction."

"Oh, no!" said the Rivertons in unison.

"He's been such a wonderful part of the community for so long! I'd hate to see him leave," added a troubled Mr. Riverton.

"He just seems so listless without her. No one to enjoy being with. No one to take care of. It's just very sad" added Suzie.

"Yes, we agree, but it's hard to know when the timing is right to reach out after someone's suffered a loss like this," mentioned Mrs. Riverton.

"You know what I think he needs?" asked Suzie. "A dog! A big, loveable, needy, silly, energetic dog." She waved her hands excitedly, bracelets jangling. "I heard the SPCA is having a special adopt-a-pet day next week. I'll bet he could walk right in and have his pick of whatever they've got."

Charlie had been standing nearby, absorbing everything that was said. *What a great idea!* he thought. As the chimes struck noon, the Rivertons began to say their goodbyes and headed to Joe Weldon's Deli for their post-church takeout lunch of Joe's feted roast beef wedges and assortment of other deli delights. While Mrs. Riverton ordered different things to take home, Charlie talked hockey with Mr. Weldon who was also a Rangers fan. They both especially enjoyed trading thoughts when Eddie Giacomin had a good game in goal.

"Big game coming up against Montreal this week!" Charlie said excitedly.

"Yes, sir! The Canadiens are in first place, as always," replied Mr. Weldon as he stood behind the counter slicing cold cuts.

"I know. And they've had our number for a while now."

"That's okay. This one's at Madison Square Garden, so we'll have home ice advantage." Mr. Weldon dropped a handful of sliced turkey breast on the scale.

"Home sweet home!"

On their way out, Mr. Weldon, as usual, told Charlie to help himself to the canister of Bazooka Joe bubble gum. He seemed to enjoy offering it as much as Charlie enjoyed receiving it.

"Thanks, Mr. Weldon! I'll save this for dessert!" Charlie picked a few pieces.

"Atta boy, Charlie. See you next week!"

"Okay, Mr. Weldon. Go Rangers!"

Once home, Charlie set up three folding tray tables in front of the TV in their den. He and his parents liked to enjoy their lunches while watching the *The NFL Today* pregame show with Brent Musburger, Irv Cross, Phyllis George, and Jimmy the Greek. Neither the Giants or Jets were particularly strong that season, but it was football and that was a staple at the Riverton house on Sunday afternoons. He turned the dial to Channel 2, adjusted the antennae for a clearer picture, and sat back to watch.

Charlie was richly blessed, and he knew it, even at such a young age. Nothing was taken for granted. He was part of a loving family, lived in a safe, comfortable home, and always had enough food to fill his stomach. As he paused to reflect on these things, he was also glad that they had a nice church to attend. His dad always said the week began with Sunday morning worship—"Best hour of the week!" *True enough,* Charlie thought. *And this week was off to a very good start.*

CHAPTER 5
COMING OF AGE

*Let your light shine before others so that they may see your good
works and give glory to your Father who is in heaven.*
—Matthew 5:16

Looking out the second-floor window of Mr. Hunt's social studies
class, Charlie could see Gooseneck Pond in clear sight, which sometimes caused his mind to drift a bit during class. No longer in the
sheltered confines of Todd Elementary School, Charlie and his buddies were beginning to enjoy small doses of independence, which was
actually facilitated by the location of the middle school itself. About a
quarter mile from the center of town, adjacent to the northwest corner of Law Park, it was pretty easy for them to walk to school from
just about anywhere.

In the morning, DMarks would leave his house up by Faith
Lutheran Brethren Church, cut across the four-lane Taconic Parkway
at Buckout Road where he'd meet up with BB. Then they'd walk up
Valentine Road where Charlie was usually waiting at the top of his
driveway. From there, it was out to Pleasantville Road, picking up
George on the way, then on through Law Park, and eventually to the
middle school.

To bookend the day, once classes let out at two thirty in the
afternoon, they'd walk up School Road to Weldon's for a buttered roll
and a Coke. The walk was short enough so that they'd still be back in
time to change into their football gear, basketball shorts, or baseball
cleats for afternoon practice, whatever the season might be.

On days when there was no practice to attend, they'd wander through the pine forest, which was located between the middle school and the main village area. It was a unique place with trees to climb, streams to wade, forts to build, and fish to catch. The ground was carpeted with soft, spongy pine needles and, in some sections, the sunlight was completely blotted out by lush evergreens. In fact, on summer days, they'd often retreat there from the pool area and ball fields because the temperature was at least 15 degrees cooler.

Some portions had become swampy, which caused many mature trees to uproot. They were left to lean on each other like so many half-fallen, evergreen dominoes. Still other areas were thick with tall reeds where pathways had been tamped down by foot traffic going to and from town. With an eye toward the future and a healthy concern for the environment, Mr. Saltzman, the middle school shop teacher, initiated a cause called "Project Watershed." Students were allowed to help him clear dead trees and dig trenches to channel water. The undertaking was so popular that each grade was given their own part of the project to focus on.

The main building that housed the Middle School was built in 1909 by Mr. Law. As Briarcliff grew and developed, he was always there to provide whatever services and facilities the local residents needed. "Only the best was good enough for Briarcliff," he used to say. When first constructed, it was home to K through twelfth grades and considered to be a state-of-the-art school building: two stories tall and made of brick and stucco. It had a broad front façade that gave the impression that it would stand forever. Inside, the common areas and classrooms were generous in size with huge windows that allowed for abundant amounts of daylight to shine through.

An entire wing was added by Mr. Law's son in 1928. The addition included a gymnasium and auditorium, which became the focus of many fond community events, including student variety shows, school concerts, choral productions, and meetings of the Briarcliff People's Caucus. The auditorium had a huge stage with a curtain so heavy that two people had to pull the cords to open and close it during performances.

The Monday after Thanksgiving, Charlie, BB, DMarks, and George headed up to Weldon's before basketball practice. To say that their lives revolved around sports would be an understatement. At the same time, a faint interest in girls was beginning to register. Of course, the girls were way ahead of them in this whole area, and they were getting impatient waiting for the boys to catch up.

"Did you guys watch the Rangers game last night?" asked BB.

"Yes, sir! The GAG Line came through again!" replied George. "Goal-a-game, baby!"

"Ratelle, Hadfield and Gilbert—the best ever!" inserted DMarks with his typical self-assured aplomb. "And best of all, they did it against the Bruins. I feel so sorry for all those poor Boston fans," he added sarcastically.

"Ratelle is my favorite," said Charlie.

"Gentleman Jean Ratelle. What a surprise you'd pick the guy who never gets in any fights!" responded Derrick.

"Oh, sit on it, Marks!" responded Charlie.

"I just wish he'd throw an elbow once in a while—you know, get mad out there, draw some blood."

"Stifle yourself, Marks!" responded Charlie. "I never understood why hockey players always have to fight anyway. There's a lot of contact in basketball and even more in football, but you don't see them getting in fights every time someone gets grazed by another player."

"No, duh, genius!" scoffed DMarks. "It's about passion. You know anything about that? Hockey players have passion, especially when they get caught up in the heat of the action."

"What do you think you know? The only heat out there in our games is your hot, stinking dog breath trying to keep up with us!

"Oh, so now you're a comedian? You should think about a career in comedy. Pretty soon, Bob Hope's gonna need a replacement on his USO tours."

"Yeah, well, Jerry Lewis isn't making movies anymore, maybe you can replace him, you spaz!"

Charlie was game to keep the argument going when George interrupted them to point something out. What he saw sent a bolt of lightning down his spine. Coming out of the Youth Center at the old Pump House was a group of girls from their grade. They were outgoing, confident, very pretty, and loved to flirt. That afternoon, they set their sights on engaging Charlie and his chums.

In spite of the fact that they had known most of these girls since kindergarten, the boys were terrified at the prospect of actually talking with them. Until recently, they had wanted nothing to do with girls in general. Yet none of them could deny that they each were experiencing a growing sense of attraction, which was starting to pick up momentum daily.

As the girls approached, severe cases of cottonmouth set in. The boys palms began to sweat, and their minds raced in a panicked frenzy wondering what they might say if the girls actually wanted to talk with them. It was a feeling worse than being called on to read out loud in class.

"Danger, Will Robinson!" said BB.

"Yeah, brace for impact," croaked George.

Charlie's brain had gone completely haywire. Only DMarks seemed relatively comfortable in the emergency situation. At that moment, Michelle Robins ran up and jumped right in front of Charlie. She and he were nose to nose. As she walked backward, she asked impulsively, "What's your favorite TV show? Mine's *Happy Days*."

Charlie had a crush on Michelle, but it was an incomprehensible thing to him. Michelle had a crush on Charlie and everyone knew it, but nobody was daring enough to do anything about it. Then her reinforcements arrived, and before they knew it, the boys were surrounded by a group of sixth grade girls, all of whom were chiming in with answers to Michelle's question. Clearly, this was a well-planned raid.

"*Happy Days*? How about *The Monkees*! Davy Jones slays 'The Fonz' every time!" said Andrea.

"Hello? You ever heard of *The Partridge Family*? David Cassidy is a dream!" said Connie.

"*The Waltons*! Who doesn't watch *The Waltons*?'" asked Barrie.

Finally DMarks stepped up and fired back. "The answer to your question is *The Streets of San Francisco* without a doubt, although it might be a little violent for you girls." He then added, "By the way, ladies, if you're not doing anything later, why don't you stop by my house for a game of Twister?"

George's turn. He was so nervous that he literally could not think complete thoughts. Still, he managed to eek out *Kung Fu.*

BB went the safe route. No one could criticize his choice of *Bonanza.*

Now it was Charlie's turn, and he felt like the whole world had put a spotlight on him. He froze on the spot. Michelle, who was now resorting to tickling him for an answer, eagerly waited for his response. His mind blanked. Then, bearing out his one-track mind for sports, he finally blurted out, "*This Week in Pro Football* with Pat Summerall and Tom Brookshier."

At that moment, everyone just stopped in their tracks, tilted their heads, and gave Charlie disbelieving stares for his totally anticlimactic answer. Silence fell over the entire group. The normally effervescent Michelle was deflated. Then she uttered a two-word dagger of a response: "They're hopeless."

Charlie felt his knees buckle and thought he might collapse. He didn't understand what he said that was so bad to actually kill the entire conversation. At that, the girls dropped away and headed into the pine forest shaking their heads.

"You guys are just a bunch of dumb jocks!" said Michelle. "Someday, you'll realize that there's more to life than sports!" The boys just stood there, heads down, until DMarks broke the silence.

"Great, just great. We're walking along with four of the best-looking girls in our grade and all you got is *This Week in Pro Football?* Thanks to you, they think we're *hopeless.* There goes our chances with them at the skating party next week."

Even George, the most mild-mannered one in the group, was nonplussed. "There are tons of great shows on TV and you picked that one? Of course they don't want to hear that stuff. Girls don't even really play sports...except maybe tennis, field hockey, and swim team."

"Lay off, you guys. It's the truth! My dad and I never miss it. Sometimes I like that show on Sunday nights better than the games themselves," replied Charlie.

"That's not the point, Einstein," said DMarks. "At times like that, you have to think on your feet. You have to anticipate the best answer. You have to tell them what they want to hear. Sometimes, you even have to make something up!"

"I think your nickname should be George Washington," said BB, laughing at Charlie. "I cannot tell a lie."

As terrifying as it was, Charlie realized it was a missed opportunity. He wanted badly to actually talk and walk with Michelle and the other girls, but like most boys his age, he just wasn't there yet. *Why was it so difficult to think and speak in complete sentences around girls?* he wondered.

On their way back from Weldon's, they were once again on School Road when the girls appeared from the pine forest. But this time, they were in a sarcastic mood. As they walked past, Charlie heard Michelle say, "Let's make believe that I'm Pat Summerall and you're Tom Brookmeyer or whatever his name is."

"I hope you're proud of yourself," DMarks blamed Charlie. "You totally deserve that! Dissed by a bunch of girls. Pitiful!"

"Stick it in your ear, Marks! If you want to talk to them so badly, why don't you just go hang out with them, you cake eater!" retorted Charlie.

"Why don't I hang out with them? Because even though they're cute, they aren't as cute as you!" he said, blowing a kiss to Charlie. He then broke into a sprint knowing Charlie would want to pound him for that.

"Go ahead and run! I'll see you on the basketball court in a few minutes! We'll settle it then!" yelled Charlie.

"The thrill of victory and the agony of defeat!" yelled back DMarks, quoting the famous tagline from *Wide World of Sports* while sprinting straight for the boys' locker room.

Just then, Sky drove by in his pickup truck. "Hi, guys! Want to jump in the back of my truck? I'm heading right past the locker rooms." The boys literally leapt at the opportunity. It was a short ride, but it was something fun and different. They all felt special as onlookers called out to them, wishing they had the same opportunity. As Sky dropped them off, he asked Charlie if he had spoken with Mr. Olson lately.

"Actually, no. I've been meaning to, but he hasn't been outside whenever I've walked by."

"His phone isn't working?" asked Sky good-naturedly.

"I guess I didn't think about calling him."

"Couldn't hurt. I bet his phone doesn't ring very much these days."

"It probably doesn't ring at all," replied Charlie sadly.

At that moment, Charlie thought he heard Sky suggest that Reverend Higgins might be able to find opportunities for him to participate in church-related activities. But Sky wasn't speaking; his mouth was closed, his lips weren't moving, except to form that full-of-life smile he had.

On impulse, Charlie uttered, "Hey, do you suppose Reverend Higgins could invite him to get involved with some of the committees at church?"

"I think that's a great idea, Charlie. Why don't you mention that to him at coffee hour this Sunday?"

"I think I will! There's always room for extra help on the fellowship committee. For that matter, I think he used to be an engineer, maybe he could help out with the trustees."

"I like the way you're thinking!" Sky smiled at Charlie and slapped the dashboard to show his enthusiasm.

The boys hopped out of Sky's truck and bounded into the locker room in the back of the middle school building. But Charlie lingered behind, watching Sky's truck as it slowly pulled down School Road and around the corner of the building. Once it was out of sight, he shrugged his shoulders, scratched his head, and headed up the steps to the boys' locker room.

CHAPTER 6

SOLDIER DOWN

*For He will command His angels concerning
you, to guard you in all your ways.*
—Psalm 91:11

So much was happening in the world and popular culture during the 1970s. Charlie and his buddies were just about old enough to pay attention, but it was hard for them to make sense of it all. The biggest thing on the minds of the adults around town was Vietnam. Everyone wanted peace with honor. Shuttle diplomacy and the Paris Peace Talks became a fixture on the nightly news, and Henry Kissinger became a household name.

Watergate was also starting to attract more attention. In anticipation of the televised congressional hearings, Mr. Hunt asked the A/V team to hook up a special black-and-white TV so his social studies class could watch as top presidential advisors raised their right hand, took the oath and fielded questions about the break-in and subsequent cover-up.

It was all so difficult to understand. President Nixon had just been reelected by a landslide, yet his administration appeared to be under siege. Toss in the Cold War and the Space Race and it just seemed like there was a dark cloud hanging over the whole country.

For their part, Charlie and his friends resorted to lighter fare as they made the fifteen-minute walk each morning to school. For a while, one of their favorite pastimes was to see if they could sing the entire long-form version of Don McLean's seminal anthem,

"American Pie." They didn't understand all the lyrics, but the refrain was as good as it got when it came to sing-along material: "So bye-bye, Miss American Pie/Drove my Chevy to the levee/but the levee was dry." Even that caused them to wonder. They knew what a Chevy was, but what on earth was a levee?

On Tuesday mornings, their exchanges were almost entirely dedicated to repeating one-liners from the prior night's episode of *Rowan and Martin's Laugh-In*. Of course, every time someone said "Sock it to me," someone got socked. The show's off-color, politically edgy humor didn't sit well with all of the parents around town, but it was fun and innovative. Plus, the boys liked to debate about who was better looking in a bikini: Goldie Hawn or Judy Carne.

Schoolwork was also a common topic of conversation. The current assignment in Mr. Van Antwerp's English class was to finish a book report on Jonathan Livingston Seagull before Christmas break. This was an unpopular assignment because none of them could understand what the book was about or why they had to read it.

"What is with this book they're making us read?" complained DMarks. "Such a drag. I mean, a book about a seagull that doesn't fit in? C'mon! Some older seagull should just tell him to straighten up and fly right!"

"I know! I think there's supposed to be some hidden message, but I can't figure out what any of it has to do with us and our lives," said BB. "Why can't he have chosen a book on Daniel Boone or Davy Crockett?"

"I'm in left field with this one," said George. "A seagull with identity issues! Bummer for him!"

"I can't figure out what we're supposed to get from it," added Charlie.

"Torture. Pure torture!" cried DMarks. "We might as well be sitting around talking to my sister's Barbie doll!"

"It's like this 'New Math.' When Mr. Stevens talks about two squared and two cubed, my focus goes out the window," said George, pointing to the pine forest. "One time, he brought me up to the front of the class, put a piece of chalk in my hand, and told me to work out an equation. I stood there frozen. Couldn't think straight and thought I might throw up!" He bent forward and pretended to gag.

"I remember when he did that to you!" recalled BB. "I felt for you, man. That wasn't right."

"Being up there with everyone looking at me was the worst! But you know what made it really bad? I clearly wasn't getting it, *and* he kept making me try it again and again! I swear I wanted to whack him with my slide rule!"

"Right! And then he just shook his head and sent you back to your seat. That was not cool," said Charlie.

"Sometimes I wish we could tell some of these teachers and other adults how we really feel," said DMarks, holding up his two hands. "I would have looked right at him and asked him to count how many fingers I was holding up with my left hand and then I would have decked him with my right. Haymaker! Windmill! Down for the count! End of lesson."

"Do you have any idea how completely idiotic you sound sometimes?" asked Charlie.

"Hey. It's a dog-eat-dog world out there. You have to stand up for yourself and you don't take anything from anyone. Push or be pushed!"

"Oh, good grief! If I just nod my head in agreement, will you shut the heck up?" Charlie covered his ears.

"Why do they think we need to know all that stuff anyway?" asked BB. "How is it relevant to anything we do in our daily lives?"

"I hear ya, man," said Charlie. "It's not like when we go to the lunchroom and pay for our chocolate milk we're told that we owe five cents to the fifth power."

"The only good class is gym," said George. "Coach Nutson's the best! When he pulls the curtain in the middle of the gym and lets us play Bombardment, that's as good as it gets!"

"Did you guys see how I accidently nailed Mr. VanHoven?" asked DMarks.

"You gave him a bloody nose! I can't believe you pegged the principal and drew blood!" said George. "Tell the truth, that was no accident!"

"Listen ding-dong, he shouldn't be sticking his head in the gym like that during a game of Bombardment!" said DMarks. "That'll teach him."

"Good thing you throw like a girl!" said BB. "You might have broken his nose!"

"Look who's talking!" responded DMarks. "The reason you play second base in baseball is because you have a rag arm!"

"Oh, mellow out, Marks," said Charlie. "You're always so uptight!"

"Speaking of gym class, did you see that the girls got a new gym teacher?" asked DMarks. "Her name is Ms. Donahue and she's really pretty!"

"I did notice. She went to King's College. Really nice. The girls love her," said Charlie.

"I can't wait till June when they start having gym class out at the pool in the park," said BB.

"I know! That's the best," seconded George. "And when Coach Nutson dives in and wrestles with us, it's so great. He's the man!"

As they cut through Law Park, Charlie glanced up at Mr. Olson's house as he was wont to do. In the light of the cheerful morning sun, the house looked a little less doleful. To his surprise, he noticed the gentlemanly old man shuffling up the driveway as he brought his garbage cans up from the street. He seemed to be in a trance as he robotically plodded along. Charlie's heart sank. Then, in the blink of an eye, Mr. Olson slipped on black ice and fell hard on the asphalt.

"Quick, Charlie. Mr. Olson needs help!" said Sky urgently. Charlie froze, looking all around him wondering where Sky had come from. But he wasn't there. *How could that be?* "Did you guys hear that?" asked Charlie.

"Hear what?" said DMarks.

"I could swear I just heard Sky tell us to go help Mr. Olson."

"My man, I know you like the guy, but maybe when we get to school you should pay a visit to the guidance counselor's office. You're hearing things!" said DMarks.

Charlie dropped his book bag and ran across Pleasantville Road to help. The boys followed right behind him, stopping traffic in both directions. When they got there, Mr. Olson was a bit disoriented. They couldn't tell if it was from the fall or from all the grief he had been experiencing, or both. BB, George, and even DMarks were all shook up as they gathered around him protectively in a circle.

"Are you okay, Mr. Olson?" asked Charlie.

"I think so. What hit me?" he replied slowly.

"You slipped on black ice, sir," said George. "Want me to go inside and call my dad? He can come over with the ambulance if you want."

"Oh no, I'm fine. But thank you," he said, feeling around his back to be sure.

"I'll go in your garage to get some rock salt for the driveway. We don't want you slipping like that again," BB offered helpfully.

"Bless you, boys. It's on the right, just inside the door. I feel like a prize fool."

"It was an accident, Mr. Olson. You can't see black ice. DMarks is always slipping on it," said Charlie.

"It's true! How do you think I got a face like this?" he said as he contorted his face into an ugly expression. DMarks's self-deprecating humor lightened the mood.

The boys held Mr. Olson by his arms and walked him into his house through the back door. It was cold and forlorn inside. The air was stale. Unread newspapers seemed to be piling up everywhere, and dirty dishes overflowed in the kitchen sink. A small black-and-white TV in the corner was tuned to the morning news. Their spirits took a nosedive as they looked around.

"Bless you, boys. Bless you. If you could just help me to my chair, that would be great. This seems to be where I spend most of my time these days."

"Is there anything else we can do? Would you like a glass of water? Maybe an extra pillow?" asked Charlie.

"No, I'll be fine. You boys should run along, you'll be late for school."

Reluctantly, they began to leave. On the one hand, they wanted to get out of there; it was too depressing. On the other hand, they didn't want to leave Mr. Olson alone. Not a word was spoken as they headed across the park to the middle school, heads down, shoulders slumping, spirits flagging. They all felt badly for Mr. Olson and how lost and lonely he was.

This departure from their normal routine made them late for homeroom. They dashed through the south doors of the 1909 building and up the stairs to the sixth-grade floor. After quickly hanging up their coats in the side cubby area, they tried to quietly sneak into the back of Mr. Hunt's classroom. However, when he saw them, he asked that they come stand in front of the classroom near him. *Okay, lay it on us,* Charlie silently thought.

That morning, Mr. Hunt happened to be sipping his coffee, looking out his window in advance of the 8:00 a.m. homeroom bell. From that vantage point, he witnessed the entire episode unfold while looking out across Law Park. When he saw Mr. Olson fall, he jumped to his feet and was about to run over there. But then he saw the boys doing the same, so he decided to let them handle it themselves.

Mr. Hunt explained to the class what they had done and then led everyone in a round of applause. The boys were super shy about the attention they were receiving. Only DMarks seemed comfortable up there. He grabbed his hands together and lifted them above his shoulders, shifting them from one side to the other like old-time ballplayers used to do after hitting a homerun. Thankfully, Mr. Hunt was ready to dismiss homeroom, which quickly ended DMarks's theatrics.

As the day progressed, word got out to other teachers and most sought the boys out to give them an extra pat on the back. Coach Nutson even took them over to Pizza Beat in his white '69 Camaro—which was beyond cool. Of course, DMarks had to ride shotgun.

Ms. Donohue told them that a lot of people would have acted like they didn't see anything and kept on walking.

"Oh, it was nothing," said DMarks. "As soon as I saw him slip, I knew what had to be done. I'm just glad the boys followed my lead." Charlie was about to kidney punch him when George urged him to just let it go.

"The old man was a little banged up, but he'll be fine. Although, I was a bit surprised he didn't dish out a little moolah for our efforts," said DMarks. That did it. Charlie nailed him good with a kidney punch, and DMarks doubled over coughing.

"Sucker punch!" DMarks croaked. "Was that necessary?"

"Without a doubt!" responded Charlie. "Want another?"

"Thank you, Ms. Donohue," Charlie humbly replied. "Mr Olson recently lost his wife, and he's kind of lonely these days. We were just in the right place at the right time. Glad we were able to be of some help."

Ms. Donohue commended the boys. "You give me hope for the future. Chocolate milks and Ring Dings are on me tomorrow during lunch period!"

It did feel good to have helped someone in need. But for Charlie, the sight of Mr. Olson down on the ground and all by himself stayed etched in his mind, along with the bleak, dreary atmosphere inside the house. Once again, that yearning to make a difference rose up in Charlie's heart as he remembered the things Sky had told him. He thought maybe he'd ring Mr. Olson's doorbell later that afternoon to check up on him. He had to do something, but what?

After school that day, the boys made their usual stop at Weldon's before basketball practice. On the way back to the gym they passed Suzie Berkshire coming out of the Yates Real Estate office.

"Hi, Charlie. Hi, boys. How we doin'?"

"Hi, Ms. Berkshire, all's well," replied Charlie. "Looks like you're in a hurry."

"Never a dull moment, Charlie! I'm heading to Mr. Olson's, he wants me to put his house on the market. Should sell pretty quickly I'd say, given its location and size. Great for a young family!"

Charlie was crestfallen with this news. "But he can't leave the town he loves! And that house! He and Mrs. Olson lived there since forever!"

"Well, a fresh start might be just what he needs. He still has a lot of living to do and getting away from all those memories might help him to turn a page."

Young as they were, the boys were a little put off by Suzie's business-minded attitude. *Is she in the business of helping others or just helping herself?* Charlie wondered. All he could think was that Briarcliff wouldn't be the same without Mr. Olson and his upstanding, coat-and-tie presence. He dug his sneaker into the ground and looked away.

Suzie could sense a tinge a tension. "Oh well, I have to get over there," she said, exhaling. "Such is life! Plus, you can't pass up opportunities like this!"

She jumped into her Mustang convertible and a few minutes later was parking in Mr. Olson's driveway. Sitting there in her car, she took inventory of the house. It was large and attractive but had a depressing aura about it and seemed deserted. It made her feel a bit uneasy, and she even considered canceling the appointment. But that would go against her take-charge nature and overarching commitment to her profession. "Oh well, here goes," she said under her breath.

Grabbing her listings book from the back seat, she bounded up the walkway to the front door. After ringing the doorbell, she waited, tapping her foot with nervous energy. Nothing. She looked in a window, but there was no sign of life. *Did he forget I was coming over?* she wondered. She rang the doorbell again, not knowing whether she should be concerned or annoyed. Walking around the side of the house she noticed his car was in the garage, which confirmed she should now be concerned.

Straight to the back door she went, rapping loudly and peering in the window. Then, focusing her eyes, she saw Mr. Olson sitting at the kitchen table, hunched over, head down, white handkerchief in hand. There in front of him, spread across the table, were several opened photo albums and a few shoeboxes full of handwritten letters. He seemed unresponsive. Suzie's mind raced. Never one to stand on ceremony, she gripped the door handle, flung it open, and stepped right in.

"Mr. Olson, Mr. Olson, are you okay?"

Hearing her voice suddenly shook him out of his dazed state. "Oh, Suzie. Thank you for coming over. I was expecting you. Must have lost track of time." He slowly rose to his feet and took off his glasses. He was in his normal white button-down shirt and navy blue tie.

Suzie was temporarily stunned as her eyes scanned the room. It was disheveled and unkept. Mr. and Mrs. Olson had always been meticulous homeowners: neat home, well-attended yard, robust gardens, and Christmas lights galore this time of year. Yet Mr. Olson didn't even seem to be aware of or care about how things had slipped. At a rare loss for words, Suzie remained still and just listened to him.

"I was just reading through some of the letters Mrs. Olson and I exchanged while I was serving in Europe during World War I. We had quite a special love." He sighed through red eyes and a forced half-smile.

Suzie teared up, and a major lump formed in her throat. She looked at Mr. Olson with glistening eyes, cleared her throat, and softly apologized for interrupting at a time like this. "Mr. Olson, if this isn't a good time, I can always come back. Really, maybe I should just be leaving?"

"Not at all! We had an appointment. Thank you for keeping it—and for keeping me honest about it!" He wiped his glasses and put them back on to give her his full attention. She was about to launch into her patented "Million Dollar Club" realtor spiel when the worries Charlie expressed moments before about Mr. Olsen began to fill her head.

She hesitated, thought about what she was doing, and drew a deep breath. "Mr. Olson, are you sure you want to sell your home? You've been here for fifty years. This home must hold so much meaning for you. Plus, you're surrounded by friends and people who love you, right here in Briarcliff." As she talked in a voice she didn't recognize at all, she tried to discreetly straighten things up for him: picking up magazines and sections of newspapers, fluffing cushions on chairs and couches, opening curtains and raising shades.

"You're right about all those things, Suzie." He sighed heavily again. "Mrs. Olson and I had a wonderful life here in this house. I've always enjoyed looking out at Law Park, sitting on the front porch in our rocking chairs, and waving to friends and children going to and from the park."

"Sure, right you are! This is your home, and homes become an extension of the people who live in them!" As she spoke, she made her way to the kitchen sink to put cups and plates in the dishwasher.

"I miss our daily walks uptown. Winter, spring, summer, or fall, we made that daily walk." Mr. Olsen distractedly fiddled with his tie.

Suzie's eyes welled up again. With an unsteady voice, she reminded him that not everyone enjoyed a home that allowed for a convenient five-minute walk to town. Mr. Olson paused at this comment and looked out at his backyard. In that moment, Suzie was struck by an unusually warm sensation as both her mind and heart opened up with great understanding and affection. It almost made her feel light-headed.

"Mr. Olson, I'd be glad to list your home—and I'm sure I could sell it quickly and pick up a nice commission. But I'm not sure that's in your best interests just yet. Why don't you think about it a little more before you make up your mind?" That she was now full-out trying to convince a client not to sell was absolutely a first for her! Mr. Olson just continued to look out the window, seemingly transported to another world of happy memories.

"Tell ya what, Mr. Olson. If you don't mind, I'm actually going to decline the opportunity to list your home. You still have some things to think about before you get to the point of putting this on the market."

As Suzie said that, he turned to her with a warm, wistful smile. His eyes were on the verge of a few tears. They looked at each other for a long moment. He understood the sweet overture she was making.

"Okay then. Thanks for having me over, Mr. Olson," she finished, straightening things up as tactfully as she could, then began to leave. "See ya around town?"

"Yes, Suzie, I'll see you around town." They stepped toward each other and embraced. Suzie detected a slight change in Mr. Olson's demeanor. He seemed visibly relieved at the prospect of not moving—and his smile was now brighter, as though the sun might be starting to come out inside his broken heart. It made her feel good, like she had orchestrated something positive.

She turned and walked toward the back door. As she closed it behind her, she glanced down and saw a long, slender snow-white feather on the doorstep. *How pretty,* she thought, curious that she hadn't noticed it on the way in. It seemed unique from other feathers she might randomly spot while out and about. She picked it up, turned to wave at Mr. Olson, and headed to her car. As she put the key in the ignition, she paused to take a closer look at the feather, then put it up under the passenger side visor for safekeeping.

CHAPTER 7
BOYS WILL BE BOYS

A time to weep, and a time to laugh; a time
to mourn, and a time to dance.
                    —Ecclesiastes 3:4

It was always a packed house for a Bears varsity basketball game at the Todd School gymnasium. That Friday was no different as people streamed in to support the team. Charlie's dad dropped the boys off about fifteen minutes before game time. They made their way through the school entrance and skipped down the glass-enclosed corridor which led to the gym. After scanning their options," they found a spot at the top row of the bleachers around mid-court.

They were all very excited to be getting yet another small dose of newfound freedom, and as the Bears took the court they cheered wildly, stopping only when the National Anthem was played. The Bears were having a great season, dominating the Class C league in Westchester County. Anchored by 6'8" Gary O'Hagan and the speedy backcourt duo of Kevin McFadden and Tommy Whiting, they were the pride of Briarcliff and the talk of the town.

At halftime, the team was up by fifteen points under the conservative but steady coaching of Doc Prewitt, who played for the Bears himself while growing up in Briarcliff. With a full forty minutes before the second half tip-off, the boys headed out to the main hallway outside the gym near the District Office. They visited the concession stand and tried to act like being out at night and on their own was a regular thing for them.

"Hey. Do you guys remember gym class back here at Todd School with Coach Cadman?" asked DMarks.

"Of course!" said George. "Who could forget? It was the best class of the day!"

"Then you'll remember what's behind the red curtain up on the stage?" He raised his eyebrows at them in an exaggerated way. In addition to the row of bleachers lining one whole side of the court, there was a large, elevated stage with a thick, heavy curtain on the other.

"That's where Coach Cadman kept that huge trampoline," DMarks continued. "And I'll bet it's still there...just dying for someone to use it."

"Oh, no!" said BB. "You're not going to get us all in trouble for the sake of sneaking onto a trampoline."

"Can it, fool! If we do this right, we can sneak through the Music Suite, go down to the boys' locker room, and then up the stairs to the back entrance of the stage. Who wants to have some real fun?"

"You're such a jerk! This isn't enough fun already?" said George. "Besides, the reason the curtain is closed is to keep people from wandering around up there."

"Yeah, we're having a great time just being here. Did you see when O'Hagan dunked? The backboard's still shaking!" said BB.

"What's the matter, ladies, you scared?" replied DMarks. "Why would you sit on some hard wooden bleachers in a super loud, sweaty gymnasium when we could be up on that stage, behind the curtain, doing somersaults and having wrestling matches on the trampoline?"

"Maybe because our parents told us to stay on the bleachers," replied Charlie. "Don't you get it? This is a test. We have to pass it to keep earning their trust. That way, they'll keep letting us go out at night for stuff like this."

"No, duh, Charles. However, you apparently have yet to realize that rules are meant to be broken. I guess you guys are all show and no go!"

"Go ahead, Marks. Go play on your stupid Todd School trampoline. We're going back inside. And oh, by the way, don't call us if you get hurt!"

"Fine! You puppies stay in your cages. I'm making my move."

"Okay, but you won't have a spotter and that's one of the cardinal rules for using the trampoline!" said George.

"Here's an idea. Why don't you guys just go home and play with your Lite-Brites! Catch you dorks on the flipside!" DMarks spun around and down the hall he went, past the library, all the way to the Music Suite, trying to look as innocent and inconspicuous as possible.

As the second half tipped off, the boys headed back up to the bleachers where they had been sitting, shaking their heads over their friend's latest shenanigans. When they got there, they were slightly concerned to see that Parker Jones had arrived and was sitting in the same place. He looked them up and down, then moved slightly to his left as the boys, with some hesitation, reclaimed their seats.

Parker was a former star of the Bears varsity basketball team, recently back from Vietnam, trying to piece his life together as best he could. He silently nodded to the boys as if to say that he was in a no-nonsense frame of mind, which made them even more uncomfortable about DMarks and what he was up to.

The flow of the game seemed to help Parker's mind-set. He loved basketball and even began to engage the boys. "Did you see that play? That man was open for a layup because the other coach switched to a 1-3-1 zone on defense."

"Wait, so our coach ran a give-and-go to counter what the defense was doing? asked Charlie. Parker was impressed that one of the boys actually spoke with him and even more impressed by the question itself. "Right, he put Ozzello out on the wing so he could receive a pass from Borho, who then could cut behind the defender and straight to the basket for a high percentage shot."

"Cool. I know they run plays on the football field, but I didn't realize you could run plays like that on a basketball court too." Charlie slapped his knees with excitement.

"Absolutely! You never want to just play street ball out there. It's not about who has the best athletes…it's about who has the best game plan." He paused, then looked Charlie straight in the eye. "I'm Parker, by the way," he said, reaching out to shake hands.

We know very well who you are! the boys thought. "I'm Charlie." The boys all nodded and threw out their names while waving in Parker's direction. He was a bit intimidating and known to be unpredictable. Most people felt it was better to just avoid him, but for that night Parker seemed to be in a good place.

Meanwhile, the crowd was so loud and the stage curtain was so heavy that no one was aware of any trampoline activity behind it. By all indications, DMarks' daring plan was working out just fine. But as the game wore on, he didn't return.

"Is anyone else getting a little concerned about DMarks?" asked Charlie.

"He's probably having so much fun that he lost track of time," said BB.

"Or do you suppose that the jerk might actually have gotten hurt?" asked George.

"I get that nothing's more fun than jumping on a trampoline, but he's been back there now for almost an hour. He should have had enough fun by now," reasoned Charlie.

"You're right. I hate to admit it, but I'm kinda worried about him." George gazed hard at the curtain as though trying to see through it. "He's such a pain!"

"Listen, this game is pretty much over. The Bears are up by twenty. Maybe we should go check on him," offered BB.

"I was just thinking the same thing," agreed Charlie.

With that, the boys waited until the next whistle blew to stop play. They quickly got up and made their way down the bleachers and over to the gym exit. By then, no one was out in the main hallway so it was easy to hustle unseen to the boys' locker room. As they made their way up the stairs to the back of the stage, their concerns increased. They should have been able to hear the sounds made by the springs of the trampoline if DMarks was jumping on it, but there was complete silence back there.

They accelerated their pace up the steps. As they got out and onto the stage area, they found the single most hilarious sight any of them had ever seen. There before their eyes was DMarks, suspended in midair above the trampoline, swinging back and forth like a pendulum. He was wearing a hooded sweatshirt and managed to somehow get it hooked on a gaff that was hanging down from the ceiling. It must have been used during the recent holiday play and, apparently, the stage crew neglected to hoist it back up to the rafters after the show.

The boys could not contain their laughter. George slid halfway down the steps laughing so hard he could barely hold on to the railing. In time, they composed themselves enough to allow the razzing to begin.

"You are such a spaz," said BB. "You look like the Sputnik, just kind of floating up there in outer space!"

"Shut. Up. You!" said DMarks. "What took you guys so long to come look for me? I might have been seriously hurt back here!"

"Hey, good buddy, what's your twenty?" said George, quoting the CB Radio phrase that had become all the rage.

"Ha ha. With friends like you, who needs enemies?" said DMarks sarcastically.

"Hey, Marks, how's it hangin'?" Charlie spit out his words with laughter.

You guys are cruisin' for a bruisin'. Now get me down from here!"

"All right, all right, we'll get you down," said Charlie. Truth be told, Charlie was relieved that he was okay.

As the boys began to look for a way they could lower the gaff, it puckishly occurred to them that this whole scene presented a priceless opportunity to create an unforgettable episode. Instead of hunting for the rope to lower the gaff, they decided to head to the ropes that opened the stage curtain.

"Hey! Get away from there," said DMarks. "Don't do it! I'll make you pay!"

"Now try to understand, we don't want to do this, but it's for your own good." Charlie smiled, recalling a phrase they all heard from their parents and teachers whenever they were about to be punished.

"Right," said George. "Now let this be a lesson to you."

"Drumroll, please!" said BB with a straight, solemn face.

As the curtain slowly opened, the game came to an immediate halt. The players just froze wherever they were on the court, and everyone in the bleachers sat in stunned silence. DMarks was red as a poppy in the sun. After a prolonged hush, the crowd erupted into bleacher-shaking laughter. To Derrick's extreme irritation, a reporter from the *Citizen Register* was there, camera in hand, and quickly snapped a photo for the Saturday paper. Also in the stands was Hank Kaufman, a detective on the Briarcliff Police Force. He was a good man and decided to take charge in a way that would scare some common sense into DMarks. Hank hurried down from the bleachers, across the court, and up onto the stage.

"Oh, great. It's the fuzz!" said DMarks.

Hank flashed his badge to the referee, then he told the boys to shut the curtain so that the game could resume without distraction. What followed was a performance worthy of an Academy Award. Hank proceeded to give DMarks the third degree. One after another, he ticked off the criminal violations that were involved with what he had done: trespassing, misuse of school facilities, and reckless endangerment. The list went on as DMarks continued to spin slowly in midair.

The detective went on to describe the kinds of punishment that might come from a stunt like this after appearing in juvenile court. By now, the usually defiant DMarks was looking alarmed and the boys actually began to feel sorry for their friend. They all fell for everything Hank was saying…hook, line, and sinker.

Finally, Hank found the rope to lower the gaff so he could unhook DMarks, who was now showing a rare degree of humility.

"I know you boys and your parents. You each come from very good families," Hank said. "Because of that, I'm going to let you off *the hook* this time." Hank discreetly winked at Charlie, BB, and George but kept the heat on DMarks. "Consider this a warning, Marks. This sort of thing will not be tolerated in the future. Marks, you in particular better walk the straight and narrow. The entire police force will be keeping an eye on you." He flashed his badge again for emphasis.

"Yes, sir. Thank you, sir," stammered DMarks.

"Okay then," said Hank. "The buzzer just sounded, so the game is over. Make tracks out of here and up to the parking lot. I'm sure your parents will be outside waiting for you." With that, the boys took off. Once they got outside, their relief spilled over.

"We warned you, Marks!" said Charlie.

"Yeah. We told you not to do it!" said BB.

"You got what you deserved, Marks!" said George.

"Relax, fraidy-cats. Seems to me the trouble is over," replied a surprisingly overconfident DMarks. The boys couldn't believe his arrogance.

"Are you forgetting about the reporter from the *Citizen Register?*" asked Charlie. "He clicked a highly frameable picture of you hanging in midair above the trampoline."

"Yeah, I think he got your good side too!" hooted George. "Your rear end!"

"Should make the front page of tomorrow's morning paper," added BB.

DMarks was both angry and deflated by that key reminder. He knew he'd be in for it once his parents saw the incriminating photo. Unrepentant and crafty as usual, he shifted into damage control and began scheming on how to intercept the paper once it was delivered to their driveway in the morning. Not only would he swipe his parents' newspaper, he was determined to steal their neighbor's for good measure.

CHAPTER 8

NEW YORK CHRISTMAS AMBLE

*For when two or three are gathered in my
name, there also am I among them.*
—Matthew 18:20

The next day, Charlie's dad woke him up early. "Rise and shine, buddy. Or, as they used to say in the military, act lively and do well!" He pulled open the curtains in Charlie's bedroom and the morning sun came streaming through.

Each year, Reverend Higgins took the church youth group to Manhattan for the annual Christmas Amble and everyone had to meet at Scarborough Station by eight thirty in the morning. Charlie pulled himself out of bed, stepped into his Levi's, and put on a warm turtleneck with his Eddie Giacomin jersey over it. He then made his bed and started downstairs where Barnes and Noble were eagerly waiting to give him that special kind of rescue-dog greeting. After feeding and letting them out, he had a quick breakfast of Tang and Pop-tarts, then headed out the front door with his dad. As they got into the car, Mr. Riverton couldn't wait to engage Charlie.

"I heard your buddy Derrick might be in for a grounding after last night."

"To the max! Wait, how did you know about that?" asked Charlie.

"Aside from this being a small, close-knit town where everybody knows each other's business? I ran into Hank Kaufman getting coffee and donuts at Weldon's this morning."

"What did he tell you?"

"That DMarks was feeling his oats and decided to take advantage of an unsupervised trampoline at Todd School."

"We told him not to do it, Dad, but he wouldn't listen. We only left the bleachers because we were concerned when he didn't come back."

"I know, son, you were checking on a friend. I'm proud of you for that. Meanwhile, when his dad finds out, I think he'll probably apply the board of education to the seat of knowledge!"

"I know! Mr. Marks is really old-school too.'

"By the way, had I been in your shoes, I don't think I could have resisted pulling the curtain open either," grinned his dad. They slapped five with each other.

As they drove down Scarborough Station Road, they could see Reverend Higgins standing by the train platform like a sentry, complete with Scottish Tam O'Shanter and mutton chops.

"Top of the morning to ya, Charlie!" boomed Reverend Higgins.

"Good morning, sir. Thank you for doing this," replied Charlie.

"Thank you for coming! I'd be lonely without you and your friends!"

Charlie walked up the steps, over the tracks, and down to the southbound platform. The December air was fresh and cold as the blustery wind whipped across the Hudson. On cue, the 8:45 a.m. train pulled in at Scarborough.

"ALL ABOARD!" bellowed Reverend Higgins. "I always wanted to say that!" he declared to the conductor who was mildly amused.

Winthrop Smythe was also on the train platform, clad in suit and tie. Saturday was usually a workday for him. He impatiently rolled his eyes at Reverend Higgins, tossed his half-smoked Chesterfield on the ground and stamped it out, twisting his foot for good measure. As he boarded the train, he brusquely cut in front of the kids to grab his normal seat. None of the kids actually knew him, but they all were aware of who he was and his mean-spirited, toffee-nosed, arrogant ways. That morning he cast a particularly cool, condescending gaze in their direction over the top of his Saturday edition of *Barron's*.

Michelle was also in youth group. As all the kids slid into the two- and three-seaters, she made sure to glide in next to Charlie. Now he'd have to talk with her as the train headed south toward Tarrytown, Yonkers, and eventually, Grand Central Terminal. Charlie couldn't help but notice how pretty she looked that sunny Saturday morning. She was wearing bell-bottom jeans with an oversized tie-dyed shirt over a wool turtleneck. A navy blue pea jacket with the collar turned up kept the wind off her back. He thought the matching earmuffs and mittens added a smart accent. As good-looking as she was, it was her glowing smile and exuberant spirit that Charlie found most attractive. She had one of those rare personalities that lit up a room and made everything seem a little brighter whenever she was around.

The attraction between the two of them was mutual. But Charlie wasn't quite yet able to figure it all out, let alone know how to convey the way he felt. He was slowly getting more comfortable talking with girls, but it still made him anxious and he found it difficult to think clearly when in those situations.

As the train started rolling, several in the group opened cans of Coke to wash down the Pop Rocks and Razzles they brought for the ride.

"What on God's green earth are you wayward children eating and drinking?" thundered Reverend Higgins.

"Breakfast of champions, sir!" responded Charlie.

"Great Prince William in a can! I've never heard of such a thing!" The reverend was set in his ways on most things including the importance of starting the day with a balanced breakfast. "I don't think your dentists would approve! Then again, what you're doing is probably good for their business!"

The kids loudly laughed it off, as they often did, when he caricatured the generational age gap. Smythe was sitting nearby, increasingly unamused by the presence of a boisterous group of young kids on his Saturday morning commuter train. *How did these brats get on this train anyway?* he wondered.

"Hey, Reverend," he called out. "Let's keep it down over there. A little consideration for others would be appreciated."

"Why, Mr. Smythe, I apologize for this display of cheerful enthusiasm, joy, and merriment. However, it is Saturday morning, which is the one day when most of us can relax and have fun." He paused, then stood up, looked at Smyth, and added, "By the way, this is a train, not a library."

Smythe didn't like it when someone stood up to him. All the kids sat silently with concerned looks on their faces. The two men locked eyes, then Smythe shuffled his paper and held it up over his face in a huff. Reverend Higgins turned back to the kids and right away engaged them on all the things they wanted to do in the city that day.

Soon after, Michelle broke the ice with Charlie. "I heard you guys had some fun with the trampoline over at Todd School last night."

"Were you there?" asked Charlie. "That was so funny to see DMarks turn red in front of the entire crowd."

"No, I wasn't there, but Patty's brother was dribbling the ball across midcourt when the curtain opened. He told her and she told me. I bet DMarks ends up in the principal's office on Monday morning!"

"Totally will. He's pretty mad at us right now, but we told him not to go backstage like that."

"He clearly has a knack for finding trouble."

"And he never seems to learn!"

"I noticed! So what are you planning to do today in the city?" asked Michelle.

"A few of us want to head over to Rockefeller Center to skate under the tree. Want to come?"

"Love to!" said Michelle. "But I also want to go to Tower Records to pick up Carole King's new album."

"That's all you girls listen to! What's it called?

"Tapestry."

"Funny name for a record. By the way, where's Tower Records?"

"Times Square, silly!"

"Oh. That's not far. I'm sure we can find it."

"You can't miss it. Kinda dominates over there."

"Okay then, we'll just follow you!" Charlie said with a mock salute and a smile.

"Groovy!" Michelle was always the first to use the popular new buzzwords.

Charlie was happy that she would be in his group, although it also kind of terrified him. Then again, if anything could help him overcome his fear of talking with girls, it would be her playful and lively personality.

The Christmas Amble was a very popular thing with the youth group. New York City was an exciting place, and there were so many great seasonal spots to visit, like the giant Christmas tree at Rockefeller Center, FAO Schwarz, Central Park, St. Patrick's Cathedral, Macy's, the animated windows at Saks Fifth Avenue and Lord & Taylor to name just a few. But Reverend Higgins always insisted that there be a service connection to youth group activities. So each year, the group held bake sale fundraisers with the proceeds going to The Salvation Army.

It was an easy equation. Once their train arrived at Grand Central, they'd head out to midtown and listen for the first bell ringer they could find. Then, each kid would help stuff the money raised from the bake sales into the red collection pot. This allowed Reverend Higgins to mix a little practical theology with the fun of spending a day in Manhattan. After that, the group was allowed to split up into clusters to go wherever they wanted. Senior high schoolers helped keep tabs on the younger ones.

Charlie, Michelle, and a few others headed up to Rockefeller Center. Reverend Higgins enthusiastically went along with them. Growing up in the Berkshires, he loved outdoor winter activities, so it wasn't surprising that he ended up first on line at the skate rental area. Soon, everyone was lacing up their skates and getting ready to stride out onto the iconic ice rink.

Concerned she might fall, Michelle asked Charlie to hold her hand. That was all it took to set off an explosion of head-to-toe anxious feelings for Charlie. Then, something amazing happened.

The moment he had her hand in his, the nervousness and anxiety began to subside and everything seemed totally fine as they glided around the rink. There was a nice chemical reaction bubbling up, and Charlie felt incredibly relieved. He and Michelle both were smiling inside and out. After a while, she got used to the rented skates and felt comfortable on the ice.

"I think I'm okay now. You can let go," said Michelle.

He squeezed back harder. "You better hold on for just a while more. I don't want you to fall."

Michelle had a gift for reading people and their motives. Along with her ultra-honest outlook, nothing got past her. "Liar! You just want to keep holding my hand," she said, now locking her arm around his, which Charlie found greatly enjoyable.

Charlie felt he was absolutely living his best life as he and Michelle skated, stopping here and there to lean up against each other on the side rail and take in the classic holiday scene. He felt like he could have skated with her the rest of the day, but soon enough, the forty-five-minute session came to a close. Charlie, Michelle, and the rest of the group reluctantly left the ice, returned their skates, and got back in their street shoes. From there, they made their way up the Promenade and out to Fifth Avenue.

Reverend Higgins then led them across the street to St. Patrick's Cathedral. The soaring rib vaulted ceilings and stained glass windows were awe-inspiring. Everyone slid into a pew on the south transept while Reverend Higgins gave a brief history lesson on the basilica. While he was talking, the organist began to play the huge pipe organ, making a sound unlike anything they had ever heard before. It also drowned out Reverend Higgins' resounding voice, which was not easy to do.

After spending a little time enjoying the sights and sounds at St. Patrick's, they exited out the huge bronze doors and went across 49th Street to see the decorated windows at Saks Fifth Avenue. That year, *Swiss Family Robinson* was the theme for the renowned animated window displays. Michelle enthusiastically noted it right away.

"Remember last summer they showed that movie at one of the outdoor movie nights at the middle school? Me and my family were on a blanket next to you and your mom and dad."

"Yes! One of my favorite movies! Those summer movie nights are the best!" Charlie didn't even realize it at first, but they somehow had begun holding hands again.

Off to the side of the last window, there was enough condensation for Michelle to draw the shape of a heart with their initials in it. From there, they turned north toward Central Park and Reverend Higgins pealed off to go to one of his favorite bookstores. After crossing 57th Street at Columbus Circle, they strode to the park through the southwest entrance near the endless rows of holiday gift kiosks.

The group was walking along happily steeped in holiday cheer when, all of a sudden, a tattered, hulking homeless person stepped out in front of them. He was wearing layers of threadbare coats and towing a small shopping cart behind him with a broken wheel. It overflowed with discarded odds and ends. As they stood face-to-face with him, he made eye contact with Charlie, held out his soiled hand and, in a barely audible voice, asked for spare change. None of them had ever seen a homeless person before, let alone been approached by one. They were confused and frightened; after all, New York City could be a dangerous place at times. Just then, Charlie experienced a head-to-toe warm feeling and heard Sky reassuring him, "It's all right, Charlie. He won't hurt anyone. He's just looking for some help so he can get something to eat."

Charlie turned around to reply but realized that Sky was not there. It happened again! He had clearly heard Sky's voice as though they were standing side by side. Without further thought, he reached into his pocket. All he had was the five-dollar bill his dad had given him for food that day. He glanced at it in the palm of his hand. It was a lot of money, but he didn't see any way he could just ignore this person. His mind raced, and his heart ached. Not only was this man without a home, he had somehow gotten to the point where he was asking complete strangers for money. *How could it be?* he wondered.

It occurred to Charlie that he didn't have any idea what it might feel like to have an empty stomach. Nor did he have a clue as to what it might be like with no place to call home. *Doesn't this man have any family he can turn to?* he wondered. These thoughts played off Sky's words. Bible lessons that placed an emphasis on being mindful of those who are less fortunate also flooded his mind.

Time seemed to slow down as they all looked into the eyes of the homeless man, who now seemed ashamed to be asking. It stunned each of them to the point where they couldn't quite think or act with any kind of intention. All except Charlie. He reached out to the homeless man with his five-dollar bill. "Here you go, sir. It's all that I have." The man took the money, glanced down and away, then moved on with a nod and a quiet "bless you." The young group just stood there, trying to digest what had just happened. It took a while before they regained their composure.

Finally, Michelle broke the silence. "That was your lunch money!"

"It's all right," replied Charlie. "I think maybe he needed it more than me."

"But you'll be hungry later!"

"It's okay, I'll survive."

"I've heard of homeless people, but I've never met one. Weren't you scared?" She looked back over her shoulder to make sure he had continued on his way.

"Kind of at first, but then I heard Sky giving us encouragement."

"What? *The Sky?* What does that have to do with anything?" She looked up.

Charlie realized he was causing still more confusion and just decided to let it go.

"Come on, let's just keep walking. There's lots more to do before we catch our train home."

"Wow. You know what? I think you're out of sight," said Michelle. As they started walking, she happened to glance down and noticed a smattering of beautiful white feathers near where they had been standing. *Now where did they come from?* she thought.

One of the others in the group mentioned that his parents told him not to give money to homeless people because they might use it to buy alcohol. "I don't know what he'll do with that money, but I do know that I'm no worse off for having given it to him," responded Charlie. "Hopefully, it will help get him through another day."

They kept strolling along, stopping at different places like the Central Park Carousel, the zoo, and Wollman Rink. Charlie remained preoccupied by the encounter. He tried to shake it off but couldn't quite get over the unsettling experience. They looped around to the west side of the park and came out on 72nd Street and Central Park West.

"See that building? That's the Dakota, where John Lennon lives with Yoko Ono." Charlie, of course, knew who John Lennon was but had not yet developed much of an interest in the music culture. He probably couldn't name more than one or two Beatles songs if his life depended on it.

"Paul's my favorite Beatle. Who's yours?" asked Michelle.

Here we go again! The question left Charlie stammering, but he was game to play along. "Um, I kind of don't really have one. What's the drummer's name? Bingo? I'll pick him. Bingo." Michelle gave him a bewildered look.

"Okay, I realize that I said you were hopeless with all that sports stuff all the time. And actually, that comment kind of confirms it. But ya know what? I'm going to make you a special project anyway. When we get to Tower Records, you're taking a crash course on popular music and I'm going to be your teacher!"

The group walked south down Broadway and eventually reached Times Square and Tower Records. Michelle picked up her Carole King album and then took Charlie around the store.

"Let's see. Do you like rock music? Like, you know, loud stuff? If so, try Deep Purple."

"I've heard of them. 'Smoke Over the Water,' right?" Another cringe-worthy moment for Michelle.

"Okay, I'm going to just ignore that one. You could also try Grand Funk or Led Zeppelin."

"Funny names for musical groups. I don't get it, a lead blimp? Makes no sense."

"Okay. Just work with me here. Let's see. Do you like Southern rock? If so, you should try The Allman Brothers or Lynyrd Skynyrd."

"Huh? Leonard Who?"

Michelle just looked blankly at Charlie for a moment. "Stay with me here. Maybe easy listening is your thing? If so, try James Taylor and Carly Simon. They're married, you know. Personally, James Taylor is my favorite."

"Really? Then shouldn't it be James and Carly Taylor?" That one kind of caught Michelle off guard, but she just plowed forward.

"If you like really innovative stuff, try this band." With that, she pulled out the latest album by Emerson, Lake & Palmer. "There's also Yes and Genesis."

"Genesis? There's a band named after the first book of the Bible? Do they play hymns or something?"

"This might be a bigger project than I thought," Michelle looked at Charlie and sighed. On the way to the cash register, she grabbed a copy of *Tiger Beat*. She couldn't resist the head shot of Bobby Sherman on the cover.

"C'mon, you guys," Michelle said to the group. "We only have about twenty minutes to catch our train home. We better book!" It would take ten or fifteen minutes to walk back to Grand Central. They got there just in time to catch the 4:30 p.m. train. Standing right outside the first car on the boarding platform was Reverend Higgins, pocket watch in hand, checking the time.

"Rule of thumb. If you're on time, you're five minutes late!" he said as the group hustled onto the train just as the doors began to close.

In the back section of that train car, a lively exchange of stories was underway from the rest of the youth group on the places they had been and the things they did. Some went to the observation deck of the Empire State Building. Others went down to Greenwich Village. A few wandered around the Theater District while others visited the United Nations. One group of girls went to Macy's, but, to their disappointment, none could find anything they wanted to buy; Reverend Higgins immediately dubbed this "The Miracle on 34th Street!"

Charlie, Michelle, and the others from their gang sat in a six-seater with Reverend Higgins. "Well, that was a long, tiring day. As my friend Dr. Cook likes to say up at The King's College, *I feel like a missionary before furlough!*" said Reverend Higgins as the train began to roll north out of the Park Avenue Tunnel. "So tell me, what did you do after St. Patrick's?"

"We hiked through Central Park, then made a stop at Tower Records in Times Square," said Charlie.

"You didn't waste your money on the infernal thing they call music these days!"

"What's wrong with our music?" asked Michelle.

"Torture. Pure Torture! If it has to be plugged in, it isn't an instrument and it doesn't make music. It makes noise!"

"Cat Stevens has a new song out, and it's all acoustic. Plus, I heard it sung in church recently. It's called 'Morning has Broken,'" said Michelle.

"So now they're stealing from our hymnal? I might have to call the church's copyright office," said Reverend Higgins in jest.

Then Michelle quickly changed the topic. "We met a homeless person in Central Park. He seemed so sad and so broken. He asked if we had any spare change."

"Well, yes, there is a bit of a homeless issue in Manhattan these days," said Reverend Higgins. "That's one reason why we do the midnight run every other Saturday night."

"Charlie gave him a five-dollar bill!" said Michelle. "It was his lunch money!"

"It was all I had! I couldn't just ignore him," Charlie chimed in.

"Generous as the sun in springtime! Well done, Charlie. You must be hungry! Here, have a piece of my pretzel." With that, Reverend Higgins pulled off a hunk of the soft pretzel he had just purchased from a street vendor outside Grand Central.

"The Bible says that God loves a cheerful giver, so three cheers for Charlie!"

Charlie managed a tiny bit of a smile but still was preoccupied by his newfound awareness of how some people live without adequate food, shelter, family, and friends. He wondered why it was that he was so blessed to live in a warm, safe home with a loving family. The fun rush of being with friends on a day's visit to the city collided with this unsettling new bit of insight.

"Remember, Charlie, our Lord and Savior didn't have a place to call home," mentioned Reverend Higgins. "He often slept under the stars and relied on the generosity of others for things like food and shelter. I believe it makes him smile each time we help someone in need. So always try to err on the side of generosity!" Charlie absorbed that and realized it was true. Jesus himself was without a home.

"The Bible also tells us that when helping others you might be entertaining angels without even knowing it. I'd say it's a very good thing you did," added the reverend.

"Thank you, sir. But I still feel bad for that man and for others like him. I just don't know how he could have ended up like that. I had heard of homeless people but kind of figured that, ultimately, everyone at least had a place to live."

"He does have a place to live! It's called Central Park."

"But I meant a warm, safe home with a family and food and TV."

"Well, yes, I see what you mean. I'm tempted to lean back on what Paul the apostle told us—that in this world, we see through a glass darkly. Things won't always make perfect sense to us, and some things we'll have to wait till we get to heaven in order to understand. In the meantime, Charlie, count your blessings, give God credit, and try to live in step with him and his ways. That's all we can do for now."

"I guess so," said Charlie, still feeling like there must be something that could be done. The rest of the train ride continued with talk about the day's activities. As they approached Tarrytown, a cobalt twilight sky slowly melded with the orange glow of the west leaning sun. On the eastern edge of nightfall, a handful of stars began to sparkle. Charlie and Michelle were looking out the window across the Hudson as one of the stars suddenly shot across the horizon.

"Did you see that?" asked Michelle.

"The shooting star? Yes!"

"Far out! Quick, make a wish!" she said, closing her eyes. After a brief pause, she enthusiastically asked what he had wished for. "C'mon, spill or I'll tickle you!"

"Okay, okay. I wished that the man we met in Central Park will have a warm place to stay tonight and from now on."

Michelle just looked at him with wonder. "And that, Charlie Riverton, is what makes you different from everyone else."

As the train approached Scarborough Station, everyone began to gather their things and exited onto the platform. Charlie suddenly and happily realized that he and Michelle were holding hands. He had no recollection of reaching out for her hand, nor her for his. It must have just happened naturally as they got ready to detrain. The feeling was indescribable. He thought about it, smiled, and decided to consider it an early Christmas gift.

CHAPTER 9
TREE TRIMMING

===

For he will command his angels concerning you to guard
you in all your ways. On their hands, they will bear
you up, lest you strike your foot against a stone.
—Psalm 91:11–12

It was a brilliant Sunday morning as Sky arrived at Briarcliff Congregational Church for worship services. In fact, the sun was shining so brightly that it was melting some of the snow and ice, even though the temperature was well below freezing.

Reverend Higgins spotted Sky and welcomed him with one of his trademark long-lost brother greetings. Charlie was also happy to see him and hopped out of his pew to say hello.

"Hi, Sky! Glad you made it!"

"Thanks, Charlie. Where else would I be on a Sunday morning?"

"Right on, Sky!"

"If there's a better way we could be using our time—it hasn't been discovered yet!"

Charlie began to enthusiastically point out a few things about the noteworthy sanctuary. "Did you know that this sanctuary and manse were built by Walter Law himself?" he asked. "The stained windows are real Tiffany glass, and the cobblestone Norman tower was modeled after the church Mr. Law attended growing up in England."

"Outstanding!" said Sky. "And the exposed wood beams in the ceiling remind me of the Briarcliff Lodge building at King's College."

"That makes sense, Mr. Law built that too! They have a copy of his original pledge card in a glass case. Five dollars per week! That was a ton of money back then."

"Freely he received, and it sounds like freely he gave," replied Sky. "Just like the way you're ministering to Mr. Olson." As the processional hymn began, Sky settled into the pew alongside the Rivertons. Once again, Charlie was left wondering exactly how Sky knew about his relationship with Mr. Olson. And, once again, Sky timed his comment so that the situation didn't lend itself to further inquiry from Charlie.

That day, the sermon's theme was based on the Good Samaritan. Everyone present had heard this text preached many times before. However, Reverend Higgins gave it a slightly different context. Instead of using the story to illustrate *how* to do the right thing, the emphasis was on *why* we should do the right thing.

"No one in history was more mindful of those who were in need than Jesus himself. And his loving example should inspire us to live in the same compassionate way," he began. "The Good Samaritan showed that love has no prejudice. His heart didn't just pump blood. It pumped compassion. It would have been easy for him to pass by, but he felt the needs of the injured person and he took action."

The reverend looked around the congregation. "How many people do we pass each day who are in need? If you want to love and serve God, then love and serve others! People begin to heal when they know someone cares. The example set by the Good Samaritan gives us the ultimate standard of living!" He raised his hands to the rafters for emphasis.

"And by the way," he continued, "give from the heart. Make it real. Do it as though you're doing it for Jesus himself! Don't go out there looking for a pat on the back. Remember, this life is not all about *this life*, and your life is not all *about you*."

The sermon resonated deeply with Charlie. It was easy to see how that theme could apply to people like Mr. Olson. He was a good and decent man who had been an active contributor to the local community. But everyone had acquaintances and even family members who just seemed driven to make things more difficult for others. It was a whole other story when it came to people like that. A "biblical conundrum," as Reverend Higgins used to say.

Sky was equally keen on what he heard. As he was leaving, he stopped for a brief greeting at the back of the sanctuary. "You know, Reverend, I met the Good Samaritan once!" said Sky, smiling broadly. Reverend Higgins paused, cocking his head sideways looking at Sky, then broke out in knee-slapping laughter. Sky flashed his megawatt smile as he shook hands and made his way out the back of the sanctuary. Charlie rushed outside to catch up with him as he walked across South State Road.

"Are you going to begin to attend church here, Sky?"

"Yes, I think so. It's really convenient for me, and I like the pastor a lot," replied Sky as he bent down to make a snowball, then threw a perfect strike—hitting the trunk of a giant Maple tree about fifty yards in front. Charlie couldn't believe his eyes. No one can throw a snowball that far, let alone hit their target squarely. "Nice throw! Bet I can hit the STOP sign at the exit of the parking lot!"

"You're on!" Charlie packed a tight snowball, took a few steps, and let it fly. Direct hit!

"That's some mighty fine shooting, partner," deadpanned Sky.

"By the way, Sky, where are you living while you're in town?"

"Up at The King's College. Dr. Cook had an extra room in the president's mansion, so he offered it to me."

"Dr. Cook is really nice. I'm not surprised he did that. How did you come to know him?"

"Oh, let's just say it was an answer to a prayer."

"A lot of us had babysitters who were students at King's. They were all such nice people."

"Not surprising, considering that many are studying to go on to seminary or missionary work."

"Yeah, right. So will you be at Gooseneck this afternoon?

"Sure will!"

"You should come to coffee hour across the street at Beebe Hall. They have all kinds of refreshments and stuff. I'll walk over with you."

"Sounds good, Charlie. Tell me, were you as impressed with that sermon as I was? I've heard a lot of sermons based on the Good Samaritan, but never one in that context."

"Yeah, I guess we sometimes try to do good works in order to impress others or to score points with God, but what God wants is for us to simply treat others the way Jesus did, with honest compassion and kindness."

"Right you are, Charlie. So what are you up to this afternoon?"

"Actually, me and my mom and dad are going over to Arcadian Gardens to get our Christmas tree! It's our favorite family tradition."

"Sounds fantastic, Charlie. Have fun!"

"We will, Sky. Thanks! It's an all afternoon thing that includes lights, decorating, Christmas music, and some of my mom's Christmas cookies too."

"What could be better? Say, by the way, I wonder if Mr. Olson will be decorating a tree this year?" asked Sky. He knew the question landed squarely upon Charlie's heart.

As they entered the Parish Hall, Charlie pointed to the north wing and mentioned that was where all the Sunday school classrooms were. He then walked Sky into the large common area where Bob and Joan Beicke, Dave and Jelane Caspar, and Jim and Karen Neel were serving up cups of coffee—and great conversation as well. Charlie introduced them all to Sky, knowing they'd make him feel completely comfortable on the spot.

"So where are you from?" asked Bob.

"Oh, I'm from up north," said Sky.

"Me too! Buffalo. Born and raised. Anywhere near your neck of the woods?"

"Actually, you'd have to go farther up than that to get to where I'm from."

"North of Buffalo? You're a better man than me," said Bob

"Some good skiing up that way," chimed in Jim and Karen.

"Oh yes, lots of things to do all year round."

"So you're from north of the border?" asked Jelane.

"Yes, you could say that," answered Sky.

"I'm from the Detroit area, and we used to drive up north to go camping each summer. It's God's country up there!"

"We call it God's country where I'm from too." Sky smiled broadly.

"Sky, you seem familiar for some reason. Is it possible that we've met before?" asked Dave.

"Gosh, Dave, I'm new to these parts, so I have to doubt it."

"Actually, I was thinking of the west coast of Africa. I realize it's that's kind of out of left field, but Jelane and I were serving in the Peace Corps, and our village lost access to fresh water."

"Oh wow, what did you do?"

"Well, it was the pumping mechanism—which was ancient— and it just gave out, so there wasn't much we could do except pray!"

"Sounds like a desperate situation, Dave."

"It was! Then, out of nowhere, a tall, muscular man showed up in the village. No one had ever seen him before, but he asked if he could take a look at the water pump."

"Was he in the Peace Corps too?"

"We never did find out who he was, but we showed him to the well. He knelt down as though to pray, then reached in to try to retune the pump. In just a few seconds, clean drinking water came bubbling out! In the midst of all the celebrating, the handsome stranger disappeared."

Joan interrupted with a plate of donuts. "Here, Sky, I picked these up fresh at the bakery before church. They go great with a cup of coffee!"

"Why, thank you, Joan. Don't mind if I do. But please cut me off if I try to come back for seconds!" Others began to come over to introduce themselves to Sky, who, as usual, was beginning to draw a crowd. Dave would have to pursue his conversation with Sky another Sunday.

After church that day, the Rivertons made their way over to Arcadian Gardens in Ossining to pick out a Christmas tree. As they strolled down the rows of trees, Christmas music was being piped through the outdoor PA system. Throughout the lot, there were metal barrels filled with smoky fires so people could stop to warm their hands as they looked for the perfect tree. The aroma of burning tinder added to the rustic scene.

Every year it was the same. Mr. Riverton preferred a Norway Spruce, but Charlie and Mrs. Riverton were partial to Douglas Firs. Midway down the fifth row, they found a Scotch Pine, which made for a good compromise.

"I think we have a winner!" said Charlie.

"Good find, son! Looks like a full, healthy seven-footer," said Charlie's dad.

"A perfect fit for our picture window. We'll take it!" said Charlie's mom. One of the workers made a fresh cut at the bottom of the trunk, and Charlie helped his dad haul the tree to the cashier. After paying for it, they took it to the car where Mr. Riverton meticulously tied it to the roof for the short ride home. Charlie's mom also picked up a wreath and some poinsettias.

They pulled out of the parking lot and drove north on Route 9. Charlie's mom wanted to go up and over Ridgecrest Road so they could enjoy the soaring views of the Hudson River. They turned left at Scarborough Presbyterian and headed up Ridgecrest to a small parking area near the intersection with Long Hill Road West. There, they could look out at the widest part of the river at one of the prettiest views on the East Coast. They all agreed: It never got old.

"If you ever know someone who doesn't believe in God, just take them to this spot," said Charlie's dad. Charlie and his mom glanced at each other with a half-smile. He made it a point to say that every time they stopped here, but the sentiment was not lost on them. As they continued to drive down Long Hill Road, an idea came to Charlie. It was a little bold, but he was full of conviction.

"Mom, Dad, do you remember the conversation we had with Ms. Berkshire after church? You know, about the adopt-a-pet-day at the SPCA?"

"Sure, Charlie. But if you're thinking about adding to our family, I don't think there's any more room at the inn!"

"Actually, I wasn't thinking about us." He paused and drew a breath. "I was thinking about Mr. Olson." Charlie's parents turned to each other and exchanged a knowing glance.

"Um, so you want to adopt a dog for Mr. Olson?" asked his dad reluctantly.

"Well, yeah. It makes a ton of sense to me. We were inside his house the other day after he slipped on the black ice. It seemed so cold and empty. It makes me think Ms. Berkshire's right…a big, happy dog would add life to his home."

"Son, this is one of the reasons why we love you so much. You have a very good heart, and I'd say this will make for a great conversation over dinner tonight," replied his mom.

"Well, okay, but we're all here in this car and the SPCA is open until four this afternoon, and it's just up the street from where we are."

"Right, Charlie, but it's kind of unusual to just adopt a dog and give it to someone without warning," his dad pointed out.

"But this is the season of giving! Not only could we do something nice for Mr. Olson, we could save a dog that needs a home too! Why don't we just drive over and see what dogs are available now?" His parents looked at each other again. Their son had a special knack for being gently persistent with people—and even though he might be putting them on the spot, he never made them feel uncomfortable and they'd usually end up doing things they otherwise might wait on. Still, they tried one more diversion.

"Now? But we have a tree to decorate," said his dad.

"Right, and we have all the lights and decorations to take down from the attic," added his mom.

"But think of how much more we'll enjoy decorating our tree knowing Mr. Olson won't be alone tonight." Checkmate. There was no way Charlie's parents could ignore that last comment. Without saying a word, they took a left turn and headed toward the SPCA.

After parking their car, they strolled over to where the dog runs were. This was not going to be an easy task. There had to be twenty-five fantastic dogs to choose from and all of them had a "pick me, pick me!" look on their face. In the midst of all the rambunctious pups, most of whom were barking and jumping toward the fence on their hind legs, they came across an older chocolate Labrador Retriever. He was the only one that wasn't bounding around woofing and yapping. Instead, he just casually looked up at them in a totally unflappable way as if to say "Hi there, Rivertons. I'm glad you made it…I've been waiting for you and I'm ready to go to my new home." It immediately did a number on them.

"Mom, Dad, how do you like this one?" asked Charlie.

"What a beauty!" his mom exclaimed.

"That's a fine-looking dog. And he has a great temperament!" added his dad.

"Can I help you with anything?" asked one of the staff.

"Yes, we think we'd like to adopt this chocolate Lab," replied Charlie.

"Oh! Great choice! He's the sweetest dog we've had in a long time. He was brought in two weeks ago, but we had to put him through a battery of vaccinations. Today is the first day we were able to put him up for adoption!"

"Oh wow! Seems like it was meant to be," cheered Charlie.

"If you'll follow me, we just need to fill out a few adoption papers, then you can take him home with you." The worker opened the fence, put a leash on the pooch, and handed it to Charlie, who got down on both knees to give out hugs and ear scrunches. Then, they all headed to the office.

Charlie's mom was beaming. "I think I'm getting a very good feeling about this. The look on this dog's face is amazing. It's as though he's reassuring us that this is all according to plan. If he could talk, I think he'd be asking us to tell him about Mr. Olson!"

"And what would the suggested donation be?" Charlie's dad asked the worker.

"Actually, we don't really have one. Whatever's in your heart will be completely fine." Mr. Riverton paused, smiled, wrote out a check, and handed it to him.

"Whoa! Your heart is pretty full today! Thank you very much!"

"No … thank *you*! It's a very good thing you're doing with our four-legged, fur-bearing, flea-bitten friends here."

Charlie was overjoyed. Down again he went on his knees exchanging hugs with their new chocolate-colored friend. Mr. Riverton tossed a throw blanket over the back seat so their living, breathing Christmas gift could hop in. Human and canine passengers were euphoric as they drove over to Mr. Olson's house

"So, Charlie, when we get to Mr. Olson's you should be the one to ring the doorbell. By the way, we haven't even given him a name. Any ideas?" asked his mom.

"Not really. Wait. How about Taylor?"

"Taylor? That's a nice name. Where did you come up with that?" inquired Charlie's dad.

"Not sure. It just came to me." Charlie decided not to mention that it was James Taylor's last name, who was Michelle's favorite singer. Soon the Rivertons were parking their car and walking Taylor up the steps to Mr. Olson's front door. He answered in his customary white dress shirt and tie.

"The Rivertons! What a nice surprise! Please come in. Hey, who have you got there, Charlie?"

"Hi, Mr. Olson! This is Taylor. We just adopted him over at the SPCA."

"Well, he's a beauty! I used to have Labrador Retrievers when I was a boy."

"Oh, wow! What a great coincidence!"

"So Barnes and Noble are going to have a new brother?"

"Well, actually, we brought him here for you. We thought he could help keep you company." Mr. Olson was stunned and speechless. His eyes instantly misted over, and his lower lip trembled. Mr.

and Mrs. Riverton stood off to the side, politely looking down at the ground. After a long pause, he dropped to one knee, cradled Taylor's head and face in his hands, and looked deeply into his new dog's eyes. Their bond was immediate, full of warmth and meaning as though Taylor was saying, *I understand and I'll be here for you from now on.* Mr. Olson gathered himself and stood back up.

"I...I...I don't know quite what to say. How can I ever thank you for a gift like this? In my entire life I—" His voice tapered off, unable to complete his thought.

"I'm so glad you like him! Merry Christmas, Mr. Olson!" shouted Charlie. "I can't wait to visit him when I come to work in your yard." The Rivertons bent down to pat Taylor's forehead one last time, then turned to get back in their car.

"This will give me a few extra things to take care of this afternoon. I'll have to run over to the A&P for some dog food and supplies," said Mr. Olson. "Then after that, you're going to get a nice, warm bath, Taylor." The Rivertons could see how energizing this was for Mr. Olson. It wasn't just that he'd have another living soul under the same roof. He now had a purpose, something to take care of every day. As they backed out of the driveway, Charlie saw Mr. Olson take out his handkerchief to blot away tears of joy.

"Thank you, Charlie. That was a beautiful idea you had. We're very proud of you," his mom said, reaching over the car seat to squeeze his hand.

"I agree, son. You might have saved two lives today," concurred his dad. Charlie felt good inside for sure. But he wasn't completely satisfied. The wheels were turning, and somehow he felt there was more to be done. *There are other Mr. Olsons out there*, he thought.

Once home, Charlie helped his dad muscle the tree off the top of the car, through the front door and into the living room. It filled the whole house with the crisp, breezy scent of pine. Decorating the Christmas tree each year was a time-honored and highly anticipated tradition at the Rivertons' house. Charlie hauled ornaments and lights down from the attic, while his mom made eggnog and played Christmas records by the likes of Frank Sinatra, Nat King Cole, Bing

Crosby, and Burl Ives. Meanwhile, his dad got the fireplace going with a warming kindle.

In particular, Charlie loved taking out the crèche his dad made by hand years ago, then carefully setting up the figurines, which were individually wrapped in newspaper. Some of the newspapers were older than Charlie, and he enjoyed scanning headlines and stories from before he was born. Charlie's dad was a very capable man with tools and anything that required being put together. With ease he had the tree standing perfectly upright in the stand and started to drape the string of old-time large bulbs. Charlie followed behind, uncoiling the wires as they went.

"Got to have an even distribution of lights, son. And when a bulb needs to be replaced, mind the succession of colors—red, white, blue, orange, green."

As they attached the last portion of lights to the tree, Charlie and his dad stepped back to review the work they had done. After making a few minor adjustments, they stood side by side and Charlie's dad draped his arm across Charlie's shoulder.

"Nice work, son. Couldn't have done it without you. You want to climb under to pour water in the stand?"

"Yes, sir!" said Charlie. This was one of his favorite responsibilities in the whole process. Once the lights were up and in place, Charlie's mom started to hang the ornaments. Many were heirlooms passed down through at least two generations of Rivertons. Charlie loved the familiar, musty scent of the boxes from being stored in the attic all year round. Of all the ornaments they had, the one made of glass depicting the manger scene was his favorite. They also had two ornaments with pictures of Boxers for Barnes and Noble. Just a few years ago, someone had left them in the park without collars or tags. Once the town identified them as strays, Charlie convinced his parents they had to adopt them. They were part of their family ever since.

After the ornaments were hung, it was time to place the individual strands of tinsel, which Mrs. Riverton did in the most painstaking way, one at a time. All three drew back to enjoy the fruits of their labors while they soaked in the joy of this annual moment.

"Mom, Dad, do you think Mr. Olson will be decorating a tree this year?" Charlie asked.

"Wow, Charlie, that's an incredible question. I hope he'll continue their family traditions, even though now he'll have a curious pup on his hands," replied his mom.

"Maybe we could bring one to him?"

"I like the way you're thinking, son," said his dad. "If it's not too late, maybe the youth group could make that into a service project?" Charlie promised to take it up with Reverend Higgins and the rest of the youth group at church. With the glow of the lights from their tree in the foreground, Charlie soaked in the warmth of Christmastime. He felt blessed for his parents, his friends, his home, and his community. Then, for no apparent reason, his thoughts turned to Sky. He couldn't get around the notion that they had crossed paths for a reason…*but why, and for what?* he wondered.

Chapter 10

Best-Laid Plans

Put on then, as God's chosen ones holy and beloved, compassionate hearts, kindness, humility, meekness and patience.
—Colossians. 3:12

It was a blustery December day, which made a relatively mild temperature reading feel more like the high 20s. In spite of the wind chill, Charlie and his friends walked uptown after school for their usual buttered roll and a Coke at Joe Weldon's. On this particular day, there was no practice after school, so the boys headed to Gooseneck Pond afterward.

"Have you guys heard about this new movie channel that's coming out on TV?" asked DMarks.

"You mean Home Box Office?" asked George.

"Yeah, HBO," replied DMarks. "You can get all kinds of movies right on the TV in your home!"

"Why would you need that? Don't you have enough to watch? Besides, in case you haven't noticed, our homework assignments are getting more involved all the time," said BB.

"I've heard of it, but they're mostly offering R-rated movies, so that's not going to get very far at my house," said Charlie.

"Oh, here we go. You mean to tell me that if you had an opportunity to watch movies like *M-A-S-H*, *Shaft*, or *The Exorcist*, you'd pass just because they're rated R?" asked DMarks.

"As a matter of fact, I would. I have no desire to see people getting beat up, tearing their clothes off, using bad language, and doing all kinds of other things that aren't right."

"You are such a Richie Cunningham!" said DMarks.

"Thank you for that compliment! Besides, who wants to watch TV if you can be out doing this kind of stuff."

"I'm with Charlie," said BB. "I don't think this whole cable TV/HBO thing is going to fly. Most of what they show is junk anyway."

"Junk? Obviously, you losers don't have the same level of appreciation for the arts that I do!" said DMarks.

"Do you believe he's actually trying to tell us that he has an appreciation for the arts?" said George. "His idea of art is doing stuff on his Etch A Sketch!"

"Oh, sit on it!" As they crossed behind the middle school, past the tennis courts, and over to Gooseneck Pond, they spotted Sky working the fire pit.

"Hi, guys," said Sky. "How goes it?"

"It goes fine. What's up, Sky?" said DMarks. "I was just having a word with my associates on the virtues of the arts."

"Somebody stop him. Whatever it takes, just stop the blathering idiot!" said BB.

"DMarks thinks this HBO thing is going to be big. But he just wants to be able to watch dirty movies," volunteered George.

"Shut up, you meathead!" replied DMarks.

"Come on over here and make us," said BB. The result was a three-man pile up rolling on the ground, testing out moves from the Saturday morning pro wrestling matches they watched on TV. Charlie and Sky watched from the sidelines, amused by all the play-acting and clowning around.

"Charlie, I might be off base here, but I was wondering if everything is okay? Seems like something might be troubling you." Sky knew full well that Charlie felt distressed about people like Mr. Olson, but he needed to engage him in order to help him come up with a solution. Charlie didn't expect Sky's query, but his dad always told him that if someone asked an honest question, it required an honest answer. So a bit reluctantly, he began to answer Sky.

"I know that the Advent season is supposed to be joyful. And I feel it. I honestly do. But at the same time, I can't stop thinking about Mr. Olson and others like him. He just seems so painfully lonely these days. And now, with Christmas coming, I wonder where he'll be and if he has anyone to be with," said Charlie.

"Ah. Right. That's a tough one," said Sky. "You guys did good when you helped him that morning when he slipped on black ice. Do you know if he has any children or relatives?"

"I don't think so. His house is right over there," Charlie pointed across the park. "Wait, how did you know about us helping Mr. Olson?"

"Oh, well, it's hard to hide our good works," responded Sky, gesturing with his palms up. "You were saying?"

Charlie paused, shrugged his shoulders, and continued, "Well, I've never noticed any visitors or cars in the driveway, not even on the days after Mrs. Olson passed away. Now, he just seems to stay in his house or sit over there on that park bench looking out across the ball fields. It shouldn't be like that. No one should be alone, especially at Christmas."

"Yes, I've noticed him sitting by himself, staring out toward the pine forest. He does seem lost right now. Although that dog you adopted for him was a fantastic idea! That had to have helped."

"Yeah, he seemed really happy when we surprised him. But still, I think he really misses his wife and their daily walks uptown. Wait, how did you hear about the dog we adopted and gave to him?"

He had done it again. *Am I getting too old for this?* Sky wondered. "You live in a pretty small town here, Charlie." Sky quickly jumped up to stomp some errant sparks from the fire. "Let's both just keep him in our prayers," he added casually, knowing full well that prayers alone would not satisfy Charlie's need to do something to help.

"I do pray for him, and I'll continue to do that. But I also feel like I should be doing something real for him."

Sky looked at Charlie with a gratified look. "Well, Charlie, God relies on us to do his handiwork here on earth. If you keep thinking like this, you'll be building up treasures in heaven before you know it."

"But…I haven't done anything."

"You've done more than you think. Plus, I'm sure your all-in feelings on this will lead to something really good. It's a can't-miss! Just keep thinking and praying about it."

"I'm glad you think so. I just want to try to help people like Mr. Olson to feel like they're not alone."

"You're a man after God's own heart, Charlie. The way you're thinking is a great book of James example of putting our faith into action in this world."

"Do you really think so?"

"I know so! Tell ya what, it's almost dark and there's no school tomorrow. Do you think it would be okay with your parents if you and I split a pizza over at Vinny's in Pleasantville? My treat. It will give us a chance to continue our conversation."

"I think that would be a great idea!" exclaimed Charlie. "My mom should be pulling into the parking lot in a few minutes, I'll ask her."

That night at Vinny's, Charlie told Sky how this whole thing with Mr. Olson seemed to open his eyes to lonely people wherever he went: the lunchroom at school, around town, by the youth center at the Pump House. And he felt it all the more against the backdrop of houses glowing with Christmas lights and filled with the warmth of family and friends.

"I bet that there are tons of people who wish they had some companionship at Christmas."

"Charlie, I think you're right. Not just on the point you made, but in wanting to get hands-on involved. You're never more like Jesus than when you're focusing on the needs of others rather than your own." The longer they talked, the more inspired they became. Sky did his part by asking leading questions, one after another.

"So there's a problem out there for us to try to solve. It's sad, but lonely people are a reality, even here in Briarcliff," said Sky. "We can't reverse the reality of their lives, but do you think there's a way we can try to help them feel less lonely?"

"Maybe we can get people to send extra Christmas cards to people who are going through a tough time?"

"What a nice idea, Charlie! And it would definitely help lift people's spirits as they visit their mailboxes." Sky's response made Charlie think that he had to go further. "How about if we raise money to buy a bunch of Christmas hams and deliver them on Christmas Eve?"

"Another great idea! A full stomach always makes a person feel better. Not sure how much fun it would be to eat Christmas dinner alone, though."

"Christmas caroling!" Charlie added, humming a little tune. "We can organize a group of carolers to go to homes where we know there are shut-ins."

"I love it! A few carols should cheer up anyone, at least for a little while."

"Right...a quick visit won't really solve anything. Wait, I've got it! What if we set a goal to make sure that no one in all of Briarcliff is alone on Christmas Day?"

"I think we're reading each other's minds! So what's our plan?" There were more leading questions from Sky; he wanted Charlie to own this.

"Well, what if we started a campaign to encourage families to invite people like Mr. Olson to their homes on Christmas Day?"

"Perfect! If all we do is commit ourselves to being a friend to lonely people, we'll have lived a significant life. Do you think we might need help though?"

"Maybe we can try to get the different community groups involved around town."

"I think you're onto something, Charlie!"

"Reverend Higgins often mentions the ecumenical group of religious leaders he's part of—I bet he'd be glad to bring something like this to them. We could also go to the School Board, the PTA, the Boy Scouts and Girl Scouts, and even the guys doing paper routes to help publicize this." Charlie's face flushed red with enthusiasm.

"Reverend Higgins is also great friends with Rabbi Steinert. Maybe he can encourage people to open their homes during Hanukah!"

For the next two hours, they were talkative as magpies. The next thing they knew, Vinny's had begun to close for the night. It was ten o'clock! Where did the time go? They hustled out the door to Sky's pickup truck. He drove as fast as he could down Pleasantville Road to drop Charlie off at home. They hurriedly pulled into the Riverton's driveway. As soon as the truck was in park, they both got out. Mrs. Riverton was standing at the front door watching for Charlie.

"Mrs. Riverton, it's my fault," Sky called out as they rushed up the walkway. "We were having pizza and discussing an important new mission, and time just got away from us."

"That's okay, Sky, now that I know you both are safe. I was a little worried, but I figured you lost track of time."

"Thanks, Mom. Can't wait to tell you and Dad what Sky and I are going to do around town. It's going to be really cool."

"Well, you can tell us as you head upstairs to get ready for bed!"

"Good night, Mrs. Riverton. You have an outstanding son."

"Would you be surprised to know that you're not the first person to tell us that?" said Mrs. Riverton with a laugh.

"No, I wouldn't be surprised, but I'm also sure that you'd never grow tired of hearing it!"

"Right you are, Sky. Thank you for being so kind to our son. Good night. Bless you!"

"Thank you, Mrs. Riverton. And blessings to you and your family too." Sky backed out of the driveway with a broad smile and a glad heart.

CHAPTER 11

JE NE SAIS QUOI

And let us consider how to stir up one another to love and good works.
—Hebrews 10:24

It didn't take long before people all around town were talking about Sky. He stood out in a crowd, especially in a small town like Briarcliff Manor. But aside from his physical traits, everyone agreed that he had a unique and instant likeability. Something about him put people at ease and created a sense of peace and concord.

In addition, he seemed to have a *World Book Encyclopedia's* worth of local knowledge. All anyone could conclude was that he must have done a lot of research on Briarcliff before he arrived. Perhaps, he was also burning the midnight oil with Dr. Cook, absorbing as much as possible about area history and personalities around the community. He also had an inexplicable ability to see and understand what was needed in advance of any given situation. "How'd he know that?" was a commonly heard phrase all around town accompanied by quizzical looks and shoulder shrugs.

More's the pity, life in Briarcliff wasn't completely trouble-free for Sky. Being so well put together and particularly handsome, he garnered all different kinds of attention. His brand of masculinity made him especially appealing to the single women around town. This was especially the case with Suzie Berkshire.

Suzie herself was quite attractive but somehow never managed to settle down with the thing she most wanted in life: a strong, good-looking man who would bring her flowers, rub her shoulders after a long day, and most of all, be a really good listener. She dated more than her share, but for one reason or another, none of the guys were quite right. With each passing year, she seemed to intensify her search. However, Briarcliff being a town made up mostly of families with children, there never seemed to be any new, available candidates.

For those reasons, she took immediate notice when Sky came to town. Right away, she went to the Recreation Department to speak with Henry under the guise of suggesting how to handle demand for pool tags for the next summer. Henry had a great way of accommodating the people of Briarcliff. So many of the things they sought him out for were somewhere between unreasonable and frivolous. Suzie took only a minute to make her suggestion.

"By the way, I noticed you have a new person on your staff looking after skating activities this year. He seems familiar, is he from around here?" she asked not too innocently.

A telling smile came across Henry's face. Now he knew the real reason why she had come in. "His name is Skyler Northbridge," replied Henry. "He's just passing through town on his way up north. He's staying in an unused room in the president's mansion at The King's College."

"Well, where's he from? How old is he? Is he married?" Suzie said in a rush.

"Haven't had the time to ask him about his personal life. But he seems to be attracting a lot of attention from the ladies around here," said Henry, having a little fun stoking Suzie's knee-jerk exasperation.

"Is that so? Well, I don't know who you're referring to, but I think that's just very forward of them. The man has a job to do, they should just leave him alone."

"Uh-huh," mumbled Henry.

"Well, if he's staying up at the college…that means he's eating their cafeteria food. I should cook him a real dinner. The poor thing probably hasn't had a square meal since he got here."

Another "uh-huh" from Henry.

"Maybe I'll invite him over Sunday night. Do you know what kind of food he likes? How about a pot roast? No, Italian, all men loooove Italian. But that can be messy to eat, especially with his beard and all. Chicken! Roast chicken with all the fixings!"

Henry gave one final "uh-huh" out loud, then muttered "Good luck, Sky" under his breath.

Suzie was dressed up like a Christmas postcard, complete with matching ear muffs, scarf, and mittens. After she did her reconnaissance with Henry, she headed to the pond with a plan to be noticed by Sky, although it was a bit risky as she hadn't been on skates in years. She spotted him working by the fire pit and found a place to sit down near where he was.

"Excuse me, sir, can you help me tighten my skates?"

"Of course! That's well within my job description. Brand new skates? By the way, my name is Sky," he offered as he knelt down on one knee in front of Suzie. His being so close and positioned as if he was about to propose, caused her to lose her bearings for a moment. "I know. I mean…hello!" she stammered. "I'm Suzie. You're pleased to meet me. I mean, I'm pleased to meet you!"

Sky looked her right in the eyes. He was smiling broadly as he continued to lace up her skates. "Mutual!"

"Welcome to Briarcliff. Will you be staying for a while?"

"Well, we'll see how it goes, but I'll probably have to head up north after the holidays," replied Sky as he reached for his skate key.

"But we've hardly had time to get to know you. What's the rush?"

"The person I work for is very busy. He gets lots of requests, which create all kinds of projects to work on." As he spoke, he tightened each lace.

"Really. What type of work do you and he do?"

"It's kind of entrepreneurial and it's really hard for him to turn down requests, so we do a little bit of everything."

"That sounds like an awful lot for just you and him."

"Oh no, there's tons of guys like me. It's a very large operation."

"There's more *like* you?!" Suzie asked excitedly.

"Sure! We're all over the place. We just don't always get noticed. So tell me, how's the real estate business this time of year?"

"At the moment, slower than a herd of stampeding turtles."

"Yeah, I guess people are focusing more on the holidays than house shopping."

"Yep. But it's okay, people like me get a little extra time to slow down a bit. Wait, how'd you know I sold houses for a living?"

Sky just smiled that warm grin. "Okay, that should do it!" he said, standing up and putting the skate key in his back pocket. "How do they feel?"

"You're welcome. I mean, thank you, they feel good," purred Suzie.

"Fantastic! And may I say that's a nice outfit you have there. Right down to your mistletoe patterned socks!" Nothing could have made Suzie's day more than a compliment like that from Sky! The only thing she could think of is that he was even more handsome up-close! She tried to prolong the conversation as it suddenly dawned on her that she was never much of a skater and had not been on skates since she was a teenager. Still, she had no choice but to get up and head out onto the ice. Sky could tell by the way she stood up that she was a bit unsteady on her skates. Ankles curved in and knees buckling, he knew this had potential for trouble and offered to help her down the slope to the pond.

"Why, thank you, Sky, you're such a gentleman. I don't think these darned skates fit right after all. Oh well, I guess I'll have to keep my jumps and axles to a minimum," she joked.

"That would be a good idea until you break them in." What happened next did not go unnoticed by anyone on Gooseneck that day. Suzie's problem wasn't that she couldn't get going; it was that she didn't know how to stop. Although she managed to get through a couple of shaky loops around the pond, she took one lap a bit too wide and ended up skating right into the sawhorse barricades, which separated the pond from the hillside. She absorbed the impact with her midsection and spun head over heels, her momentum causing her to swirl face down, spread eagle on the ice. Sky saw the whole thing and could hardly contain his simultaneous amusement and alarm as he rushed out to make sure she was okay.

"I meant to do dath!" Suzie spit out, along with some snow, trying to hide her embarrassment as Sky reached her.

"You okay, Suzie? Any breaks or bruises?"

She looked at Sky completely mortified. "Just my ego I guess. Although, I might have banged my head."

"What part did you hit, the hard part? I was afraid you might have broken your anterior hallux!" Suzie welcomed his concern, although she didn't realize he was mostly just trying to cheer her up. She also had no idea that anterior hallux was Latin for "big toe." Sky helped her back up on her feet and got her steady again. From there, he slowly towed her off the ice as she kept her feet stationary and shoulder-length apart and tried to maintain her balance. Once safely back on land, Sky walked her up to a cozy spot by the fire.

"I guess you think I'm a bit clumsy out there." Suzie giggled.

"Not at all! You did a great job clutching that sawhorse!"

"Here's a cup of my special recipe hot apple cider. Why don't you dry off a bit here by the fire? The Briarcliff College Glee Club is getting ready for their annual carol sing." Each year, the all-girls college came to Law Park to carol for the skaters. From there, they'd wander uptown wassailing all the way.

Suzie looked sideways to see who else might have seen her gaffe, then pulled her hood up over her head, hunkered down, and wished she could just disappear. She noticed Matt Gilroy was out on the ice, repositioning the sawhorse barrier. In spite of her feeling sheepish over what just happened, her indomitable spirit compelled her to invite Sky over to her house for Christmas.

"Oh, Sky! I heard you're staying with Dr. Cook up at The King's College. Since you don't seem to be married or anything, why don't you come over to my house for Christmas dinner?" She hesitated for a split second. "You're *not* married, are you?"

"Married to my work, you might say, but otherwise unattached. As for the invitation, you're very kind and I greatly appreciate it. Not sure what my plans are just yet, but I'll let you know for sure."

"I'm known for my roast turkey! I also make my stuffing from scratch and have a special recipe for cranberry chutney." She removed her skates and put her boots back on.

"I actually think I've heard that!"

"No need to bring anything, just yourself. And your appetite," she added coyly.

"Noted. Thank you again. Very much appreciated."

"You're very much welcome." Suzie was liked by all, but she could come on a bit strong. After all, as the owner of Yates Real Estate Agency, she had to be forward when asking buyers and sellers to part with their money.

"By the way, if you'd ever be interested in buying a place around here, I'd be glad to show you around." Suzie wasn't backing down. "They just built a row of townhouses on Ash and Jackson Roads. They're charmers and perfect for a single man like you!"

"I'm all set up at King's but will let you know if that changes."

"Well, what if you just came over for dinner tonight?" she feigned being spontaneous. "I know Mr. Kenney does a good job with the food service up there at the college, but surely you'd enjoy a home-cooked meal!"

"Actually, Dr. Cook invited me for dinner tonight. In fact, I skipped lunch today to save extra room for Mrs. Cook's chicken and rice!"

On that, Suzie's enthusiasm took a hit. Nothing she tried was working. She grabbed her skates and gave Sky a breezy goodbye as she headed to her car to reconsider her plan of attack. *This isn't a lost cause,* she thought. *And I won't give up so easily!*

CHAPTER 12

PARKER AND THE PARK

And we know that for those who love God,
all things work together for good,
for those who are called according to his purpose.
—Romans 8:28

Parker Jones was a glowering, bristling, complex, tinderbox of a person. He had an above-average IQ, excellent athletic size, and basketball skills that at one time, were good enough to make the starting team on the intercollegiate level. Then, as was the case with the hopes and dreams of so many other young boys, Vietnam got in the way.

In his younger days, Parker was a model young person, popular with his peers as well as teachers and adults around town. He lettered in football, basketball, and baseball at Briarcliff High School. In the summer, he was captain of the swim team. An all-league standout in any sport he played, several upstate schools offered him sports scholarships. He chose St. Bonaventure, which was a regional powerhouse in college basketball.

It was a great decision from the beginning. He was the sixth man during his freshman year, subbing in for starters at any position except center. As a sophomore, he made the starting five. But with an eye toward the heroic generation that went before him, Parker felt compelled to "do his part" by enlisting in the United States Army. No one tried to talk him out of it. A lot of well-meaning young people were doing the same thing. In fact, it was a source of pride for many parents and adults who came of age in the World War II generation.

After moving out of his dorm room and lugging all his things back to Briarcliff, he spent about a week visiting family, friends, past teachers, coaches, and others around town until it was time to ship out. His first stop was Fort Benning for a few weeks of boot camp. From there, it was straight to Khe Sanh.

From day one, it was clear that almost nothing was the way he thought it would be. In a short amount of time, he'd become very well-acquainted with the harsh realities and brutalities of war. In spite of it all, he willed himself to remain positive with each new day.

During his second year in-country, Parker got word that his mom had been killed in a car accident crossing the Taconic Parkway at Buckout Road. He took it hard. His dad died many years prior after battling lung cancer. Suddenly, he was all alone and striving just to stay alive in a harrowing, treacherous jungle on the other side of the world.

His fellow infantrymen became his family. They tried their best to offer support and condolences. Still, he felt isolated and without a home. At the same time, fighting for his life and the lives of those around him in active combat zones each day toughened his mettle until he was able to be furloughed.

Conscientious to the core, his commitment to the cause and his keen instincts and endurance earned him a rapid succession of promotions, all the way to command sergeant major. Each day, there were intense skirmishes, snipers, and sneak attacks. But after facing the Viet Cong, they also had to be constantly aware of crocodiles, poisonous snakes and spiders, even Indochinese tigers, and other dangerous things.

He saw and experienced things that no human being should have to face. Fellow soldiers were cut down all the time, many before their twenty-first birthday. They had all arrived with visions of hope and valor but, eventually, most became hardened by the unforgiving realities of war. Worst of all was the killing of innocent civilians. After a while, Parker and many others began to wonder about why they were even there.

Because of the passing of his mother, the Army offered to end his tour of duty early. But Parker insisted on returning to his platoon after a few short weeks sorting things out back in Briarcliff. He was inspired by Captain John McCain who had been in the news recently. After his plane was shot down, he had been captured and imprisoned at the Hanoi Hilton. When his captors learned that McCain's father was an Admiral in the US Navy, they offered to free him as a publicity stunt. But McCain declined, insisting on staying with his comrades until they all were released.

As things began to unravel with the handling of the war effort, morale took a hit and drugs crept into the ranks. The GIs took note of anti-war protests back home, which led to a growing sense of aimlessness. It didn't help that the Pentagon seemed to keep holding them back from accomplishing what they were sent there to do.

By the time the Paris Peace Accords were signed, Parker had become jaded like so many others. He was angry at the world and hooked on opium, marijuana, and mescaline. At first, the drugs seemed to help him cope. But, as is always the case, they ultimately made things worse as he spiraled deeper into his bleak and cheerless reality.

After the war, he arrived back in Briarcliff feeling like a stranger and found a job as a teacher and coach at nearby Sleepy Hollow High School. But it didn't last. His behavior was erratic, and his temper unchecked at times. The school principal had no choice but to ask him to leave. For the one-time local sports hero and member of the National Honor Society, this was a ruinous blow.

Eventually, he found work at Barker's Department Store over in the Arcadian Shopping Center. He also drove a cab for Henry's Taxi and was a golf caddy in-season at Briar Hall Country Club. As the chip on his shoulder got bigger and heavier with time, his abrasive demeanor became a problem wherever he went. This left Parker with a lot of time on his hands.

One day while rummaging through boxes of long-forgotten things, he found his old library card. It was tattered and worn but still valid. He put it up to his nose and breathed in deeply. The stock scent transported him back to the days of his youth when he and his father would visit the library on Saturday mornings to bring home some reading material for the coming week. The card itself seemed to connect him to happier times and a sense of normalcy—both in stark contrast to his shattered life now.

As he struggled each day to put one foot in front of the other, he'd take that card to the library and use it to check out books on religion, philosophy, and political commentary—hoping they would help him to make sense of the world around him. He'd perch himself on a park bench and devour one book after another in a ferocious way. Every once in a while, he'd pace back and forth over by the War Memorial Monument having imaginary arguments and debates out loud with establishment VIPs. It was his way of digesting the material and understanding its practical application. He didn't care if people thought in doing so that he'd gone crazy.

After a while, he could no longer bear to live in the house he grew up in now that everything had changed so harshly. So he decided to sell his parents' home over on Whitson Road and purchase one of the wash houses on North State Road. These were small cottage-style homes that were originally built by Walter Law to provide housing for employees who took care of the laundry for Briarcliff Lodge in its heyday, hence the name "wash houses."

He reached out to Suzie Berkshire, who reluctantly got involved helping him with the whole process. "I still don't know why you'd want to sell your parents' lovely home and move into one of these little old wash houses. They're much smaller, and they don't have as big a yard, either. Plus, Chief Daggett says that the way they were built back in the 1920s makes them a bit of a fire trap. If one goes, they all go!"

Parker didn't say much in response. "I guess I just want to break from the past. Forge a simpler life. Besides, I need some bread."

"Well, if you're looking to downsize, this will do it!" Although Suzie was doing most of the talking, she was secretly assessing Parker like one of her listings. *With a haircut, shave, and some decent clothes, I bet he'd clean up nicely*, she thought. Hidden beneath the layers of his harsh experiences, she could sense a certain warmth and authenticity.

Parker mostly looked down as he talked, seldom making eye contact. His mind was made up, and he told Suzie he'd like to move forward. As they began to discuss the details, he realized that there was something he liked about Suzie, something that perhaps reminded him of his own mother. *I miss the presence of a strong woman in my life,* he thought. *And for sure, there'd never be a dull moment with this one!*

But Parker had a lot of baggage to unpack and deal with and would sometimes find himself in a restless fit. To deal with his deeply conflicted emotions, he'd pitch a tent and set up a campsite on the raised train bed left behind by the old Putnam Railroad Line. On certain nights, you could look down from the hillside by the library and see a small campfire glowing in the distance by the extreme east side of the pine forest. Somehow, the primal nature of living outdoors helped him to get centered. While there were concerns about his campsite, the village police just left him alone as no one wanted to provoke him.

He often vented his bitterness on passersby around Briarcliff. To him, they were privileged, sheltered, and shallow. In particular, he seemed to zero in on the younger set as they made their way through Law Park. He felt they were disrespectful toward their country, generally irresponsible and had it way too easy.

Increasingly, he made it a point to make his menacing presence felt. Sometimes he would do that simply by standing at a distance, glaring at the kids as they swam, skated, or played ball. Other times, he might jog or ride his bike alongside them uttering threatening comments. He would even go to the Briarcliff Police Department to file complaints based on fabricated accounts of kids acting in unruly, disruptive ways.

It was a sad display. In his short life, he had gone from being a very well-liked, exemplary kid, to a wretched, miserable being who each day strode deeper into the depths of the tormented nightmare that had become life as he knew it.

Naturally, Charlie and his buddies sometimes felt intimidated by Parker Jones. Yet Charlie tended to look on him with sympathy and even a desire to help. He couldn't relate to what Parker had been through, but he wanted to let him know that someone cared about him and the tough, trying life he had been served. Given all his issues, Parker did have a legitimate sixth sense about others and detected a sincere heart in Charlie. That being the case, he tended to leave him and his friends alone for the most part.

That night, there was a varsity basketball game at Todd School. The Rivertons decided to attend and sit with Charlie after the shenanigans that took place the last time. Not surprisingly, the Bears cruised to an easy victory behind a 22-point effort by the sharpshooting Mike Patterson. Afterward, as they were driving to the Briar's for dinner, Charlie saw Parker walking along North State Road by himself. Wanting to offer some act of kindness, Charlie was glad to hear Sky suggest that they invite him to dinner. He was about to respond, but this time, he stopped himself. He knew Sky was not there in the car.

"Mom, Dad, there's Parker Jones! Can we invite him to dinner with us? I bet he'd love someone to eat with." It was a bold suggestion, and Charlie's parents were understandably hesitant.

"Nice idea, son, but let's not put Parker on the spot. Sometimes people would rather have advance notice of an invitation like that," said his dad.

"I agree with your father, Charlie," added his mom. "Besides, we only made reservations for three."

Young as he was, even Charlie could easily counter that one. "Mom, they don't have triangular tables at The Briar's. Each table seats four."

In that moment, Charlie's parents both felt a warm composure come over them. Something was encouraging them to follow their son's lead. They looked at each other and made a snap decision. Mr. Riverton stopped the car, rolled down his window and called out to Parker, who was shocked that someone might actually acknowledge him.

"Hey, Parker! Doing anything for dinner?" asked Charlie's dad. Then his mom leaned across the front seat to encourage him to join. "We're headed to The Briar's, and we'd love to have you along. Our treat!"

At first, Parker was skeptical, locking eyes with Mr. Riverton. "Hey, man. You putting me on? If this is just some kind of game, I'm not interested."

"Not at all, Parker! Are you hungry? C'mon and join us!" said Mr. Riverton.

"Don't mess with me, man. I don't need any hassles!"

"Really, Parker, we'd be delighted to have you with us!" said Charlie's mom. Parker was a few paces from their car. He squinted his eyes and stared at them trying to take full stock of the situation, which he finally decided was cool.

"I dig that you stopped, but I think I'll just be on my way." Charlie rolled down his window and got involved. "But, Parker, we're going to The Briar's for Granny Burgers. It's just up the street!"

Parker began to let his guard down. Deep inside, he had a heart for kids. "Granny Burgers? I haven't had one of those since before Nam." He approached the car, leaned down, and once again tried to scope out the situation. After a minute or two, he shrugged his shoulders, opened the back door, and slid into the seat next to Charlie.

The Briar's was a very popular restaurant owned by the O'Hagans, a large and popular family in town. It had a special kind of ambiance that made visitors feel right at home. In the main dining room, red-and-white checkered curtains and tablecloths lent a cheerful accent, while a fireplace big enough to stand in added a touch of timeless character. Down the back hallway toward the bar area, the swinging door to the kitchen was constantly in motion with hot plates and generous portions coming out in rapid succession. And truth be told, Briars coleslaw was legendary.

That night, the place was filled with Briarcliff families. Heads turned when the Rivertons arrived with Parker. No one dared to associate with him and his volatile personality. But Charlie didn't mind, he was just happy to be able to pass along some act of kindness to a person who otherwise would be all alone.

As if to return the favor, Parker seemed to experience a bit of renewal as they sat down near the fireplace in the main dining room. He was polite, soft-spoken, and conversational. He focused on Charlie and told stories of what Briarcliff was like when he grew up there. He spoke of his experiences in Boy Scouts, summer camp in the park, and playing sports, particularly the rivalry with next-door Pleasantville. He also sprinkled in a few stories about the jacket and tie canteens they used to have in the Parish Hall at Briarcliff Congregational and how nervous it made him to ask girls to dance. Charlie was captivated, absorbing each word like a sponge.

"One time," said Parker, "we were playing basketball against Pleasantville on a Friday night. The place was packed to the rafters, literally! It was a tight game, and it was getting rough out there," continued Parker. "We all were taking elbows and jabs, but we were giving it back as good as we got. The score was tied with five seconds left...and we had the ball."

"That sounds so intense!" said Charlie.

"It really was! Coach Prewitt saw that Pleasantville had just switched to a man-to-man defense against us, so he called timeout. On the sideline, he ran through a bunch of different plays then picked one we had never used in a game before. It was called 'Student Body Trap.' That meant I'd stand at the top of the key just above the foul line, while the rest of the team was down on the blocks underneath the basket on either side of the paint. Coach wanted Gene Cadman to inbound the ball because he was always so calm under pressure. Gene held the ball over his head super high to counter the defender who was jumping up and down waving his arms. Then, he slapped the ball with his right hand...the signal for the rest of the guys to charge up to where I was...creating a pick on the guy guarding me."

"And then you pivoted and cut down to the basket?" Charlie interrupted in anticipation.

"Right! Then Gene lofted the ball up toward the rim. I leapt up, caught the ball, and laid it in at the buzzer for the winning basket.

"So cool!" said Charlie.

"And that, Charlie, is the first time anyone had ever seen an alley-oop play in the history of Briarcliff sports!"

"Far out!" said Charlie.

"Yeah, that was a great game. Got carried off the court by my teammates that night. I'll never forget it." Then, in a flash, he turned dark. After a prolonged pause, he quietly reflected. "Little did I know that I'd be carrying friends off the battlefield a couple years later." The juxtaposition of the two stories struck a painful chord as he tilted his head down and just stared at his plate.

Charlie's parents struggled for something to say. Luckily, Coach Cadman happened to be at The Briar's that night and stopped by their table. If he couldn't cheer Parker up, nobody could.

"Park!" said Coach. "Great to see you! Nice crowd tonight."

Parker brightened slightly as he stood to greet Coach Cadman and his lovely wife, Peggy, who was a cheerleader at the game Parker just described.

"Parker was just telling me about the time you tossed up a game-winning alley-oop at the buzzer," said Charlie.

"What a play that was! All credit to Coach Prewitt for calling it. But Parker was the only guy who could have pulled it off," said Coach Cadman.

"Don't be so modest, Gene. It took a perfect pass," said Parker, pointing at him.

"Pass? I was trying to shoot the ball. It was wide right like most of my shots!" Coach responded, laughing out loud and pretending to shoot.

"Your time will come too, Charlie," said Parker.

"Charlie, this guy was our go-to whenever we needed a bucket," said Coach.

"Yeah, but Gene was our coach on the court. He ran the offense and called the plays," said Parker. "He always knew exactly how we needed to set up on offense and defense."

"We had another play called 'Park It,'" said Coach. "Parker would position himself on the right wing, then cut down the lane off the Cincinnati Double Stack—our bread and butter offense—and around to the far left corner. I'd hit him with an overhead pass just as he pivoted to shoot the ball. It was money in the bank every time!"

"Too bad they didn't have a three-point line back then!" said Charlie.

"He would have averaged fifty points a game if they did!" said Coach. The conversation went on like that for a while. Charlie was captivated by the stories and felt really good about how animated Parker had become. After dinner, the Rivertons walked outside and offered him a lift home. Feeling high on the positive evening and fun recollections, and full of uncharacteristic optimism, Parker decided to walk the short distance to his house.

As they waved goodbye, Mrs. Riverton looked down at Charlie who was sporting a very gratified and contented smile. She reached out to give him a hug. His dad joined in with a warm pat on the back. Looking over Charlie's shoulder, Mrs. Riverton noticed a few feathers scattered around in the parking lot. *Wherever did those come from?* she thought, as they all headed to their car.

CHAPTER 13

CAROLS AND LIGHTS

*Therefore, welcome one another as Christ has
welcome you, for the glory of God.*
—Romans 15:7

The annual tree lighting ceremony and carol sing was always a twice-circled event on most people's calendars. It was a true community event that made room for people of all faith backgrounds.

The tradition was started almost one hundred years ago, when Walter Law himself planted a Norway Spruce just inside the park at the corner of Pleasantville and South State Roads. Over the years, it grew to about eighty-feet tall. Each year, the Public Works Department would string the tree with lights, and it would stay illuminated through New Year's Day.

Before the ceremony began, Mr. and Mrs. Holmes headed over with batches of "Old Man's Milk," their special eggnog recipe which had been handed down through generations. On the way, they stopped at Mr. Olson's house to see if they could coax him into coming out for some holiday cheer. They rang the doorbell and, to their glad surprise, they found him in the midst of a good day. Mr. Olson had answered the door in his customary shirt and tie, a dress code he held over from his days working at IBM.

"Hi, Jack, how we doin'?" asked Mr. Holmes.

"Oh, fair to middling," replied Mr. Olson. Just then, Taylor came trotting to the front door to enthusiastically greet the visitors as only rescue dogs can.

"Wow! Who's this?"

"This is the latest addition to my family, Taylor!"

"When did you get him?"

"I didn't! Charlie Riverton adopted him at the ASPCA and brought him here as an early Christmas gift for me." Mr. Olson got slightly emotional as he recalled this act of kindness and reached for his handkerchief.

"Wait a minute, Jack, I'll join you!" said Mr. Holmes, all choked up and pulling out his own handkerchief. "I wish someone would give me a dog someday!"

"Well, beware what you wish for! You never know what can happen with young Charlie Riverton around town."

"Anyway, we're heading to the tree lighting and we wondered if you might like to join us?"

"Plus, we also wanted to park in your driveway, if you don't mind!" Mrs. Holmes smiled.

"How nice of you to think of me! I was going to just watch from my living room window but I can't resist your eggnog, so count me in! C'mon inside while I get my coat." They stepped inside and noticed that he was playing Christmas records on his portable Victrola, which they took as a positive sign that he was beginning to turn a page.

"Do I need my scarf? How cold is it out there?" asked Mr. Olson.

"How cold? Cold enough so that lawyers have their hands in their own pockets!"

They all laughed as Mr. Olson put Taylor on a leash, and the group headed across the street and down toward Gooseneck Pond. Once there, they mingled and sipped and shared, which made them even more—and more—popular as the evening wore on.

Other residents got into the act dressing up like shepherds and wise men. One gal who worked over at Muscoot Farm in Katonah brought a goat and a lamb along to try and create a manger scene. The Cliff Notes acapella singing group from Briarcliff High School was also on hand. They strolled around in poinsettia-red scarfs and stovepipe hats with sprigs of holly fastened to the brim. Their job was to lead the Christmas chorusing, and they always succeeded at getting everyone involved, especially when they corralled groups of people to sing and act out "The Twelve Days of Christmas."

Troop 18 of the local Boy Scouts, under the stable leadership of Joe Laylak, started and kept the bonfire going so that everyone could warm up as needed. Of course, Joe always used it as an opportunity to teach lessons on outdoor fire safety, and the scouts responded with the utmost sense of duty and responsibility. Just in case of an emergency, the volunteer fire department was also on hand with their pumper truck, which was parked over by the library.

Suzie Berkshire was making her happy presence felt, bouncing from one conversation to another and laughing all the way. At one point, as Sky was walking by, she happened to turn from a conversation, stumbled over a pinecone, and tripped right into him. That his chest was rock solid did not go unnoticed. She looked up, he looked down.

"Merry Christmas, Mr. Northbridge," she said softly, looking up in an almost star-struck state.

"And Merry Christmas to you, Ms. Berkshire!" Sky nodded, hands braced on her shoulders from their sudden fender-bender. Suzie was smitten and stayed put, not backing off an inch. She almost felt light-headed standing so close to him, and wished she could stay there like that for the rest of the night. After an awkward few moments, Sky cleared his throat. "Um."

"Yes? Is something wrong?" inquired Suzie.

"Not really, but ah, you're standing on my foot."

"Huh? Oh, sugar honey iced tea! Why am I always so clumsy around you?"

"It's okay, I have another foot!" He gave a little hop to prove it.

"You always say the nicest things. Meanwhile, I'm clumsy as a blindfolded, drunken mule!"

Sky smiled broadly, gave Suzie a quick hug, and they both continued mingling.

Considered somewhat of a local celebrity, Brooke Astor came down from her estate, Holly Hill up on Scarborough Road, to join the festivities. She was one of the most prominent socialites and philanthropists in the country. That year, she was driven in a Ford Model 30 Roadster, the same one her father-in-law, John Jacob Astor, drove while winning the inaugural Briarcliff Manor Trophy Race in 1908. She came partly to enjoy the warmth of Briarcliff's extended family and also to donate the car to the Briarcliff Historical Society in memory of her husband, Vincent.

Tradition called for the mayor to provide a brief speech, then lead the countdown to the tree lighting. Amusingly enough, there always seemed to be a problem with the lights themselves. For one reason or another, at least one strand on the tree usually failed to illuminate, leaving a large, dark gap of unlit evergreen. Because of that, everyone always held their breath when it was time to flip the switch.

Once it was sufficiently dark, Mayor Kennard stepped onto the platform to offer a holiday greeting to one and all. "How blessed we are to be here in this safe and beautiful place we call home, to enjoy the bonds of fellowship with friends, family, and neighbors. May the special joy of the holidays be with you all. Now, it's my distinct honor to continue the tradition started by our esteemed founder, Mr. Walter William Law. Let the countdown begin for this year's lighting of the oldest tree in Briarcliff!" He gestured to everyone to join in. "Ten. Nine. Eight. Seven…"

Mrs. Finnie was on the podium with the mayor. She was born in Briarcliff and a descendant of one of the original families. She and the mayor both had their hand on the switch. When the crowd roared out a final "Zero!" they did their part, and, on cue, the top and the bottom of the tree lit beautifully, but the strands covering the middle section remained dark. The team from the Public Works Department looked on in dismay, scratching their heads. Meanwhile, the usual cheers and jeers rose up from the fun-loving crowd.

"Try kicking it!" yelled the Glascott brothers.

"Hey, let's get this tree lit before my clothes go out of style!" needled another well-meaning townie.

"Humbug!" heckled another.

The mayor and Henry looked at each other in a blushed state of panic. Then, Sky calmly sprang into action. With his trademark smile and can-do way of approaching things, he strode right over to the tree. After checking a few connections and then laying his hands on the fuse box, he asked the mayor to flip the switch off and on again. In an instant, the entire tree lit up. In fact, it didn't just light up, it was brighter than anyone could ever remember. It was the same tree and the same amount of lights as every year, but somehow, some-way, it seemed a hundred times more vivid. Everyone was enchanted by the dazzling radiance.

"I bet they can see it all the way to the North Pole!" said Mr. Marville.

"Well, then, let there be lights!" said Mayor Kennard over the loudspeaker. He put his hand over the microphone, leaned over to Henry, and whispered, "How'd he do that?"

"I don't know, but it doesn't surprise me one bit!" replied Henry.

"Let's hear it for Sky, keeper of the lights!" said the mayor. A splash of applause broke out as Sky smiled, waved, then tried his best to fade into the background.

"Bravo, Sky. Well done!" said Reverend Higgins. "The light shines in the darkness, and the darkness has not overcome it!"

"Thank you, Reverend. Love the reference to John 1:5!"

"Well, now, I'd say that's a right special knowledge you have of your Bible!"

"Where I come from, it's required reading!"

"I'd love to know where that is! Sounds like heaven to me." Sky gave a chuckle, then made his way over to Troop 18 to see if they needed a hand with anything.

Next up was the lighting of the Menorah. To do the honors, Rabbi Steinert from Congregation Sons of Israel stepped up to the podium to stand alongside Mayor Kennard. "Shalom! Welcome everyone! It's my privilege to now light the Shamash candle. In light-ing this candle and with the illumination of this splendid Christmas tree, I'm reminded that we bring light into this world when we do good for others. May God bless you all with peace and light!"

Thankfully, there were no mishaps. As the center candle of the handsome menorah lit perfectly, the mayor and the rabbi embraced with hearty pats on the back. Reverend Higgins was nearby the platform and helped his older and greatly esteemed friend down the steps.

"How'd I do, Reverend?" asked the rabbi.

"Ya done good, Rabbi! Now c'mon, let's go toast the holidays!"

"Well done, Rabbi!" Sky called out, hustling over to shake hands. "Got to let our light shine whenever we can!"

Rabbi Steinert looked deeply into Sky's eyes. "Something tells me you have a great deal of experience in doing that."

"Glory be to God, sir!" replied Sky as the two men embraced.

The evening went on from there: neighbors acted like family, acquaintances became friends, and friends felt like one's nearest and dearest. By the end of the evening, there was a virtual town-wide hug-fest as people began to say good night. A few free-spirited people got a bit slapdash overindulging that night, so Sky walked them to his pickup truck and helped lift them into the payload to drive them home in the frosty night air.

"Bundle up, guys, and hold tight," said Sky, tossing them a few fleece blankets. Just as he was about to put the truck in gear, he noticed Lady Astor waving, indicating that she wanted to have a word with him. Sky rolled down his window as she approached.

"Young man! Most impressive how you got Mr. Law's tree to light up so magnificently."

"Why, thank you, Mrs. Astor. All it needed was some hands-on attention. No big deal."

"And you're modest too. I like that in a man. Lovely. Skylar, I believe that's your name, can I ask you to give me and my man Ferguson a lift to my home? We just gifted the vehicle we drove here in, and now we have no way of getting back up to Holly Hill."

"I think the payload is kind of full back there, but if you're willing to ride in the cab with me, I can have you home in a matter of minutes."

"That would be fine, young man. Ferguson, help me into this lorry, won't you? I'll sit next to Skylar, you can get in after me." Even Mrs. Astor found something uniquely attractive and compelling about Sky. She felt strangely uplifted as they drove along. "I'm told you're staying with Dr. Cook over at The King's College," she said.

"Yes, ma'am, Dr. Bob has been very generous opening his home to me."

"Well, that's just down the street from me, you know. You're welcome to call on me any time if you'd like."

"Mrs. Astor, I'm sure I'd enjoy that immensely. I'm kind of focused on my task here in Briarcliff for now. But if I get a day off anytime soon, I'll absolutely take you up on that. Thank you!"

"But of course...perhaps high tea one afternoon?"

"I've always been a teetotaler, so I'll try my best to come for a visit."

"Lovely. I shall be looking forward to that." Soon, they arrived at the circular entrance of the Astor estate. Ferguson got out and helped Mrs. Astor off the bench seat.

"Lovely time tonight, Skylar. Thank you for the lift," she said.

"Quite all right, Mrs. Astor. I have a few more stops to make now," Sky said with a smile. As he drove along, he reflected on how happy everyone seemed who had attended the event that evening— and all just because it was an opportunity for friends and families to come together. *People needed people,* he thought. Fellowship brought joy. Of course it did! God designed human beings to relate to and help care for each other on this earthly journey.

He noticed that the guys in the back of the truck had begun singing Christmas carols. They couldn't have been much more off-key, but it was music to his ears. He enjoyed a good laugh over it and decided to join in. *There were all kinds of ways to celebrate the season,* he concluded.

CHAPTER 14

BOYS ABOUT TOWN

==

Bear one another's burdens, and so fulfill the law of Christ.
         —Galatians 6:2

Charlie, DMarks, BB, and George left Saturday morning basketball at Todd School to walk uptown for roast beef wedges at Weldon's. Along the way, Charlie told them about bringing Parker to dinner.

"Okay, that's it!" declared DMarks. "Certifiable!! That's what you are. Stark raving certifiable...I still think you need to go to the school guidance counselor for evaluation."

Charlie looked at DMarks and just shook his head, "You don't get it, and you never will. When did it become a crime to try to do something nice for another person?"

"You never heard what happens to nice guys? They. Finish. Last!"

"I don't know about that, Marks," said BB. "Keith Partridge, Greg Brady, Davy Jones...they're all nice guys, and they usually end up fine."

"Okay. First of all, they're all dorks. Secondly, I hate to break it to you, but none of them are real! Third, of course they end up fine—it's scripted that way! They're thespians!"

"They're what?"

"Look it up in your Funk and Wagnall, airhead!"

"Did he just say a bad word?" asked BB.

"Time out, DMarks. Not only are you officially off the rails, you're wrong! The Bible says, *As you sow, so shall you reap.*' If you're a jerk, it will come back to you, which if you'd care to take a look in the mirror, you might notice the truth in what I just said!" lectured George.

"Oh, so now you're a philosopher? Sometimes you have to act like a jerk in order to get what you want. Then, when you get it, you tell me, who won?"

"If we all agree with you out loud, will you shut the heck up?" asked Charlie.

"Try me." With that, all three boys looked at DMarks and told him he was right and they were wrong. "There. See what I mean? Another check in the Derrick Marks win column."

Now that the argument was over, they could get to their regular dribbling contest as their walk continued. There always had to be some kind of competition between them, and seeing who could dribble the ball the farthest without losing control was the key challenge. Extra points were earned for creativity: alternating bouncing the ball off the sidewalk and back onto the road was one drill; bouncing it off cracks in the sidewalk while still maintaining control of the ball was another.

Thomas Mannix was a couple of years older and exceptionally talented at basketball. He took a liking to Charlie and helped him develop his ball-handling and dribbling skills. The latest thing was to dribble the ball back and forth through your legs as you walked along without looking down. It was a very difficult skill to master, but Charlie was ready to unveil it to the others as they headed down Ingham Road.

The guys were in awe and immediately began to attempt the feat, but none of them could go more than one or two steps without losing control of the ball.

"Where'd you learn that?" said DMarks incredulously.

"Thomas Mannix. He can dribble this way better than others dribble regular!" DMarks was jealous and couldn't stop trying to duplicate what Charlie was doing. The boys however were concerned that if he lost control, the ball would bounce into oncoming traffic.

"Dream on, Marks. A spaz like you could never learn this trick," said George.

"Stick it in your ear, *nerd*. I got this."

"Dude, you're about to sink your own battleship. You should take a break until we get into the park," said BB.

"Why are you guys raggin' on me? You jealous of this new ball my parents got for me?" He wouldn't listen. As they made it to the 9A overpass, he bobbled the ball, and it slipped off his fingertips, traveling over the stone barrier and down into oncoming traffic. The ball bounced once, twice, then ricocheted off the front bumper of a car going fifty miles per hour. They couldn't look away as it flew forty-five yards in the air, finally landing near the northbound lane, where it promptly dunked itself right into the headwaters of the Pocantico River. There was no way to retrieve the ball as the current took it speedily downstream.

"My parents just got that ball for me last week!" he croaked out. "I'm so dead."

"A brand-new Spaulding ZiO Excel—gone!" said George. "Those go for forty-five dollars!"

"Well, it should wash ashore down in Elmsford where the current merges with the Saw Mill River. Hopefully someone there will put it to good use!" said BB.

"Yeah, with our luck, it will be one of the guys we'll be going up against when we play Alexander Hamilton in basketball next month!" said Charlie.

"Wait, maybe you can get someone to drive you down there, then buy it back from whoever finds it!" George chimed in.

"You guys are a regular riot. I'm so getting grounded for this," said DMarks, shuffling slowly along with a hangdog look. They made their way through the park, up School Road, and past the pine forest. At Weldon's, they ran into Coach Cadman who was also getting lunch.

"Hi, guys! Give me five," said Coach. "What are you up to?"

"We just came from Saturday morning basketball at Todd School," said Charlie.

"That's great! You going back to the open gym?"

"Yeah, after we get something to eat."

"I'm heading up to King's for the afternoon basketball game against Nyack College. You're welcome to join me if you want to come along!" They were all free until dinnertime, so they jumped at the opportunity. Naturally, DMarks called "Shotgun!" as they piled into Coach's Ford LTD.

"Did you ever think that sort of thing might explain why you have no friends in life?" asked BB.

"Ha! You're just jealous that you didn't call it first!" Once again, the boys just looked at each other and shook their heads. Soon enough, they drove through the entrance and across the campus, where Coach found a parking space by the gymnasium near The King's College Pond. As Coach parked his car, they saw something that caused them all to do a double take.

"Look, you guys! Down by the pond!" shouted George.

"What the?" said BB, as he strained for a closer look.

"How the heck?" said DMarks. While entering campus through the west entrance, the driver of the bus carrying the visiting basketball team must have had trouble negotiating the narrow causeway by the pond. Somehow, the left rear wheels of the bus had gone fully off the pavement and were hanging over the edge as the bus teetered. Sky happened to be walking with Dr. Cook down the hillside from the student center when they saw what was going on.

"Oh, no! It looks like the bus is about to fall into the pond!" said Dr. Cook. "God bless it, it is! Do you think it could tip over sideways?"

"I don't know, but we need to do something fast!" replied Sky. Dr. Cook sprang into action, calling for everyone to quickly get off the bus. But Sky had something else in mind; taking charge, he asked the players and coaches to tack hard on the passenger side. He then swiftly climbed into the driver's seat, put the bus in gear, and gunned the engine. In no time at all, he pulled the entire bus back onto the causeway and up into the parking lot. The redistributed weight had given him the traction he needed to get the bus righted. The boys just stood there with their mouths wide open. It was like a scene from an action hero movie.

"Okay, what just happened?" asked DMarks.

"Banana shenanigans! There's no way—" added BB.

"That bus was on three wheels, and the underbelly was touching the rocks on the edge of the pond. You can't just drive it out of a situation like that," said George, pretending to turn a big steering wheel.

"Uh, that's exactly what he just did. Do you figure there's anyone else who could have pulled that off?" said Charlie, shaking his head. Equally astonishing was the fact that there was no damage at all to the underside of the bus or to the stonework lining the edge of the pond.

"I'm going to have to ask the high school physics teacher about that one," said Coach Cadman. "Even if he was able to drive that thing out of there, how is it that the bus doesn't even have a scratch on it?"

As the visiting team and coaches stepped off the bus, they all paused to take a good look at Sky who just stood by smiling and wishing them a good game. They thanked him, then hurried to the locker room to change into their warm-ups. Dr. Cook glanced over at Sky and grinned. *Of course he did that,* he thought as they both headed into the gym.

"Nice going, Sky!" said Charlie, reaching out to slap five.

"Hi, Charlie! Thanks, buddy," said Sky, slapping the palm of his raised hand.

"You going to the game?" asked Charlie.

"Yep. I'll be sitting with Dr. Cook in the faculty section."

"Awesome. See ya in there."

There was something about the sights, sounds, and scents of a gymnasium that preteen boys found naturally appealing. Admission was free so they walked right in, but DMarks stopped at the phone booth outside the entrance. He picked up the receiver, dialed the 914 area code, then quickly hung up the phone. Some thought that in response, you could trick the phone into dispensing a dime. But it didn't work.

"This pay phone is lame!" he said in frustration.

"You're lame!" said BB.

"Oh, stuff it, you geek!"

"Now, now, let's use words that heal not harm," said George with just the right touch of sarcasm.

The game tipped off, and the boys had a great time sitting with Coach, rooting for King's. With a few minutes until halftime, Charlie decided to head to the boys' room. As he stepped down the bleachers, he passed right where Sky was sitting with Dr. Cook, so he stopped to hang out with them.

"Hello, Charlie. How in the world are you?" asked Dr. Cook. "And thanks for coming out to cheer on our team." Charlie was always amazed how Dr. Cook could remember everyone's name.

"Hi, Dr. Cook. Hi again, Sky!"

"Back at you, Charlie. No hockey today?" asked Sky.

"Well, Saturday is kind of a basketball day for us and when Coach Cadman offered to drive us here to the game, we didn't want to pass it up."

"You should have brought your skates, the ice on our pond is in great shape," said Dr. Cook.

"And it's so big!" said Charlie. "You could have five hockey games going all at the same time! Plus, it's cool to skate over to the island in the middle. Sometimes we find old mittens, scarves, and hats there."

"And knowing you, Charlie, you probably take them to the lost-and-found afterward," said Sky with a broad smile.

"Of course! It's just inside the Lodge building up the hill," said Charlie.

"Good man, Charlie. By the way, let me know if you find any money out there!" said Dr. Cook, laughing. "Say, are you and your friends going to shoot around down on the court at halftime?"

"If it's okay, sure!"

"It's more than okay, but no dunking please," joked Dr. Cook.

"You don't need to worry about that. We couldn't dunk even if we were wearing our moon shoes!"

"Well, you and your friends have fun. And remember to walk with the king today and be a blessing!" Dr. Cook was also a well-known radio evangelist. He used that phrase with his daily radio broadcasts, and it had become his signature sign-off at the end of each program.

As Charlie got almost to the front lobby area, he heard Sky say, *"Bring Mr. Olson home to your house for Christmas."* It startled him and he immediately looked back at Sky, but he was way too far away to be heard. And anyway, Sky was looking down at the action on the court. In spite of the high noise level from the crowd, Sky's words had been loud and clear—and firm as well, like some kind of clarion call. *How did I hear him?* Charlie wondered.

Then, as though by design, Sky deliberately turned and looked straight at Charlie. His face was expressionless, and his eyes locked in on Charlie's. Sky held the gaze, then just nodded his head, as if to confirm that Charlie had heard him right. It jolted Charlie, but it also provided a breakthrough moment. When he got back to his seat after visiting the boys' room, the idea of inviting Mr. Olson over for Christmas totally occupied his thoughts.

As the game continued, the McCandless brothers dominated with their inside-outside game and Kings won by twelve points. As the boys headed out of the gym, Coach Cadman asked if they wanted to stop at Briarcade Diner for a hunk of their famous Boston cream pie.

"Shotgun!" yelled DMarks.

"There he goes again," warned George. "Sometimes I wish I had a shotgun!"

"I'm rubber, you're glue—whatever you say bounces off me and sticks to you!" replied DMarks.

"Okay. You've sunk to a new low." BB sighed.

"I haven't heard that since second grade!" added George. "Seriously, you need professional help."

As the others razzed each other, the wheels were turning in Charlie's mind.

CHAPTER 15

CHRISTMAS VILLAIN

*A new spirit I will put within them. I will remove the heart
of stone from their flesh and give them a heart of flesh.*
—Ezekiel 11:19

Winthrop Smythe was not a likable man in any sense whatsoever. He
grew up in a poor family on the hardscrabble streets of South Boston.
Early on he learned to take what he could get—and take he did.
He trusted no one in his arrogant, disdainful, and calculating ways,
always adopting a no-holds-barred approach to life.

Friendships meant nothing to him and, in fact, he had no
friends to speak of. The only person he had any kind of a committed
relationship with was his wife, and that was mostly a perfunctory,
emotionless thing. For Smythe, it was all about looking out for himself; fighting and winning was all that mattered. So what if rules got
broken and people got hurt? It was survival of the fittest, as far as he
was concerned.

In 1941, he took a job with a real estate speculator based in
Briarcliff Manor. While most of his peers were enlisting in the Army,
he managed to gain 4F status due to the fact that he was legally
blind in his right eye, the result of a severe beating he once absorbed
from his alcoholic father. The company was called Briar Cliff Land
Development and Properties. The original partners, who themselves
were friends of Walter Law, made dozens of land purchases back in
the late 1800s when the area was still undeveloped. They had the

foresight to see that the choice geographical area would one day become a very valuable suburb of New York City.

They were astute investors. One piece of land they owned was the parcel adjacent to Scarborough Train Station. It was the size of a football field and, although not suitable for residential subdivisions, they speculated that the village might need parking for people who wanted to live in the suburbs and commute daily by train to work in Manhattan. Years later, when the village tried to purchase the land, the owners of Briar Cliff Properties insisted on a lease agreement, whereby they would receive a portion of daily parking proceeds in perpetuity. Eventually, this created an enormous annuity for the company and involved little or no overhead.

They also owned the land that the old Putnam Rail Line was built on, which allowed them to charge rent to the railroad. Each time a train pulled into the Briarcliff Train Station, the railroad was obligated to pay them a fee.

The Putnam line also ran along the border of the John D. Rockefeller estate in Pocantico Hills, to the businessman's great dislike. He found the trains to be dirty and noisy. For years, he tried to get the tracks rerouted, but it was of no avail. Finally, he purchased the railroad himself and shut it down. This meant a total loss of revenue to Briar Cliff Properties and a lengthy tract of land that was completely unproductive financially. In response, they floated the idea of selling the land to the State of New York for expansion of the Taconic and Saw Mill River Parkways, which Mr. Rockefeller disliked even more. In turn, he was forced to buy the land at a price many times the market value and with the stipulation that it would be made into a bike and walking path for local residents up and down county. It was a rare thing to take on Mr. Rockefeller and win.

Briar Cliff Properties also owned the land along Route 9, on the border between Scarborough and Ossining, and developed it into the Arcadian Shopping Center. One of the partner/founders was Greek and wanted a namesake from his ancestral home. This was a significant move as it launched the company into real estate development. All in all, Arcadian boasted a department store, a movie theater, a bank, a barbershop, numerous mom and pop stores, office space, restaurants, and the expansive Arcadian Garden Center and Nurseries.

Losing no steam, the company went on to buy the scenic properties all along the top of Ridgecrest and Quinn Roads, as well as up and down both sides of Scarborough Road—all the way to the Astor estate. They foresaw that someday they could subdivide the land into one acre plots and sell them at inflated prices to wealthy families wanting Hudson River views.

Yet another wise acquisition was the many acres of land adjacent to the old Rockwood estate, now home to Phelps Memorial Hospital. In the late 1940s, Briar Cliff Properties was visited by a development committee, headed by John D. Rockefeller Jr., that had forward-looking plans for a community hospital. They were given a more than fair price for the property, which did much to assuage any lingering hard feelings from the Putnam Line land deal. Notwithstanding this generosity, they still made a hundredfold profit on their initial investment and were sure to benefit from a public relations windfall.

Smythe started off as a clerk at Briar Cliff Properties and rapidly worked his way up to vice president. He was uncommonly shrewd, which caught the eye of the original founders, many of whom were beginning to think in terms of retirement. When the last of them passed away in the 1950s, Smythe had already leveraged a majority ownership position in the company and began to run it lean and mean in a cold, calculating way. People's jobs were strategically terminated with the minimum severance, even after years of loyal service. To him, they were mere entries on the ledger.

By this time, the company had stopped purchasing and developing properties and was mainly in the rent collection business. Smythe was so cunning that when some of the businesses could not pay their rent, he would negotiate a paid position on the corporate boards, then exert his power to eventually acquire stock equity positions.

One day, he and Mrs. Smythe left their imposing home on Ridgecrest Road and drove down into Briarcliff for some early

Christmas shopping. They went to Whiggs, which was a favorite boutique for the latest fashions. Mrs. Smythe happily tried on one outfit after another, each time asking her husband for his opinion. For his part, Smythe sat on the leather couch in the middle of the store smoking his Chesterfields and reading the *Wall Street Journal.* "How much is that one?" was about all he said in response, barely even lifting his head up to look.

After the better part of an hour had passed, Mrs. Smythe decided on several garments and accessories and Mr. Smythe went to the cash register to pay. As they were leaving, Skeezie Schutte, the store's top sales girl, mentioned that a new line of Lizzy Gingham flats had just arrived.

"They're flying out of here!" she said.

"Do you have a pair in my size?"

"As a matter of fact, we do," answered Skeezie. "Have a seat and I'll be right back."

"Oh hell's bells. Haven't you shopped enough? I don't have all day for this!" seethed Smythe.

"Tickety-boo, Winthrop. This won't take long."

"We still have to stop at Weldon's for lunch and, by now, the place is probably packed," complained Smythe as he retreated back to the leather couch.

Mrs. Smythe tried on the shoes, but they didn't fit quite right. She walked around and looked at them in the mirror but finally opted to put them on hold. Smythe was characteristically incensed that she made him stay an extra five minutes, and all for nothing.

"Time is money," he began a familiar lecture as he grabbed her purchases, "and let's make up for lost time *if you don't mind.*" Mrs. Smythe meekly followed him out the door, looking over her shoulder at Skeezie with an apologetic half-smile.

At Joe Weldon's, they gave their usual order and, when it was ready, Smythe reached into his pocket to take out his wallet. It was missing. Instantly enraged, he looked around and locked his cold stare on Rafael Ortiz.

"Hey, you little immigrant, what did you do with my wallet?" accused Smythe. Rafael was completely caught off-guard and so stunned that he was momentarily speechless. He looked around to see if Smythe might be addressing someone else.

"I…no…have your wallet, sir. Here, I have my own money," he said as he reached into his pocket and held out a bit of cash. Rafael and his beautiful young family had emigrated from South America and lived modestly in one of the wash houses. He worked at The King's College in the maintenance department and was considered one of the most honest, decent, and gentle people around. As Raphael stood there panicking, Smythe continued to run roughshod over him in front of a growing number of onlookers.

"You don't fool me trying to make yourself look so innocent!" He then raised his voice louder and addressed the rest of the patrons in the deli.

"You all better check for your wallets. This little Spanish-speaking thief might have robbed you too." Mrs. Smythe was beyond mortified over her husband's caustic behavior. She was so upset that all she could do was shrink in the background and look on. Mr. Olson also happened to be there and was equally dismayed at what was happening.

"I've got my wallet right here!" he said, stepping over to Raphael in a show of support. "Leave him alone, Winthrop," he added gently. "He's an honest man, and he would never take what didn't belong to him."

"Stay out of this, Olson. This is none of your business!" Smythe said, jabbing his finger in Mr. Olson's chest. Fortunately, Mr. Weldon had thoughtfully called the police, who now arrived to diffuse the commotion.

"I have reason to believe this little foreigner stole my wallet," Smythe told Officer DiLoreto, again jabbing with his finger. "I want him brought in for questioning."

"Mr. Smythe! I no have your wallet! I swear on the cross!" pleaded Rafael, pulling his pockets inside out to prove it.

"Don't fall for that trick. He probably already stashed it some-place. I want this store combed until my wallet's found and then I want him brought up on charges!" roared Smythe.

"Now just a minute, Mr. Smythe. Did anyone actually see Rafael take your wallet? What proof do you have?" asked Officer DiLoreto, the beloved local cop better known by his first name, Eddie.

"Oh, come on. Isn't it obvious? The poor bastard needed money to buy his kids Christmas gifts…so he picked my pocket," responded Smythe.

"Mr. Smythe, you don't have the right to accuse Rafael of this sort of thing if you don't have any proof."

"Listen here. I have a lot of pull with the mayor and police chief in this village. Maybe they should investigate *you* as well!" threatened Smythe.

By now, Rafael was shivering with fear. To make matters worse, he didn't have a firm command of the English language, so he couldn't follow everything that was being said. Then, quite unexpectedly, he was overwhelmed by a feeling of goodwill, as though a caring friend was giving him a hearty hug. His fear resided, replaced by a calm, even peaceful feeling.

"All right, if you won't do what's necessary, I will." Smythe turned and shoved Rafael against the wall, starting to frisk him.

Suddenly, Skeezie Schutte came running into Weldon's calling out to Smythe, "You won't get far without this!" She held up his wal-let. "You left it by the cash register."

Smythe turned crimson with rage and embarrassment, but he was too petty to apologize for his actions. Instead, he let go of Rafael, snatched his wallet from Skeezie, and dashed out to his Lincoln Continental in a fit of pique. Again, Mrs. Smythe followed contritely.

As he drove off in a rage, his emotions inexplicably and sud-denly flipped. He began to feel badly for the way he acted and even thought about going back to offer an apology. He couldn't relate to or understand in any way what these thoughts and feelings were or where they had come from. But they were real, and he knew it. Still, he kept driving, just wanting to put some distance between himself and what had just happened.

Meanwhile, Eddie and Mr. Olson offered to take Rafael for a cup of coffee to help him to calm down.

"Don't worry, Mr. Ortiz," said Eddie. "He's not a very nice person. We on the police force don't like him either."

"I have to agree with Eddie," said Mr. Olson. "I've known him for decades, and he's always been that way."

"I no want trouble with anyone. I so sorry for this whole thing."

"You did nothing wrong, Mr. Ortiz. You're a good man, and you didn't deserve that."

"Thank you, Officer Eddie. *Dios te bendiga*!" said Rafael. "God bless you too, Mr. Olson."

"No one really knows why he's that way. He just doesn't seem to like other people. I don't even think he likes himself!" said Mr. Olson.

"Me and my wife. We will pray for him," said Rafael.

Eddie looked at Mr. Olson. "If the rest of the world could be more like this man—" he said.

"We'd all get along a lot better," Mr. Olson completed Eddie's thought.

As they started to head out of the store, Eddie noticed some random feathers scattered around where Rafael had been standing. *The guy must have torn open poor Rafael's jacket*, he thought.

Chapter 16
When A Plan Comes Together

Therefore encourage one another and build one another up.
—1 Thessalonians 5:11

After church that Sunday, Charlie and Sky eagerly picked up their conversation about Jesus' example by helping others. Charlie raised the idea to encourage people to invite folks over who would otherwise be alone on Christmas Day.

"I think you've got something there, Charlie," said Sky. "Let's push back on loneliness right here in Briarcliff!"

"It's really simple, but I think it would work! Plus, who doesn't like when company comes over?"

"Nothing better! Especially around the holidays. That's the way God wired us. We all have the desire for fellowship."

As coffee hour was winding down, Sky said a few goodbyes, then headed across the street to Law Park. It was an ideal December afternoon for outdoor fun. Not a single cloud in the sky, no windchill to cope with—just crisp, refreshing air and lavish sunshine, bright as heaven.

In the following days, Sky and Charlie sprang into action putting up signs on storefronts and telephone poles, visiting the local PTA and rotary clubs, and handing out flyers. They also talked with the editor of the *Citizen Register,* who was more than happy to give front page attention to the feel-good cause. It was a big deal to get your name and photograph in the local newspaper, let alone an entire article.

"Can we have your autograph?" kidded DMarks on their way to school the day after the article ran.

"Yeah, can you sign it 'to the best friends a guy could ever have?'" tossed in BB. Charlie turned a bit red but just kept walking and tried to ignore them.

"Chill out, you guys, can't you see he's embarrassed by all this attention?" said George. "By the way, Charlie, if you get any free stuff for all this, I get first dibs!" That did it. Charlie started swinging, administering dead arms and charlie horses all around.

To help get the word out, they decided to make a community announcement at the annual Holiday Craft Fair. This was a huge event hosted each year by the Women's Auxiliary of the Briarcliff Volunteer Fire Department. It was a brave thing for Charlie to do, as hundreds of people usually showed up. When he arrived at the high school and took stock of the overflow crowd, he began to freak out a little bit. DMarks was there and could see that Charlie's anxiety level was rising.

"Break a leg, old man!" he said, then kneed him with a gentle charlie horse to try to get his mind off of what he was about to do. It didn't really help. Charlie was growing numb with anxiety to the point that he didn't even acknowledge DMarks and his thoughtful attempt to lighten the mood.

Mrs. Nelson, who chaired the Woman's Auxiliary, found Charlie in the crowd. "There you are, Charlie, I've been looking for you! Are you all set with your big speech?"

"Well, actually, I think I just forgot everything I had planned to say," stammered Charlie.

Mrs. Nelson felt for him. "Too bad you can't do what I do when I have to speak in front of a crowd…take a shot of whiskey!"

"How much longer before you need me to talk?" he asked.

"Oh, about five minutes. Let's head to the platform now so we can get things started."

Charlie's heart began to race, his mind went blank, and his palms were sweating. Mrs. Nelson began her general welcoming remarks. As she talked, Charlie looked out to see if he could spot

Sky in the crowd. No luck. The gym was absolutely packed. He had expected Sky would be there for moral support and was now both nervous and crestfallen when he realized that there was no sign of him. Charlie was waiting anxiously on the side of the platform when, out of nowhere, that now familiar warmth enveloped him. It was as though someone had wrapped him in a warm blanket. He began to feel calmer and more comfortable. He heard Sky's voice. "Don't be nervous, Charlie. You've got this in your heart, and God will bless your words."

He spun around to greet Sky. "Where have you been?" he whispered excitedly. But Sky was not there. Still, his confidence began to rise, his thoughts were suddenly clear, and he felt a peaceful accord with what he was about to do.

"Now, I'd like to introduce you to young Charlie Riverton, who has a few words about how we can all help to make this a special Christmas for everyone," Mrs. Nelson announced to the welcoming crowd. Charlie stepped up to the microphone and began a brief but heartfelt appeal for people to consider opening their homes on Christmas Day.

"We all know someone who might be hurting or lonely for one reason or another. Let's bear each other's burdens and find someone to bless with the gift of companionship at Christmas." In particular, he emphasized the shut-ins, the elderly, and those who might have suffered a loss of some kind over the last year.

Not everyone knew how to respond to what Charlie was asking them to do. People liked to keep Christmas with their immediate family. At the same time, there were those in the community, like Mr. and Mrs. Vossler, who didn't have family nearby and welcomed the opportunity to fill their home with others on the most holy day of the year. After Charlie made his appeal, he walked off the platform to the side and circled around to the back of the gym where the water fountain was.

"That took guts," declared DMarks to BB. "I have a big mouth, but getting up in front of five hundred people ain't easy."

"No way I could have done that," said BB. "I would have frozen up."

"Ha!" said George. "You would have peed in your pants!"

"Nice, real nice," responded BB. "And you would have cried for your mother."

"Dang right. I don't mind admitting it!" said George. "Hey, Marks, what's it like to be up on a stage in front of a few hundred people?" He laughed, referencing his recent incident with the trampoline at Todd School.

"Oh, you're just a regular riot, aren't you?" he said. "Milton Berle, better watch out, he's got competition from comedians like you."

"Lighten up, Potsie!" said BB. "You never could take a joke."

Just as Charlie got to the water fountain, he looked up and there was Sky. He was looking down at him, smiling and nodding his head in approval. "You did great, Charlie! You should be proud of yourself!"

"Wait, where did you come from? I looked out from the podium and couldn't see you anywhere."

"Well, Charlie, there's hundreds and hundreds of people here. Joe Namath and Mickey Mantle could have walked in, and you wouldn't have been able to spot them."

"Thanks for the words of encouragement by the way. It helped calm me down up there." Charlie looked at Sky, waiting for a reaction. He wanted to let Sky know that he was onto these unusual occurrences.

"I'm not sure what you're referring to, Charlie. I got here just as you were starting to talk," said Sky with a smile. As the two of them walked back to the gym, Charlie knew in his heart that he had heard Sky's voice. And there had to be something to this warm aura he kept feeling whenever he needed special support or help. He was still searching for a better grasp of it, but he was sure that Sky was somehow involved.

CHAPTER 17
THE WAY THE (BOWLING) BALL BOUNCES

Behold, children are a heritage from the Lord,
the fruit of the womb a reward.
—Psalm 127:3

That Friday night, Michelle's parents were throwing her a birthday party at Briar Lanes. Everyone loved to bowl, plus the snack bar there had the best French fries in town. The guest list was pretty large, enough to fill up eight lanes with teams of four. Everyone traded in their street shoes for bowling shoes as they arrived, then made their way over to where the bowling balls were stacked. Some made their choice based on color, others on weight, and a few on how old the ball looked.

Kids could bowl with whoever they wanted, but Michelle made sure that she and her partners were on the lane adjacent to Charlie, BB, George, and DMarks.

Whenever possible, the boys loved to show off their athletic abilities in front of the girls. Although bowling wasn't hockey, basketball, or football, it did prove that you had good eye-hand coordination, balance, and agility if you could speed the ball down the lane and knock a few pins down with authority. Of course, whenever one of the boys bowled a strike, their feigned reaction was cool, detached, and completely aimed at making the girls think it was normal and entirely due to their superior athletic ability.

The flirting began early and often. "Charlie, can you show me how to hold this ball?" asked Michelle. Of course, Charlie pretended he was mildly annoyed, as though he was more interested in bowling than he was in Michelle. Meanwhile, he literally jumped at the opportunity.

"Here," he said, standing shoulder-to-shoulder with her looking down the lane at the pins, "you put your two middle fingers and thumb in the holes like so. Then, you hold it up using your left hand to kind of balance it." As Charlie talked, Michelle just looked at him and smiled. In reality, she couldn't have cared less about whether or not she could bowl a strike.

"Then, you get centered on the lane, take a few steps, wind up, and let it fly. Here, I'll show you." With that, Charlie nailed all ten pins, prompting Michelle to dramatically throw her arms around his neck laughing and shouting, "My hero!"

DMarks, eager to do some flirting of his own, got up and walked over to Andrea. "What my clumsy friend didn't demonstrate was the importance of balance. As you stride up to the line, you have to kind of glide to it. In the process, you swing the ball back like you're pitching a softball, then bring it forward in a pendulum motion. As you finish the forward motion, just let it go." Andrea was amused and happy to play along.

"Now the key is to make an athletic move with the ball. Here, give me your ball, I'll show you," said DMarks. Andrea picked up her ball and was reaching it out to DMarks but lost her balance at the last moment, dropping the ball directly on his big toe. DMarks yelped in pain as he hopped around on one foot muttering bad words under his breath.

"Oh man, that had to kill!" BB doubled over in laughter.

"Nice aim, Andrea!" yelled George.

"Yo, DMarks, is that what you meant when you told us all about the thrill of victory and the agony of DA FEET?" crowed Charlie.

"You guys are bogus," growled DMarks. "Can't you see I'm in pain here? I think she broke my toe!" The boys helped him take a seat and carefully untied his shoe. As they slipped it off, there was a bit of blood on his sock. He probably cracked his toenail.

"Dude, you need to hang it up for tonight. Go get some fries and play Pong at the snack bar," said George.

"Oh, that's just great. Can't think of something I'd rather be doing on a Friday night," replied DMarks.

"Maybe we can kind of put a chair up there on the bowling lane and you can bowl sitting down?" said BB.

"Yeah, you'll be safe from these girls up there," said George, fighting not to laugh.

"Just shut up and help me over to the snack bar," said DMarks. He draped his arms across George's and BB's shoulders, and they walked him over to the snack bar in dramatic fashion like an NFL highlight reel. No question, his toe had to hurt, but it was highly comical to see DMarks pogo-ing around on one foot while trying not to let on how much pain he was in. His night was over before he bowled a single frame. As he sat with his foot raised watching the others have all the fun, Andrea felt bad for him and paid him regular visits. Each time it was her turn to bowl, she'd shout to him, "This one's for you, DMarks!"

Charlie, BB, and George also looked in on him as much as they could. "How's your toe? Do you think it's broken?" asked George.

"How am I supposed to know? Do I look like a doctor?" responded DMarks. "All I know is that the average man could not handle the pain I'm in."

"Such drama," replied BB. "Maybe we should drop a ball on your other foot, you know, to even out your pain."

"Maybe I should drop a ball on your head!" replied DMarks. "I could have stayed home and made Creepy Crawlers with my little sister for all the fun I'm having here."

"Look on the bright side, Marks. I don't think they'll have to amputate." BB mimed a sawing motion.

"Very funny. Just wait till you see all the sympathy I'm going to get from the girls when I show up at school with crutches."

"Yeah, right. Any minute now, they're going to be pushing us aside to feed you French fries," said George, flicking one at him off the plate.

"Very funny. Somehow, I don't recall asking for a cup of your opinion!"

While checking on DMarks, Charlie noticed that Sky, Henry, and some of the others from the Rec Department had just arrived and were starting to bowl down at the other end of the lanes. He went back to Michelle's parents and asked if he could go down to visit with them. Of course, they were totally fine with that.

"Hi, Sky! Hi, Henry," said Charlie.

"Charlie!" said Sky. "Wow, you really are all-sports. Now you bowl too?"

"Actually, we're just here for fun. It's Michelle's birthday party."

"Well, go bowl her a strike!" said Henry.

"Already did!" he offered up proudly.

"Good for you, Charlie! Then I'd say the rest of the evening is gravy."

"Or he could go bowl a strike for Michelle's mom," challenged Sky.

"Ah! That would be a nice touch," replied Henry. Charlie's face was getting red but in a good way.

"What's up with your friend, Derrick?" asked Sky.

"He was trying to show off, and a bowling ball was accidentally dropped on his foot."

"Ouch!" said Henry. "Hope that won't keep him off his skates. You guys are like the four musketeers of hockey!"

"He'll be okay. His toe is bruised but not as bad as his ego." Charlie laughed.

"I bet his toe heals sooner!" said Sky.

"You got that right, Sky. And all the girls were watching when it happened!"

"Which only magnifies the pain!" said Henry.

"Hey, you should get back to your group," said Sky. "You don't want Michelle to think you've got another girlfriend." Charlie smiled and turned red as a cardinal, then headed back to the other end of the bowling alley.

By the time he got there, Michelle's dad had set up a slide projector and was showing family pictures of her first swimming lessons at the Briarcliff Pool, first day of Kindergarten in Todd School, Michelle in a Brownie's uniform, marching in the Memorial Day Parade, photos from Family Fun Day in Law Park, and more. The kids all shouted out in delight; most of them were also in the photos. Charlie noticed that even as a small child, she had a radiant smile and an outgoing spirit.

Soon pitchers of soda and slices of pizza were being passed around. After singing "Happy Birthday," the party went on for a while more. Michelle picked up two slices of birthday cake and made her way to where Charlie was sitting with the guys. As they saw her coming, George and BB helped get DMarks to his feet and drifted over to another table, leaving Charlie and Michelle by themselves.

"My mom makes this cake for me each year from scratch. I brought a piece for you," said Michelle.

"Just when I thought this night couldn't get any better!" said Charlie. "Cake with Coke is the best!"

"Right?" said Michelle.

"It's so much fun being here. Thanks for having us," said Charlie.

"Being out at night is so great, isn't it?"

The two sat together, leaning up against each other and chatting comfortably. Charlie was happily surprised at how far things had come with regard to his nervousness around girls. He glanced at Michelle. "Um, since it's your birthday, I think…um, you're entitled to a birthday kiss." A short time ago, it would have been inconceivable that he would have thought, let alone said, something like that.

"I like the way you're thinking, Charlie Riverton." With hearts galloping, they shared a brief, innocent kiss.

"I guess that makes it official?" said Michelle.

"Um, not sure what you mean," said Charlie.

"That we're going out, silly!"

The first real kiss had happened. Both survived and both were thrilled inside. Soon it was time for everyone to go home. They held hands as they walked to the front door. Once outside, they found a spot to the side of where everyone else was standing and kissed again. This time, they lingered, wrapped in each other's arms. More fireworks, more seismic activity, more chemical reactions.

"I like this better than watching *This Week in Pro Football*," said Charlie quietly.

"I knew you'd come around," Michelle said, smiling.

CHAPTER 18
COUNTY CENTER ENCOUNTER

Judge not, that you be not judged.
—Matthew 7:1

The boys were psyched. The Harlem Globetrotters were at The Westchester County Center, and tons of kids were going. Best of all, it was only a fifteen-minute drive down the Bronx River Parkway to White Plains. Mr. Riverton and Charlie picked up DMarks, BB, and George and made the short drive south. The guys wanted to get there early for warm-ups because the Globetrotters were known for interacting with the fans. They were looking forward to some big laughs.

"My favorite is Curly Neal," said Charlie. "Someday, I'm going to dribble a basketball like him."

"Meadowlark is the man!" said DMarks. "I like how he keeps things loose."

"You like him because he's a wise guy," said BB.

"Shut your face!" said DMarks.

"Who's your favorite, BB?" asked Charlie.

"Probably Geese Ausbie," replied BB. "I like how he just quietly goes along with the antics."

"Me too," said George, "but you gotta like the way Meadowlark can pull off a half-court hook shot!"

Mr. Riverton, who was a basketball fan himself, drove along listening to the chitchat, enjoying every minute. He knew that time was fleeting and, soon enough, he'd be handing his car keys to Charlie so that they could go places like this on their own. He parked and the boys bounded out of the car. After crossing the parkway, it was straight up the steps to the main entrance. The aromas of the concession stand filled the air: popcorn, hot dogs, and cotton candy.

Anticipation was building in the stands, and they could hear the familiar whistling of "Sweet Georgia Brown," the team's theme song, on the PA system. They found their seats up in the second tier and, as soon as they got comfortable, the Globetrotters came out and broke into their famed magic circle, dazzling the fans with their trick passes and ball-handling skills. The boys were laughing and slapping fives as the Globetrotters poured on the entertainment. Of course, that included the gag when Geese tosses a bucket of water at Meadowlark as he hides near the crowd in the front row, but instead of water, it's just confetti.

The County Center, a small venue with a big-time feel, was a safe place with only about 5,000 seats. So Mr. Riverton didn't mind when the boys asked if they could go exploring. Of course, their journey quickly found them at the concession stand for Twizzlers, Milk Duds, Snowcaps, and soda fountain Cokes.

"Yo, lend me some bread," said DMarks to Charlie. "My mom and dad forgot to hit me up with my allowance this week."

"Bummer for you, Marks. Maybe that had something to do with your general attitude?" said Charlie, half in jest.

"C'mon, man, don't leave me hangin'," begged DMarks.

"All right, don't have a canary. Here, two bucks. Don't spend it all in the one place," he joked in a serious parental voice.

"Whoa. Two whole dollars? You're like Jed Clampett! A pocketful of cash and you don't want to part with any of it," said the always sarcastic DMarks.

"And now you're down to one!" said Charlie, snatching back one of the bills. "Would you like to try for ZERO?"

"What a dweeb!" said BB. "The guy gives you money without hesitation, and you complain?"

"Hey. In life, you have to set your expectations high," said DMarks, raising his hand above his head.

"High *and* rude in your case," pointed out George. "Seriously, you should come with a warning label!"

"Go ahead, aim low. See where that gets you. It's like hitting to right field!" said DMarks. "Besides, I know this guy here. He'll never let me down. Hey, Charlie, who loves ya, baby?"

The three others just stared back at him blankly. But he was right, Charlie just didn't have it in him to let his friend feel left out at the concession stand. He handed back the dollar and added two more. BB and George shook their heads.

"What's crazier?" BB asked, beaning Charlie with a Milk Dud. "That DMarks asked for money or that you gave him more than he asked for?"

As they began to return to their seats, they encountered a disheveled older man shuffling along, sweeping up with a dustpan attached to a stick. He seemed forlorn, never looking up or making eye contact with anyone. Unkempt, hunched over, and in need of a shave, he had a tattered New York Knicks cap balanced slightly off-center on his head. As they watched him, he hobbled over to the benches lining the exterior walls of the area where he was sweeping, all the while chewing on the stub of an unlit cigar. He sat down, exhaled heavily and wiped his brow with a handkerchief.

The boys couldn't help but notice. They all instinctively looked at Charlie to gauge the expression on his face. "Go ahead, Charlie. Take a minute to say hello to him," said Sky. "A simple greeting can make a big difference in someone's life."

"That's exactly what I was thinking!" said Charlie out loud.

"Who the heck are you talking to?" asked DMarks. Charlie paused and tilted his head, trying to figure out if he was hearing things, then turned his attention back to the old man. The boys could see what was coming.

"Oh no, not here, not now," said DMarks. "Leave the man alone, he's working!" With that, he tried to nudge Charlie back to the arena and their seats. It was too late. He was on his way over to the old man.

"Guys, I just want to see if he needs anything," Charlie called back over his shoulder. "He's all out of breath. Maybe we can get him some water or something."

"Water? That old man looks like he needs a beer!" answered DMarks.

"That was cold, man," said George.

"Yeah. That was so cold it gave me brain freeze," agreed BB.

"I was just trying to lighten the mood," said DMarks.

"Dude, have some class. The guy is struggling. Charlie's right... let's go talk to him," said BB. DMarks was spitting nails but went along with the others. As they got closer, Charlie was already inquiring if he was okay and if he needed anything

"Oh, thank you, boys. I'm just taking a rest. Are you enjoying the game?" the man asked.

"Very much, sir, thank you," said Charlie.

"The Globetrotters have been coming here for years. I remember when Wilt Chamberlain was on the team. He barely had to leave his feet to dunk the ball."

"He's on the Lakers now. My favorite player!" said BB.

"He's unlike any other player in the game," said the man. "If I were starting a team from scratch, he'd be my first pick."

"I'd go with Jerry West," said George.

"You guys don't know what you're talking about!" said DMarks. "Pistol Pete Maravich. Greatest. Player. Ever!" This made the man smile and come more alive as the boys bantered back and forth. There was suddenly color in his face and a sparkle in his eyes. He seemed so glad that someone was actually showing an interest in him.

"There's a new player you boys should watch for—Ernie DiGregorio out of Providence College. He's going to be your 'Rookie of the Year!'" said the man, joining in.

"I love Ernie D! I saw him throw a behind-the-back pass the length of the whole court against Chicago last week!" said Charlie.

"Yes, he'll try anything out there," said the old man. They talked basketball for a few more minutes, but when he noticed his supervisor coming in their direction, he stood up to get back to work.

"It's great talking with you boys, but I don't want you to miss any of the game. You should go back to your seats," he said. As an employee of County Center, he had voucher coupons to the concession stand, and he reached into his pocket and pulled out four of them. "Here, go have a Coke and a giant pretzel on me," he said.

"Gosh, mister, that's really kind of you," said Charlie.

"You're good boys. Have fun tonight! I'll be taking care of this area if you need anything."

The boys felt lifted up by the encounter with the old man. They were amazed at how he instantly transformed once they began to engage with him. All he needed was a human touch. As they turned to leave, Charlie glanced back and noticed the old man sweeping up a few feathers near where they were standing. Charlie took it all in: feathers, voices, random touches. *There just has to be a connection,* he thought.

"I told you guys we should chat it up with the old guy," said DMarks, holding up his coupon to the concession stand. "I'll sell mine to the highest bidder. Do I hear $2.50?"

"You know something? You're like Mondays—nobody likes you...and comments like that explain why!" declared an exasperated BB.

"Yeah. What happened to 'leave him alone, he's working,'" demanded George.

"Just ignore him. He can't help himself!" said Charlie, snatching the coupon out of D'Mark's hand. "That will cover your debt from the cash loan I just gave you."

"I think it also calls for a dead arm," said BB. And with that, he administered a perfectly landed shot that almost caused DMarks to drop his bucket of popcorn. He also threw in a world-class wrist burn for good measure.

"Now that's going to cost ya. I don't know where, when, or how, but that's going to cost ya.

"Yeah, yeah, I'm shaking with fear," said BB. "Hey, did anyone else notice those feathers back there? That's becoming a pretty common thing for us these days."

"Yes!" said George. "Did one of you guys grow a pair of wings or something?"

"Maybe there's an angel following us around?" said DMarks sarcastically.

"I could believe that maybe there's an angel hangin' with Charlie, but all you'd ever attract are fleas," said BB.

"Oh, put a sock in it!" said DMarks as he reached out to flick the back of BB's ear.

When they got back to their seats, the game was in full swing and the laughs and crowd noise was infectious. "Where have you guys been?" asked Charlie's dad.

"He was making new friends as usual, Mr. Riverton," said DMarks.

"Here, Dad, we got you a hot dog and a 7UP."

"Thank you, boys. Very thoughtful of you."

"It's the least we could do, Mr. Riverton, in return for your driving us here and taking such good care of us. I encouraged Charles to use some of his money to remember you at the concession stand," said DMarks.

"Seriously, Marks. Who let you out of captivity?" asked Charlie through gritted teeth.

As everyone continued to enjoy the game with the Globetrotters dominating the otherwise hapless Washington Generals, Charlie once again heard that familiar voice. "Well done, Charlie. You made that man feel seen and heard—and that will have a positive ripple effect in his life." In response, Charlie offered a silent prayer for the old man working at the County Center.

CHAPTER 19
HOLIDAY FIELD TRIPS

===

And above all these put on love, which binds
everything together in perfect harmony.
—Colossians 3:14

Everyone loved field trips. Each year, during the month of December, the sixth grade class boarded school buses to neighboring Irvington and Tarrytown for guided tours at Sunnyside and Lyndhurst. Sunnyside was the home of the beloved American writer, Washington Irving, and Lyndhurst was the lavish home of the nineteenth century financier, Jay Gould. Both offered unique lessons in history, industry, and the arts—and both were always decked out for the holidays.

Irving was most noted for *The Legend of Sleepy Hollow* and *Rip Van Winkle*, but he also was a prodigious writer of histories and essays, including a few Christmas tales. Mr. Van Antwerp taught English at the middle school and considered himself an authority on Washington Irving. Each year, he'd dramatically read out loud from the author's Christmas stories during the bus rides to and from the sites.

Sunnyside was located right on the banks of the Hudson River on the Irvington-Tarrytown border. It featured a charmed bit of Dutch revival architecture. The students were treated to a complete tour of the house and grounds by guides dressed in period dress. Everything was tastefully decorated for the season.

The tour guide gave a passionate recounting of some of the Christmas traditions Washington Irving kept each year. Among other things, he would hunt wild turkey in the woods to the north of his property, then personally prepare and roast them on an open fire. He also kept orchards on the south side for afternoon exposure to the sun. From apple, pear, cherry, and nut-bearing trees, he would pick, flavor, and preserve holiday-spiced delicacies that he had adopted from his travels to England and Europe.

One of Irving's traditions in particular resonated with Charlie. On Christmas morning, Irving would take his horse and carriage up to Tarrytown. After stopping at St. Mary's for morning worship, he'd canter down Main Street and park near the Music Hall. There he'd wait, looking for someone who might pass by who seemed to have no place to go for Christmas dinner. Once he got a gut feeling about someone, he'd leap from his carriage and tip his top hat to greet the person, without mentioning who he was. After a brief conversation, he'd make an enthusiastic invitation for Christmas dinner and insist that the person come home with him on the spot.

Irving always had a large guest list. Once, Mark Twain, who owned the Tappan Hill Estate on Highland Avenue, joined the festivities. Charles Dickens actually stayed with Irving one year at Christmas while visiting the states to promote his newest novel: *A Christmas Carol*. Of course, many of the prominent local families were also invited as well: Van Tassels, Knickerbockers, Mitchells, Shaws, McSiebachers, and more. In the midst of that kind of crowd, the lonely stranger soon blended in and, by the end of the day, had made merry with a host of new friends.

"Later in his career, Irving wrote an essay called 'Christmas Tidings,'" explained the tour guide. "In it, he reflected on how a simple act of inclusion could make such a profound difference in a person's life." Although Charlie realized that his and Sky's idea of doing the same wasn't exactly original, he was glad to know that they had the same kinds of things in mind as Irving once did.

As the class weaved through the charming abode, one room was more festive than the next. Clearly, Christmas was a day of warm celebration and remembrance for Irving and his family.

After the Sunnyside tour was over, it was back to the buses for the brief ride up Route 9 to the Gould estate. Lyndhurst was a veritable gothic castle set on a high bluff, brooding over its portion of the Hudson. One of its claims to fame was that it was the set of the 1960s horror soap opera, *Dark Shadows*.

That notwithstanding, it was transformed into a Christmas wonderland each year with rich decorations of all kinds everywhere you looked. Here again, the students were treated to guided tours by talkative and knowledgeable docents who remained in character as they went room to room. All the kids were in awe that they were at "Collinswood," the home of Barnabas Collins—he of vampire fame from *Dark Shadows*. The show was too scary for any of them to watch an entire episode, as vampires were the spook-d'jour of the day. As a result, Michelle insisted on holding hands the whole time, which was just fine with Charlie.

"Don't worry, it's still daylight. Vampires only come out at night!" said Charlie, giving her fingers slight squeeze.

"How do you know? Have you ever known one?" asked Michelle. On cue, DMarks came up from behind and jumped on Charlie's back. He had taken a couple of Chicklets and forced the gum up into his top molars to make it look like he had vampire fangs.

"I've come to drink your blood," he said, quoting the famous Bela Lugosi line.

"Get off me, you yo-yo!" Charlie laughed.

"Oh, don't be such a Ken doll!" said DMarks.

"You don't scare us, DMarks!" said Michelle. She held up her hands forming a cross to ward him off. DMarks let out a half-scream/half-groan and fell to the floor as though he had fainted.

The opulence of the place was amazing to the kids. Most of the original furnishings were still there. "Do you have any idea how much this stuff is worth?" asked DMarks. "A fortune I tell ya."

"Yeah, well, don't get any ideas. You already have a criminal record from your little stunt at the Todd School gymnasium," said Charlie.

"Thank you for that reminder. What, did you just join the police auxiliary or something?" asked DMarks.

"No, but I am on the staff of the student newspaper, and I'd like to be sure that you stay out of the headlines," said Charlie.

"What a guy!" replied DMarks. The fun freedom of being away from their classrooms on a school day was exciting—and these field trips always created lasting memories.

It turned out that the Goulds also had a Christmas tradition similar to Irving. Each year on Christmas Day, they paid to bring inmates from nearby Sing Sing prison to the estate where they were treated to fine food, music, board games, and other relaxing pastimes. Mr. and Mrs. Gould believed that if they could provide a modicum of encouragement to these temporarily wayward souls, it could provide the motivation needed for a better life once they were paroled.

"See that, DMarks. When you get locked up someday, maybe you can get them to revive the Lyndhurst Christmas tradition," joked BB.

"Was that called for? I think not," replied DMarks, pretending he was handcuffed.

Soon enough, it was time to get back on the buses. Mr. Hunt led a carol sing as he did each year, all the way back to Briarcliff. Being the great teacher he was, there was also always a mandatory stop on Route 9 in Tarrytown by the statue commemorating the capture of Major John Andre. Mr. Hunt would recount that it was a turning point in the Revolutionary War and ultimately the birth of our nation.

From there, the bus kept rolling up Broadway, through Tarrytown and Sleepy Hollow, past Philipse Manor and Phelps Memorial Hospital. Everyone was having so much fun that no one wanted the ride to end. Eventually, they turned right on route 117, then left onto South State Road, and soon arrived at the middle school. By then it was going on two thirty in the afternoon and everyone was dismissed to head home.

That day, Michelle invited Ellen, Laura, Gretchen, and Robin to come over after school. Charlie and the guys walked home with them chatting up a storm. What had been a terrifying thing a short time ago was now something the boys could not get enough of. Suddenly, their interest in girls was almost equal to their interest in playing sports.

CHAPTER 20

MAN ABOUT TOWN

As you wish others to do unto you, so also do unto them.
—Luke 6:31

Anticipation was building for the middle school ice skating party that night. Everyone looked forward to skating under the stars. Even the kids who didn't skate would go out on the pond and slide around in their snow boots.

Since there was no basketball practice after school, Charlie walked uptown to the Manor Barber Shop for a haircut. It was the sort of day you'd otherwise choose for running errands; the skies were overcast and the air was raw with the threat of rain or sleet. He zipped up his parka and pulled his New York Rangers baseball cap down low on his forehead.

After the short walk past the pine forest and through the town center, he was warmed on arrival by the familiar sight of the red, white, and blue barber pole out in front and the cheerful atmosphere inside the barber shop. He'd been going there since he was a little kid. John, Nick, Joe, and Nat, the group of friends and brothers from Italy were all there clipping away. Charlie hung up his coat and hat, then grabbed a copy of *Sports Illustrated* and sat in a chair near the back of the shop where the portrait of President Kennedy hung.

"Charlie, you overdo for a haircut. We give you a crew cut today!" said John.

"Leave him alone. He good boy, right, Charlie?" responded Nat.

"I'll just have a regular, if that's okay," said Charlie, playing along.

Winthrop Smythe was in Joe's chair getting a haircut and a shave, chain-smoking Chesterfields, and reading the *Wall Street Journal*. He was condescending and demeaning toward Joe, picking on him for every little thing. But Joe was able to quietly absorb it, good natured as he was.

As Nick finished with his customer, he motioned to Charlie to have a seat at his chair. "I give you your first haircut in this seat, remember? Had to put you on a leather block...two years old you were!" said Nick.

Charlie smiled and nodded. The fact was, each time he got a haircut there, no matter which barber it was, he was told the exact same thing. It made him feel special that all four claimed to have given him his first coif.

"Charlie, you have a girlfriend?" asked Nick. The question caught Charlie off guard. "Kind...of," he stammered, which made all four barbers break out laughing.

"Kind of?" said Nat. "That's not the sort of thing you 'kind of' have!" he said, wagging his index finger sideways. "You either do or you don't. Capeesh?"

"Well, then, I guess I do," replied Charlie, beaming. For the first time, he had said it out loud and his own words really hit home.

"Charlie, you need advice on girls, you come to me!" said John, pointing at his chest under his barber's smock.

"His wife no even talk to him. You come to me, Charlie! I give you the best advice on women," Nat shouted across the room.

Charlie liked the attention but saw in the mirror that he was turning red as the barber's chair he was sitting in. Nick continued to clip away, asking about school, sports, and a bunch of other standard small-talk topics. After a short time, he finished the job, so Charlie got up, grabbed his coat, and headed to the front of the shop to pay. They kept a large jar of Bazooka Joe near the cash register, which always provided a post-haircut treat.

"Take two pieces, Charlie. One for you and one for you girl-friend!" Nick winked. Charlie happily complied. Not only did he love the gum, he also enjoyed the mini-comic strip each piece came wrapped in.

Smythe had also just paid at the cash register near the front entrance. He took his change and, instead of offering a tip to Joe, he kept it all, grousing about what a terrible job he had done. Charlie opened the door just as Smythe turned to leave, clipping one of Smythe's wing-tipped Florsheim's in the process with the bottom corner of the door.

"Watch it, boy! Don't you know how expensive those shoes are? I should have you pay for them to be shined after that little stunt."

"Gosh, I'm sorry, Mr. Smythe. It was my fault. How much does a shoeshine cost? I have a few dollars left from my haircut."

Charlie's words caught Smythe off guard. He squinted his eyes and gritted his teeth as he looked down at Charlie to size him up. Hardly anyone addressed him directly, especially not in such a con-siderate way. What's more, Charlie didn't seem to be intimidated, which made Smythe even more bothered. He wondered what kind of game this little delinquent was trying to play.

"What are you up to, boy? You think talking back is going to help?" asked Smythe, trying to bully and frighten Charlie. In that instant though, Charlie was once again visited by that unique, warm presence he had been experiencing over the last week or two at diffi-cult times like this. He felt calm and centered as he stood his ground.

"I wasn't trying to talk back, sir. Honest! I'd be happy to pay for my mistake," said Charlie as he pulled a few dollars from his pocket.

Everyone in the entire barbershop was now staring at Smythe and wondering why he was harassing Charlie for what clearly was an accident. The tension was thick as Smythe kept bearing down on Charlie. He was about to unleash another reprimand when, sud-denly, he was seized by an unfamiliar pang of emotion. All at once he got a glimpse of what a mean-spirited, vindictive rogue he was. He began to feel badly for the way he had treated Charlie and Joe and even thought that perhaps he should offer an apology.

Smythe had no idea what to do with these thoughts and feelings. An act of humility from him would be a first. After a prolonged, awkward face-off, he just grabbed his coat and hat and fled through the front door without saying another word. Charlie and everyone else just watched as he strode briskly across the street to where he was parked by Manor Wines & Spirits. Nat ran over and opened and slammed the door again for emphasis, reaching up to ding the bell extra hard above the door. He glared out the window, dinging the bell again as Smythe momentarily glanced back.

Smythe sat in his Lincoln Continental besieged by a need to know where those chastened feelings had come from. After a few minutes, he decided that he wanted a drink. He vaulted out of his car and into the liquor store where he purchased a fifth of Chivas Regal. Once back in his car, he unscrewed the top and took a stiff belt straight from the bottle. The whole episode was utterly unsettling for him. He'd always seen himself as superior to everyone else and incapable of being in a situation where he'd ever owe someone an apology. Even if an apology was in order, he'd never actually entertain the notion of asking forgiveness.

He lit another Chesterfield, took a long drag, and propped it up in the car ashtray. His mind was racing. What were these thoughts and feelings flying around in his head and heart? Something was welling up inside him, but instead of allowing it to come out, he seized on it and crushed it into submission. Whatever this was, he thought, it would not get a foothold with him. At least not that day. He grabbed the bottle and took another swig.

For his part, Charlie was not that ruffled by Smythe's behavior. He looked at the guys in the shop, thanked them, and headed out the door. John, Nick, Nat, and Joe all shook their heads, muttering to each other in Italian. Joe didn't have anyone in his chair, so he grabbed a broom and began to sweep up the hair clippings in and around where each barber was working. When he got near the front door, he noticed something unusual. "Piume?" he said aloud. "Feathers?" *Where did they come from?* he wondered, then kept sweeping.

Charlie's next stop was up the street at People's Westchester Savings Bank. He had money to deposit from the snow shoveling jobs he worked throughout the neighborhood. As he was about to cross Poplar Road, Smythe drove by in his Lincoln Continental. He slowed down to take a long hard look at Charlie. *There's something about that kid*, he thought. He made a mental note to find out who he was and to keep an eye on him, then he floored the gas pedal and kept driving.

Charlie continued on his way, and soon he was handing his cash, checks, and bank book to one of the tellers so that she could process the deposit. When she handed it back to him, he reviewed it diligently so that he could see the interest he had earned since the last visit.

"Wow, Charlie, you've been working hard lately. That was a large deposit!" said the teller. "What are you going to do with all your money? Buy hockey equipment?" she kidded.

"I'm just kind of saving it up for a rainy day," said Charlie. He didn't really know what that saying meant, but his parents always stressed it to him, so he thought he'd use it. From there, he walked back down and across the street to the Penny Candy Store above Birratella's service station. He knew that Michelle liked those elastic, multicolor candy necklaces, so he purchased one to give to her later at the skating party. He also grabbed a fistful of Atomic Fireballs and a few boxes of Red Hots for him and his buddies.

Sergeant Whiting, the very popular police officer, who also worked a second job off-hours next door at Manor Wines, was outside sweeping the sidewalk as Charlie walked by.

"Seen any bad guys, Charlie?" he asked in jest and smiling broadly. Charlie paused for a moment, thinking that Mr. Smythe, in his own way, certainly qualified.

"No, sir, Sergeant Whiting, but I'll let you know if I do." Charlie continued on down Pleasantville Road past Camelot, the hardware store, Manor Valet, and Noller's Market. Officer DiLoreto was directing traffic at the crosswalk, in the center of town.

"That's a good-looking haircut, Charlie!" he called over.

"Thanks, Officer Eddie! It was a bit overdue."

"Ha! The way some of the older boys wear their hair these days, you're doing just fine."

As he passed The Briar Rose, he noticed Rabbi and Mrs. Steinert coming out laden with bags and packages. He quickly rushed to hold the door for them.

"*Thank you*, Charlie!" enthused the rabbi. "Sometimes I wish God created us with three arms!"

"Happy to help! Looks like you've got your hands full, sir," noticed Charlie.

"Just a few things for Hanukkah. Eight nights of lights and festivities, you know," bubbled Mrs. Steinert.

"Yes, right. I have a few friends at school who are in your congregation, so I know all about the Festival of Lights!"

"Maybe someday you and your family can join us," suggested the rabbi.

"We'd love to!" answered Charlie enthusiastically, as they all turned to walk down the sidewalk together.

"We're quite inspired by what you're up to around town, Charlie. In fact, these gifts are for members at Congregation Sons of Israel who live in the elder care facility up on North State Road. They have no one to celebrate Hanukkah with, so we're going to bring Hanukah to them."

"That sounds awesome, Rabbi Steinert! I hope you all have a fantastic time together!"

"Bless you, son," offered the rabbi, putting his hand on Charlie's forehead.

Charlie continued on with a pleased smile on his face. As he crossed the middle school grounds, his spirits were running high from his encounter with the rabbi. Soon enough he reached Gooseneck Pond where he ran into Sky, who was prepping for that evening's skating party.

"Sky! Hey, how's it going?"

"Walking on sunshine, Charlie."

"What are you up to?"

"I was just enjoying a few moments of prayer and reflection before people start arriving to skate."

"Really? I never thought about worshiping outside of church services."

"Actually, Charlie, as Dr. Cook often tells us, you can pray your way through the day wherever you are."

"What a great concept! Pray all day!!"

"Yes, sir! No day is complete without prayer and worship, Charlie. So, how goes it with you?"

"Just got my haircut, looking forward to the skating party tonight."

"Good call. Got to look your best for Michelle." Sky winked.

"I really like her." He blushed. "But I still get a little shy and nervous around her. I'm so afraid that I'll run out of things to say or that I'll say something stupid."

"I find that if you try to put yourself in the shoes of the other person, it usually goes just fine. Plus, once someone breaks the ice, the conversation just flows from there."

"No pun intended?"

"Ah, right, no pun intended."

"Thanks for the advice. I'll try to keep that in mind. If only she was a Rangers fan…we'd have so much more to talk about!"

"Ha! Just be glad she's not a Bruins fan!"

"Then we'd just be crying!"

"Can't have that!"

"Hey, by the way, there's a new song by a guy named James Taylor. It's called 'You've Got a Friend'…he's Michelle's favorite. Do you think you can add it to the records that will be played over the loudspeaker tonight?"

"You and Michelle have a favorite song already?"

"No!" Charlie blushed again. "But she mentioned him and this song in particular, so I kind of got to know it a bit myself."

"Chivalry is alive and well here in Briarcliff! Good for you, Charlie. We'll make sure that we play it early and often for you two."

"You're the best, Sky. I'll see you in a couple of hours."

"I'll be here!"

Being around Sky gave Charlie the same feeling as when he'd slip on his favorite, most comfy, oversized sweatshirt. Both provided a special kind of warmth, solace, and well-being.

As Charlie headed home, he glanced up at Mr. Olson's house. The lone, dim light in the back of the house was on, as usual. He had a little bit of time, so he decided to cut across the street to see if he could say hello. As he got to the back door, he peeked inside. Mr. Olson was sound asleep in his reclining chair with a copy of *Life Magazine* draped across his chest and glasses perched upon his forehead. The room was disheveled and partially lit by his black-and-white Magnavox, which was showing nothing but gray static. Charlie wondered if he should go in and at least adjust the antennae for him. He looked on for a moment more feeling sad and torn, then said a silent prayer and continued on his way home.

The lyrics to "Silent Night" came to mind: "Silent night, holy night/All is calm, all is bright/Sleep in heavenly peace, sleep in heavenly peace."

"Sleep in heavenly peace, Mr. Olson," he whispered softly into the coming night air.

CHAPTER 21

SKATING PARTY

A friend loves at all times and a brother is born for adversity.
—Proverbs 17:17

Skating parties in Law Park were always a big hit with the kids and the parents who came to chaperone. The damp weather that afternoon had cleared out to reveal a starlit sky, and the temperature also dropped a few degrees, which made for excellent skating conditions. Charlie, BB, DMarks, and George walked over from the Tree Streets, each with their laces knotted and skates hanging over their shoulders.

"You gonna try to skate with Michelle?" DMarks asked Charlie.

"Maybe. We'll see," said Charlie, trying to mask his nervousness. "How about you? You going to take another shot at Andrea?"

"As a matter of fact, I am," said DMarks, spraying a shot of Binaca into his mouth. "And if she knows what's good for her, she won't play hard to get this time!"

"Could you possibly be any more suave? I'm sure she's just waiting for you to sweep her right off her skates," said BB.

"Five bucks says you're going to get the icy mitt tonight!" said George. "And by the way, keep that Binaca handy, you could dust a crop field with your breath."

"Hopefully she won't bring her bowling ball with her tonight!" added Charlie.

"Very funny. Who are you losers, going after tonight?"

"I heard Laura was sweet on me, so I figure I'll give it a try. I've got nothing to lose!" George said hopefully.

"I'm playing the field, but by the end of the night, I bet two Cokes and a box of Bazooka Joe that I'll be skating with Robin," said BB.

"Wait, what? She's way out of your league!" said DMarks.

"Actually, I have a note from her right here. It was in my locker. Says she's looking forward to pairing with me in the group skate."

"Are you sure one of us didn't put that letter there as a prank?" asked DMarks.

"Pretty sure, unless your penmanship just went from chicken scratch to girly cursive!"

"Got ya there, DMarks," said Charlie. "You can't draw a straight line, let alone write in script like that."

"Yeah, well, good luck with that one!" said DMarks. "If you can land a good night kiss from her, I'll buy a pair of L'eggs and wear them to school on Monday!"

"He's just jealous because the only letter he ever got in his locker was from the librarian fining him for past due books," said BB.

By the time they got to Gooseneck, the party was already going strong. The boys threw on their skates and joined the fun. A little while later, Michelle arrived and sat down on a bench to put on her skates. Sky noticed and decided to spur things along as Charlie came skating by.

"Whoa there, Charlie! Looks like Michelle could use a hand getting down the slope and onto the ice, my friend."

Michelle beamed and was grateful to Sky for the assist. She was wearing a blue parka with a fur-lined hood and a long, white knit scarf with matching mittens. Her smile, as usual, lit up the night. To his credit, Charlie came right over and approached her in a very gentlemanly way. He took her hands and carefully walked her down to the ice. Once there, he held onto her left hand as they strode out to where all the fun was happening. Charlie glanced back for a moment to see Sky giving him an enthusiastic thumbs-up. He also happily recognized that Michelle didn't seem to want to let go of his hand.

There was a fun vibe that night in Law Park. The Rec Department was playing albums by Jethro Tull, Elton John, Carly

Simon, Cat Stevens, Three Dog Night, and the like. The sound of skates slicing across the ice and kids laughing and calling out to one another filled the air.

"This is groovy!" said Michelle as she and Charlie skated around, chatting with others, still holding hands.

"I know. The whole middle school is here!"

"And I love the music they're playing," said Michelle. "My favorite is the new song by James Taylor." On cue, as though Sky was listening in and taking requests, the next song played was "You've Got a Friend."

"Did you plan that?" Michelle playfully asked.

"I wish I could take credit," Charlie replied. "Thanks, Sky," he muttered, as Michelle put her arms around his midsection, and they continued to skate.

Meanwhile, DMarks had organized a skate chain and, as they passed by, he grabbed Michelle's hand and swept them along. As the chain grew longer, a whip affect began to develop resulting in five or six skaters on the tail end going headlong into a snowbank, laughing all the way.

After a while, Michelle and Charlie decided to take a break, skating to the middle of the ice to lean up against the original stone fountain that Mr. Law had scenically placed in that spot all those years ago. Once again, DMarks went into action, skating over with a playful look in his eye. He took a quarter out of his pocket and flipped it in the air saying, "Heads you kiss, tails you miss!"

"Say what?" said Charlie.

"Try it, you'll like it!" said DMarks. Before Charlie or Michelle could absorb what was happening, DMarks shouted, "Heads it is!"

Michelle looked at Charlie who was tentative. In response, a pleased smile came across her face as she leaned in for a kiss. In response, DMarks flipped the coin again and shouted, "Heads!" Charlie was acclimating quickly. This time, he was much more receptive to giving and receiving a more deliberate kiss.

This went on several more times before Charlie and Michelle finally figured out that no matter which side of the coin was up,

DMarks was going to say it was heads. Once they caught on, DMarks skated away with a laugh. "Another couple of happy customers!"

Inside, Charlie was exhilarated and grateful for what DMarks had done. Outside, he had no choice but to act bothered and upset. "Better watch your back, Marks!" he threatened. It was his adolescent way of trying to act like this whole thing about kissing girls was nothing of any great interest to him, although he knew it was a moment he'd never forget.

"What's the problem? Should I have used my Magic 8-Ball instead?" quipped DMarks as he sped around them. By now, Michelle and Charlie were leaning against each other arm in arm. Something transformational was evolving inside them. Their hearts were beating a little differently as they glanced into each other's eyes.

"You'll never need to flip a coin to kiss me again, *ever!*" said Michelle.

"Well, I'll plan to keep one handy just in case," responded Charlie.

They stayed out in the middle of the pond for a bit more, then skated in so they could sit by the fire and sip hot chocolate. As an added touch, Sky broke out some oversized flannel blankets. It was perfect, or so they thought. Just then, snow flurries began to mingle with the crisp night air.

"Look at those two," Sky said to Henry. "They give me hope for the future."

"Two of the best kids in Briarcliff," agreed Henry.

"No argument here. I'd say this whole scene is the sort of thing Walter Law had in mind when he first developed this park and pond."

"Time for some pictures," announced Henry to the crowd, pulling out his Polaroid SX-70. For the rest of the night, he skated around taking photos and handing them to kids on the spot. They all loved to watch as the picture developed right before their eyes, capturing all the fun.

Charlie and Michelle just stayed put under the blanket, snug as two parts of a puzzle. They were glowing bright as the night stars.

Chapter 22

Towering Mistake

Put on then, as God's chosen ones, holy and beloved, compassionate hearts, kindness, humility, meekness and patience.
—Colossians 3:12

A new blockbuster, *The Towering Inferno,* had just been released in theaters. Not only did it have an all-star cast lead by Steve McQueen, Faye Dunaway, and Paul Newman, but it was released with the new Dolby Surround Sound, promising a more realistic and intense movie-going experience. It was showing over at the Rome Theater in Pleasantville, and the boys had their hearts set on seeing it. They lobbied their parents to let them go on their own, which turned out to be an easy sell. The boys were responsible, and the Rome was a safe place just one town over. Their only concern was with the movie itself; it looked like a lot of graphic death, destruction, and grisly scenes.

The boys weren't worried. They had been given a taste of nighttime freedom, and they wanted more. George, BB, and DMarks walked over to the Rivertons' house, and Charlie's dad drove them over to the theater. They were each given five dollars for admission and a visit to the concession stand, and their parents expected leftover change.

"Remember, guys, you're in a public place. The way you act will reflect on your families. Be on your best behavior please," said Mr. Riverton.

"Thank you, Mr. Riverton. I'll make sure everyone walks the straight and narrow. And may I say how much I enjoyed riding in your new car? A Chevrolet Caprice Classic…such a nice family vehicle," said DMarks.

The other boys glared at him in silence. He was just fishing for a bogus way to engage Charlie's dad.

"You're such an Eddie Haskell," Charlie whispered through gritted teeth, as George and BB issued well-placed elbows to each of DMarks's arms in perfect unison.

"Why, thank you, Derrick. I didn't know you were a car enthusiast," said Charlie's dad.

"Of course. I'm particularly partial to a Ford Mustang, like what Steve McQueen drove in *Bullitt*…460 horsepower, V-8 engine. As soon as I turn sixteen, I'm going to get one of my own."

"Easy there, grasshopper. You don't want to raise your profile around town. Detective Kaufman's already keeping an eye on you." Major burn by Charlie's dad! The boys wailed with laughter as DMarks got put in his corner.

"Seriously, Marks, were you ever abducted by aliens or something?" asked BB.

"And where the heck are the aliens when you need them?" added George.

Charlie just rolled his eyes. "Thanks, Dad. We'll meet you across the street by the Pleasantville Train Station after the movie."

"Okay, son. You boys have fun," said Mr. Riverton, patting Charlie on the shoulder as he exited the car. "Including you, Derrick."

The guys tried to act cool as they entered the theater, but inside they were bursting with excitement. They stopped at the ticket window, then headed to the concession area and into the theater, where DMarks insisted that they sit in the front row.

"This is where you want to be for a movie like this!" said DMarks. "Front row, baby! Nothing between us and the towering inferno!"

"Well, my mother always says you'll get a stiff neck if you sit in the front row from looking straight up at the screen," warned BB.

"And honestly, Marks, you're already a pain in the neck, so I vote something closer to the middle!"

"Look, I know what I'm doing while taking in a picture show. I'm telling ya, this is where it's at!" insisted DMarks. "Especially for a movie like this. People are going to be jumping out windows. ON FIRE! It'll be like they're landing in our laps!"

"All right, all right. Don't have a cow!" said George.

The coming attractions were starting to roll as they sat down— all of them barn burners like *The Godfather*, *The Poseidon Adventure*, and *Planet of the Apes*. Unbeknownst to them, Michelle and her friends had found out the boys were going to the movies that night and got permission from their parents to do the same. As they arrived in the darkened theater, they eventually spotted the boys and slid into the second row directly behind them, acting surprised to see them.

"You guys! What are you doing here?" Michelle asked.

"Yeah, we had nothing to do, so we kind of just decided to go to the movies," said Diane.

"We're regulars here! They practically know us by name," added Andrea.

"Yeah, right. You all deserve an Academy Award for that performance!" said DMarks. "Just keep it down, the movie's about to start." But then, sensing an opportunity, he yelled, "CHINESE FIRE DRILL!" as the movie began to play. With that, everyone scrambled over their seats, ending up boy-girl in the front row. Miraculously, no soda or popcorn was spilled and everyone settled in next to their latest crush.

The movie was super intense from the beginning: nonstop harrowing scenes of people stranded and screaming for help. Everyone lost everything and they were powerless to stop the blaze; it was relentless destruction and despair. The boys gradually started to squirm in their seats. Some of them actually looked away from the screen, and the girls covered their eyes. It turned out that the boy-girl seating came in handy as everyone leaned in closer, overlapping like a litter of puppies.

"This movie is too intense," said Michelle, squeezing Charlie's hand so hard it was turning white.

"I know! It's almost like a horror movie!"

"The look on that woman's face when she jumped from the eightieth floor is going to give me nightmares."

"And what about the guy who got stuck in the elevator and roasted alive like he was in an oven?"

"The firemen tried everything, but nothing worked. Everything still burned down."

"I just feel so bad for all the people who lost everything in the fire. Where are they supposed to go? What are they supposed to do?"

"Going to the movies is supposed to be fun." Michelle sighed.

"It will be the next time. Let's stick with Disney movies from now on!" added Charlie.

"Deal!" She grabbed both of his hands for extra security.

At last, the movie came to an end and the house lights came up. The group left the theater feeling stressed out and exhausted. The boys hung back to harass DMarks.

"Great idea sitting in the front row, DMarks," said BB sarcastically. "My neck aches and I'm so wound up I might run back to Briarcliff to let off some steam."

"Oh, please. You didn't like it when Barrie threw her arms around your 'stiff neck?' You, amateurs, should be thanking me for getting the girls to pay attention to us!"

"The day we need your help to get attention from girls is the day we should all become hermits!" said George.

Across Wheeler Avenue they went, through the train station waiting area, and out to the parking lot near the Pleasantville Diner. Charlie's dad was already there, chatting with Michelle's dad who had come to pick up the girls.

Even though the gang was growing up and feeling their oats, the movie was upsetting for them, and they took comfort in the sight of two caring parents waiting with warm, inviting cars. They couldn't wait to get home to their own beds, although it wasn't likely that any of them would be sleeping very well that night.

CHAPTER 23
OUT WITH THE OLD

Finally all of you, have unity of mind, sympathy,
brotherly love, a tender heart and a humble mind.
—1 Peter 3:8

At dusk, a couple of days later, the boys were beginning the walk home from Gooseneck Pond. The orange glow of the sun had already faded beyond the overlooking hills of Briar Hall Country Club. These were the days when it got dark around five in the afternoon. No one really liked the loss of daylight savings, but the payback was the cerulean shimmer in the night sky that came with the winter solstice. Even the boys took notice, though they never made it a topic of conversation.

The early arrival of nightfall also put an accent on the festive beauty of Christmas lights, now on trees and homes all around town. As they walked along, the boys picked out their favorite light shows and rehashed the day.

"Can you believe that lame filmstrip we had to watch today in Mr. Macci's class?" said DMarks. "Seriously, do they think we're still back in Todd School?"

"I kind of liked it. Much better to watch a science experiment than to actually have to conduct one in Science Lab. I hate when we have to put on those goofy safety goggles!" said BB.

"I'm with you. Those goggles are for nerds," said George. "And when we get to eighth grade, we'll actually have to wear white lab coats too!"

"Guys, you have to get over yourselves and just go with the flow," said Charlie. "These are the rules. They're for our own good."

"Oh, brother. There he goes again," said DMarks. "Listen up, Charles. A man's life isn't about keeping the rules, it's about breaking them and making new ones!"

"What? Where did you get that one?" asked Charlie.

They were just about to pile on DMarks when they noticed the scent of cigarette smoke. It was coming from somewhere in the dark out in front of them. Someone was there, but who? The conversation stopped, their bodies tensed up, and their senses focused as they slowly and tentatively moved forward.

Then, without warning, Parker Jones leapt out from behind one of the hundred-year-old Maple trees. He was in a crouched position and dressed in army fatigues as though geared up for hand-to-hand combat. A half-smoked Camel cigarette dangled from the corner of his mouth. He stood up slowly, taking a long drag from his cigarette before flicking it to the side. His eyes were filled with wrath and locked in on the boys.

"You kids think you're pretty smart, making all that insufferable noise with your never-ending hockey games!" he snarled. "I'd say you all need to be taught a good lesson. Maybe I'll teach you one right here. Right now!"

He stood his ground, glaring at them and jam-packed with pent-up rage. The boys stood in silent shock, stiff as boards, unable even to think. None of them said a word for fear of what Parker might do in one of his angry outbursts. Even the overconfident DMarks was frozen in place.

"Let's split you, guys," whispered George out of the side of his mouth. "This is not cool."

"Yeah," said BB. "This is one uptight dude."

"That's right. Don't you know there's a noise ordinance here in town?" Parker growled. "I've got it all on tape. Just you wait till I take this to Detective Kaufman at the police department." He held up a cassette tape. "You and your hockey games won't be disturbing the peace much longer."

"Seriously, guys, let's book," hissed DMarks. "If we all run for it in different directions, he can't catch us all. It's every man for himself."

But just then, Charlie was comforted by Sky's voice. "Don't be afraid, Charlie. The Bible says that a soft answer turns away another's wrath." He was so relieved that Sky had shown up. *Maybe now Parker would calm down and leave them alone,* he thought. But it became immediately apparent that Sky wasn't actually there at all. At first, this realization made Charlie near nauseous with fright, but then came the now familiar warm feeling. Compassion replaced fear in his heart. He remembered that Parker had been through a lot with the war and the loss of his mom. What he needed was kindness and understanding.

Composed and empowered by this influx of strength and grace, Charlie took a few tentative steps toward Parker, looked him in the eye, and words just began to flow. "Parker, I'm sorry if we were louder than normal today. Sometimes we get pretty worked up out there and, well, you know all about what it's like to be in the middle of an intense game. Still, no excuses. We'll try to keep it down in the future."

Slack-jawed and incredulous, DMarks, BB, and George looked at their friend, eyes darting back and forth between each other, then back to Charlie, then to Parker.

"If you could give us one more chance, we'd appreciate it. Our parents would be disappointed in us if you take that cassette to the police department," added Charlie. "By the way, Parker, I've been meaning to ask you…my family and I were wondering if you might be able to join us for Christmas dinner? My mom's cooking a thirty-pound turkey, so we'll have plenty of food." He spread his arms to indicate a long, laden table. "Oh, and after dinner, we always take a nice stroll around the Tree Streets and through Law Park before dessert. If you're free, please come and spend the afternoon with us."

Now it was Parker who was speechless and frozen in place. He was stunned that someone actually had made eye contact with him— even more taken aback that someone wanted to befriend him with an invitation to Christmas dinner.

He stared back for what seemed like an eternity. *Does this young kid think he can create some kind of diversion to get him to lay off?* he wondered. *Does he think this is some kind of game?* In those days, kids weren't supposed to talk back when an adult was taking charge, particularly if there was a scolding involved.

Charlie kept going, "And for dessert, my mom makes three kinds of pies: blueberry, apple, and pumpkin. I always have a slice of each. You don't need to bring anything, Parker. Come just as you are. Okay? We'd really like to have you with us."

The phrase "come just as you are" caused Parker's knees to buckle. He was one-hundred-percent speechless now. A lot of his anger was based on his perception that people were not willing to accept him as he was; he was convinced that everyone wanted the pre-Vietnam version of Parker Jones and that he was unanimously rejected around town for the way he was now.

"So if you don't have any plans, please come over. You know where I live, right? You can help me tend to the fireplace. I know you're good with that sort of thing."

Parker felt himself rapidly thawing inside. He was so choked up that he couldn't even speak. This simple act of God-honoring kindness was more than he could handle. It was as though years of ice and stone were melting deep within him. Moved as he was, he was unable to respond in any way and simply looked at Charlie while struggling to hold back tears.

After a long pause, Charlie continued, "Well, hopefully, you can make it. You don't even have to tell us in advance. If you're free, just come over. There will be a place for you at our table, Parker."

For Parker, it had been years since anyone acted like they had a place for him in their life—in any shape or form. As the boys cautiously began to walk around him, Parker remained dazed, immobile. They picked up their pace as they got out to Pleasantville Road. As soon as they got out of sight from Law Park, DMarks could not contain himself any longer.

"That's my boy! I knew you had it in you! See, if you hang out with me, you learn how to stand up for yourself! I was about to step up and let him know how we really feel—it's a good thing you did what you did."

"Wait, what?" George did a double take. "Seriously, Marks, your mouth is like a convenience store—it never closes!" He turned to Charlie. "*That* was amazing! None of us would have had the courage to do what you just did!"

"Ditto, Charlie!" said BB. "That guy is darned scary, but you stood up to him."

"It wasn't that big of a deal, guys. I always felt Parker was a good guy inside. It's just that he's been through a lot. Besides, I was only doing what Sky told me to do."

"What, did you have a conversation with Sky earlier today or something?" asked DMarks.

"No, while we were standing there in front of Parker, Sky read me a Bible verse, and it helped put things in the right perspective. You guys didn't hear him?"

"That's it, now he's hearing things. I want you to go home, have a little dinner, and go to bed early. You'll feel better in the morning."

"Seriously, guys, that's not the first time I was in a jam when I heard his voice clear as blue water…leading me on to what I needed to do."

DMarks reached over to touch Charlie's forehead. "I think he might have a fever."

"Lay off, jerk. I'm not making this up," complained Charlie.

"I can't say I've heard his voice, but you have been like a mini-Superman lately…that speech you gave at the Advent Craft Festival, the incident in Central Park, that time at County Center," mused George.

"It's not just his voice. It kind of comes with this warm feeling, almost like someone's wrapping me up in a big, protective blanket or something," he explained.

"Okay, then. Anyone know what's on TV tonight?" asked DMarks, wanting to change the subject while making a circular motion with his finger by the side of his head as though Charlie had gone crazy.

"I wouldn't expect you to understand," said Charlie, "you're such a dweeb."

"Knock it off, DMarks. Can't you see he's serious?" asked BB as he flicked the back of D'Marks' ear.

"Watch it, bro. I'm a bad man," replied DMarks, raising his voice a few octaves to quote Muhammad Ali.

"Oh, I'm scared. Real scared," mocked BB as he tucked his leg behind DMarks and pushed him backward into a snowbank. With the mood now considerably lighter than earlier in the park, the boys dusted off DMarks and raced each other home.

Back in Law Park, Parker stood motionless, thunderstruck by the kindness Charlie had extended to him. Then, his emotions completely ruptured into a flood of sobbing, uncontrollable moans, wails, and sighs.

He dropped to his knees next to the War Memorial, where he stayed for the better part of an hour until he was able to regain conscious control of his thoughts and feelings. His mind raced through the gamut of childhood memories, the dreadful horrors of Vietnam, the loss of his parents, and the painful state he had been living in. He was wracked with emotional pain, which caused his body to heave and shake with unspeakable, grief-fueled spasms and convulsions.

Over and over, he'd incline his head down, pounding the frozen ground with his fists. Then, he'd lurch his head and shoulders backward until he was almost parallel to the ground, looking straight up at the night sky.

He cried and he wept uncontrollably until, finally, he reached a point where nothing audible could come out anymore—just silent tears, sorrows, regrets, and grief. Charlie's act of humanity had triggered a full-blown epiphany for Parker. After what seemed like forever and a day, he got back on his feet. Somehow, some way, he was reminded of a Bible verse that he took with him to Vietnam: Luke 6:32, *"If you love those who love you, what credit is that to you? Even sinners love those who love them. Love your enemies and do good. Be merciful even as your Father is merciful."*

He was conflicted about that message during his time in-country, especially when firing his M2 Carbine at people he didn't even know. But in that moment, he understood why Jesus would have emphasized the need to love everyone—those who love you back as well as those who do not. Now he realized that the ultimate weapon in this world is love. Love can change the remotest of hearts, including his own! *What a gift! Praise God from whom all blessings flow!* he thought

This was a watershed moment for Parker, and he knew it. He stood still, slowly turning and surveying the world around him. He was totally alone at the crest of Law Park, yet he felt like he was receiving a warm, beautiful embrace of some kind. *What could this be?* he wondered. There was no one else there, yet it was unmistakable. The comfort of someone's arms wrapped around him was so real. He couldn't even remember the last time he had felt something like that. It triggered a massive wave of new tears, but this time they were tears of joy. He glanced down. Feathers? It was as though someone had emptied a small down pillow around where he was standing. He bent down on one knee for a closer look, then picked one up, running his fingers along its soft, white edge. He smiled and placed it in his breast pocket for safe keeping.

Then, of all things, laughter began to bubble up from deep within him. The deepest, most cathartic and transformative laughter he had ever experienced. It was as though he was reconnected to life itself in that moment. The jaded bulk and burden of all his harsh experiences seemed to vanish. The world felt brand-new to him and joy-filled.

In his mind's eye, he found himself back in the sanctuary of the Briarcliff Congregational Church listening to a certain sermon delivered by Reverend Rapp almost twenty years ago. The subject was on how God can make all things new. Reverend Rapp's words came back to him loud and clear: "What do you call it? Call it grace."

"Yes, grace! Grace!" Parker shouted a prayer of thanksgiving out loud for the grace of God. And what better time for him to receive this wonderful gift of a new beginning than during the season of

Advent. He began to head home. As he walked, he could hardly contain himself. There was a spring in his step and, as he got to the business section of the village, he greeted everyone he passed with warm holiday cheer. He even offered gentle and patient help to an elderly couple carrying groceries out of Noller's Market. He didn't mind the sideways looks he was getting, he hadn't felt that good in years.

The air has never smelled so fresh, he thought. *Nor had the stars ever shone so brightly.* As he headed toward the north end of town, he noticed that the Manor Barber Shop was still open. The last time he had stopped in there was for a pre-boot camp crew cut. A page had been turned in his life, and he decided to mark it with a fresh haircut and a clean shave.

Chapter 24

Library Lessons

Faith is the assurance of things hoped for,
the conviction of things not seen.
—Hebrews 11:1

The next day in school found the boys sitting through a tiresome math class. The lesson matched the weather, which was lackluster and dreary. Mr. Stevens was using the overhead projector to formulate equations. He had a clever system, or so he thought, of using colored Flair pens on the transparent slide to emphasize different parts of the equations. Unfortunately, it didn't help to make the subject matter any more compelling.

Math was like a foreign language to Charlie and the guys, and they quickly lost interest as the teacher prattled on. The classroom lights were dimmed for the overhead projector, so DMarks seized the opportunity to pass notes between them. He kicked things off with a cartoon drawing of the prior day's incident with Parker Jones. It showed Parker as a three-headed monster towering over the boys and Charlie standing out in front with a halo over his head. "St. Charles" was written in block letters underneath.

George got into the act by jotting down what he was anticipating under the tree on Christmas day—a new skateboard, a transistor radio, and an Atari system—and adding sarcastically that DMarks was probably getting a pet rock. Meanwhile, BB scribbled a reminder that *A Charlie Brown Christmas* was on CBS that night at eight o'clock.

Most of it was lost on Charlie, who wasn't really paying attention to the notes being passed around. More and more lately, he had been thinking about his relationship with Sky; in just a few short weeks, they had become kindred spirits. The biggest thing, though, was the handful of incidents when Charlie heard Sky's voice and felt a warm, comforting guidance at critical moments. It was all so out of the ordinary, and he struggled to make sense of it.

He had never met anyone like Sky. There were lots of great adult role models around Briarcliff, but Sky had qualities that defied description and set him apart. The more he thought about it, the more he was drawn to what the Bible had to say about angels. Just last Sunday, Reverend Higgins preached on Luke 2:8–11: *"There were shepherds in the field, keeping watch over their flock by night, and an angel of the Lord appeared to them and the glory of the Lord shone around them and they were sore afraid. And the angel said to them: Fear not for behold, I bring you good news of a great joy that will be for all people. For unto you is born this day in the city of David a Savior who is Christ the Lord. And this will be a sign for you: you will find a baby wrapped in swaddling cloths and lying in a manger."*

Wait a minute, he thought. *If the Bible spoke in such detail about angels, then they must be real. They wouldn't be in the Bible if they were just some kind of make-believe fairytale.* He further reasoned that if they could appear in Old and New Testament times, they could also appear in Briarcliff Manor in the 1970s.

His experiences with Sky were all so uncanny. Was he really just some random guy who happened to be passing through town and took a temporary job with the Rec Department? A job which was only opened because of a completely unexpected early blast of winter weather?

Suddenly, he was struck by a daring concept: it seemed like a longshot and impossible to fully decipher. He sat up straight, his brow furrowed deeply, wondering if it could conceivably be that Sky was actually some kind of guardian angel, heaven-sent with a special purpose to carry out? He decided to visit the school library after school that day to do some research.

Since math was the last class of the day, he only had another half hour to go. Finally, the bell rang and school was over. He went straight to his locker to get his jacket and five subject loose-leaf binder, then headed to the library. As he walked through the front entrance, he was greeted warmly by Ms. Miller, the librarian.

"Hi there, Charlie!" she said. "This is a bit of a surprise. No sports this afternoon?"

"Not today, Ms. Miller. Basketball practice is suspended until after Christmas."

"No hockey out on Gooseneck?"

"Actually, they closed the pond for the afternoon to give it a rest from all the use it was getting. The ice was getting kind of chewed up, and Henry wanted to brush it off and water it down."

"Well, I'm glad to see you. Let me know if I can be of any help."

"Thanks, Ms. Miller. I will."

Charlie headed to the card catalogue where he began to search out books on the subject of angels, seraphs, and heavenly messengers. He found a few interesting selections and began to skim the pages, but they were all fiction. In one, the angel character was portrayed as an innocent, clueless, stumblebum. Another featured a fallen angel, full of faults and bad habits. Still others cast the angel as a part of a kid's fable. None seemed to have any of the characteristics found in the Bible.

He moved on to the Microfiche machine to see if he could find articles from newspapers and periodicals. That's where he hit a rich vein of material; there were dozens of recorded incidents that bore a striking resemblance to what he had been experiencing with Sky. He kept scanning article after article, getting more and more absorbed with each find. Some articles were very recent, others dated back to the 1800s.

Amazingly, he found a brief piece published in December 1898 by the *Briarcliff Daily Voice*, the local newspaper started by Mr. Law. The article referenced his generous sponsorship and support of missionaries to Japan. When asked what drew his attention to that particular cause, he responded by saying that he had experienced "a beautiful, other-worldly, yet unmistakable bit of guidance from an angelic voice calmly but definitely telling me to become involved in helping to spread God's Word in that part of the world." He added, "At random times I'd be alone in my study or walking the grounds when, suddenly, I'd be visited by an audible voice and a warm presence. No one else was nearby but, nonetheless, it was as though Mrs. Law and I had an unexpected visitor. So clear was the message that I was moved with conviction to become involved." Charlie read the rest in awe. "At about that same time, there was a handsome stranger in town, quite robust in physique and magnanimous in character. He said he was passing by on his way up north, but while he was among us, he always seemed to leave things a little better than they were before."

Walter Law himself had his own experience with a heavenly friend—right here in Briarcliff! The more he discovered, the clearer it became to Charlie: Sky had all of the qualities people noted when they spoke of their own personal experiences with heavenly visitors. Two plus hours flew by and the next thing he knew, it was close to four thirty in the afternoon and time for Ms. Miller to begin to close the library for the day.

"You're pretty absorbed over there, Charlie. What are you researching?" she asked.

"Um, well, you might be kind of surprised if I were to tell you," he said.

"Ha! I'm a librarian! I've helped people find books on everything under the sun. Your friend Derrick Marks was here just the other day trying to read up on gangsters like Al Capone and John Dillinger. And…some of the girls were here to dig out issues of *Tiger Beat* and *Seventeen* looking for photos of David Cassidy, Robby Benson, and Davy Jones."

Charlie got a kick out of hearing about DMarks looking up things like gangsters. Probably the real reason why DMarks visited the library was because Ms. Miller was so attractive and all the middle school boys had a crush on her. Either way, it made him feel more comfortable explaining what he was there for.

"I was trying to learn a little more about the subject of guardian angels."

"You're in luck! I happen to have done a fair amount of reading on the subject myself."

"Wow, really?"

"Sure! It's a very popular subject actually."

"Far out! Do you think angels still visit earth these days? Have you ever had any experiences where you felt like you might have encountered one? Do you believe they're here with us now?"

Ms. Miller smiled at Charlie's enthusiasm. "I do, I have, and I believe! For starters, the Bible absolutely confirms that angels are sent to protect us, communicate with us, and help achieve God's plans in our lives."

"So…you've actually felt like there was someone who spoke to you and gave you guidance?"

"As a matter of fact, Charlie, more than anything else, that was how I got through the loss of my dad in the Korean War."

"Oh. I didn't know about your dad, Ms. Miller. It must have been really hard for you and your family."

"It was. We were all just devastated after we received the news. It was around Memorial Day and the town pool over in Law Park was about to open for the season, so at least I had that as a go-to place to do things with my friends and keep the loss of my dad off my mind. Back then, we kids practically lived at the pool all summer long."

"Right, same as it is these days," said Charlie.

"That year, there was a new lifeguard. I have to say, he was incredibly attractive and all the girls were crazy about him. He was very tall and extremely well-built, almost like he had played pro-fessional football or something. As I recall, he also looked like he came from the beaches of Southern California with a thick head of sandy blond hair and a really cool, well-groomed beard—long before beards had even come into style."

Charlie was bowled over. It was as though she just described Sky.

"While he was in town for the summer, he lived up at The King's College in the president's mansion with Dr. Cook. Anyway, he was a super positive guy, and that made him all the more popular. He'd always say or do something that made us smile and feel good about ourselves. No one ever quite knew where he came from or where he went to after the pool closed Labor Day Weekend. But I don't think any of us will ever forget him."

Charlie was hanging on every word, practically hypnotized. "All summer long, whenever I had a down moment, I'd start to feel this really warm, comforting presence. Even though I never actually saw anything or anyone, there was this rich, soothing voice reminding me that although my dad was gone from this earth, he had accepted God's offer of grace through Christ and his faith had carried him to a wonderful, heavenly destiny. It was so beautiful and heartening to hear."

"Wow, Ms. Miller. That's awesome. So you actually heard a voice? Actual words?"

"Yes, that's right. The words never seemed to be audible to others, but I sure could hear them loud and clear."

"And did you also feel like, maybe, you were being wrapped up in a warm quilt or comforter?"

"I'd say that's a good way of putting it. Hard to describe. Almost like a bear hug, a lot like the way my dad used to wrap me up in his arms when I was a little girl."

Charlie was riveted. The parallels between his experience and Ms. Miller's were plain and clear. "There was one other thing," she said, "every once in a while, I'd notice a feather in my path or near where I might have been standing or sitting. At first I didn't think anything of it. It's not exactly uncommon. But what really got my attention was when it began to happen at times when I was indoors at home or school or places like the mall."

Charlie's mind was approaching overload. Not only did his research add insights to what he was experiencing, but now, someone who he trusted had experienced very similar things. "Gosh, Ms.

Miller, I can't thank you enough for your time. Maybe we can talk again soon."

"We absolutely can, Charlie. Anytime. You should begin to head home. It's already getting dark. I'll put those books away for you."

"Okay, Ms. Miller. Thank you. Thank you very much."

On his way home, Charlie was awash in thoughts about Sky and all that he just heard from Ms. Miller. It was a lot to digest and understand all at once. *Could it actually be that Sky had been to Briarcliff before? Was it possible that this was his third visit here?* He was onto something, and now he was even more intent on getting a better understanding of it.

As he walked, he felt very light on his feet. He was flying high with the new insights he had gained from his conversation with Ms. Miller. Others might have responded with apprehension and maybe even fear. But not Charlie. He had a heart for God and was keen on knowing more.

CHAPTER 25

MOM TIME

*Train up a child in the way he should go, even
when he is old he will not depart from it.*
—Proverbs 22:6

Mrs. Riverton was a very organized person who liked to be thoroughly prepared on all things well in advance, especially if they were going to have company. Even though Christmas was still a week away, she went to her electric typewriter and keyed out a special shopping list. She liked to shop at the A&P; Charlie had time, so he went along as well. Truth be told, he had fond memories as a young boy riding in the seat of the shopping carriage.

As they pulled into a parking space, Charlie's mom asked him to stop next door at the Rexall Pharmacy to pick up some aspirin and cough medicine. No one was sick at the Rivertons' house, but they were running low on these things and she liked to have a well-stocked medicine cabinet. Charlie was always happy to oblige. Rexall sponsored his Little League baseball team, which had won the championship at Ryder Park that past spring. Whenever he came in, the druggist and the store manager treated him like a local sports hero.

"There he is! CHARLIE HUSTLE!" shouted the store manager.

"Hi, Mrs. Bishop," said Charlie. "Merry Christmas!"

"And Merry Christmas to you, Charlie. What brings you in today?"

"Oh, just some basic stuff. Aspirin and cough medicine."

"Don't tell me someone's coming down with a cold!"

"Nah, just stocking up for my mom."

"Thank goodness! Let's see, she likes Bayer Aspirin, I have some right here. I think she also likes St. Joseph's cough syrup. She usually takes some Mentholatum and Vicks VapoRub as well."

"Oh, right, I'll take that too."

"Okay, Charlie, I'll ring you up over here," said Mrs. Bishop. "That will be $5.95. Tell ya what, give me six bucks and help yourself to a fistful of Double Bubble."

"Gee, thanks, Mrs. Bishop!"

"It's the least we can do for that homerun you hit in the championship game for our team!"

"Oh, that was just a lucky hit. Thanks again, Mrs. Bishop. I hope you and your family have a merry Christmas!"

"Same to you, Charlie!"

Charlie walked next door to the A&P. By the time he found his mom, she had already covered three aisles with her methodical way of shopping. She knew where everything was, and she strolled each aisle systematically, starting on the right and working her way to the left. Up and down the aisles they went until they made it to the far end of the store where the butcher and meat counters were.

Charlie smiled at the way his mom got so focused in on her shopping activities. It was similar to when she wrote out their Christmas cards or did her annual, all-day Christmas cookie baking marathon. It was like she was on a mission.

"What will it be today, Mrs. Riverton?" asked Harry the butcher.

"Hi, Harry. Merry Christmas to you! Can I put a couple of things on order, then pick them up on the 23rd?" she asked.

"Of course!" said Harry, pulling a pencil out from behind his ear. "What will it be?" He licked the tip of the pencil and got ready to write.

"Let's see, we need a large spiral ham and a thirty-pound Turkey."

"Hello! Wow, you must be having a lot of company."

"Well, we are expecting a few visitors."

"My mom always cooks for an army," interjected Charlie.

"So I've noticed," said Harry. "Okay, Mrs. Riverton, I'll have everything ready on the 23rd."

"Thanks, Harry!"

"You're welcome, Mrs. Riverton. Merry Christmas!"

The best part of shopping at the A&P was visiting with Doris, the cashier. Her line was always the longest as people preferred chatting with her as they paid. She never failed to send you home with a smile.

"Charlie, I remember when you were small enough to sit in the carriage seat when your mother came shopping," she said. "Now look at you! Good gracious! Growing up so fast I can't keep up with you!" Charlie loved hearing these things from Doris, even though she mentioned them most times he was there.

"I'm in middle school now, Miss Doris. It's really fun," he replied.

"Oh, Lord, bless you! How do you like your teachers?"

"Most of them are great. Mr. Hunt is the best. He's funny and seems to care so much about us."

"That's good to hear. Now you watch out with your social life. Some kids your age are smoking. Doris says, 'Stay away from cigarettes!' They're no good for you!"

"Don't worry, Miss Doris, I'm not into that."

"You're a good boy, Charlie. Your parents raised you well!"

"Thank you, Miss Doris. Actually, with parents like mine, I kind of think that I should have turned out better!"

"Oh, Lord, I wish there were more like you, Charlie. By the way, your friend Sky was just here. Such a nice man!"

"Sky? Was here? He's awesome!"

"He told me that he thought we might be related! Imagine that. He's white as milk and I'm black as midnight!" She laughed. "Said something about biblical lineage or whatnot. We had a good laugh, but you know what? I think he really meant it! Come to think of it, we're all God's children, so I guess it's true!"

Mrs. Riverton smiled at Doris as she took out her checkbook to pay. Doris handed her back a receipt and a ream of plaid stamps.

Charlie and his mom exchanged holiday wishes with Doris, then headed out to the car. It was a beautiful December day and holiday music was playing on a loudspeaker outside the A&P.

As he reached for another bag to put in the trunk, Charlie spotted what looked like Parker Jones coming out from Pircio's Dry Cleaners. Their eyes met, and Parker immediately began walking very intentionally in their direction. Charlie's heart went into panic mode.

"Mom, let's hurry up and unload the carriage."

"What's the rush, son?"

"Oh, nothing. Just some homework I need to get back to."

Charlie's mind raced. Was Parker angry from the other day? Was he going to cause a scene right there in the parking lot? He was coming on too fast to be avoided. As he closed in, Charlie observed that he looked and carried himself very differently. Clearly, he had visited the barber. Gone was the beard. Gone was the long hair. Gone was the American flag bandanna and the jeans jacket with cut-off sleeves. He was clean-cut and neatly dressed. Even the burning look in his eyes was gone; it had given way to a kind and considerate expression, which confirmed a new, peaceful countenance. Charlie's fear had now turned to curiosity and anticipation.

"Mrs. Riverton!" shouted Parker. "I wanted to thank you very much for your invitation to Christmas dinner. I'm very much looking forward to it and was wondering what I can bring."

Caught completely unaware, Charlie's mom nonetheless responded without skipping a beat. "Wonderful, Parker! That makes us very happy. I think we're good on all things food-related." She pointed to the overflowing carriage of groceries.

"So I see. It looks like you're cooking for an army!"

"Ha! That's the second time I've heard that in the last five minutes!"

"Looks like you'll have plenty of leftovers. My mother, God rest her soul, would never approve of me showing up empty-handed. Please, there must be something I can bring."

"Honestly, we'd be so glad to have you with us. Just come as you are!" Once again, that phrase registered in a deeply moving way with Parker and gave him pause as he recalled his experience in the park.

"Tell ya what, I'll bring something for Barnes and Noble," said Parker, who himself was a dog lover. "Maybe a few marrow bones from Harry the butcher."

"Great idea! They're part of the family too," said Mrs. Riverton.

"Okay, looking forward to it!" He then turned to Charlie self-consciously and lowered his voice. "Listen, buddy, I want to thank you. I wasn't very kind to you and your friends the other day in the park, and I'm really sorry. I appreciate your patience and your kindness to me. You taught me a lesson, and it made a difference, man. A really big difference. Give me five!" Charlie raised his palm to meet Parker's, and then they gave each other that new upward-clasping handshake popular with the younger set. Parker then headed into the A&P.

Mrs. Riverton watched him go, then looked at Charlie. "Did someone maybe forget to mention something?"

"I guess I kind of did, Mom. We bumped into Parker the other afternoon on the way home from Law Park. He was really bummed out, so I tried to cheer him up by inviting him over for Christmas dinner."

"That was a very nice gesture, Charlie. I'm glad you did. By the way, when did Parker get all cleaned up like that?"

"Well, he wasn't that way when we saw him in the park, so it must have been in the last forty-eight hours or so."

Charlie was completely amazed at Parker's transformation. As the afternoon sun cast a wonderful warmth across his back and shoulders, he reflected on how far a simple act of kindness could go in the life of another person.

"Tell ya what, Charlie," said his mom. "Do you think this might be a good time to go over to Bob's Army-Navy in Ossining? I know you wanted a new pair of Bauer Black Panther skates for Christmas. If we drive over now, you can try them on to make sure we get the right size."

Bauer Black Panthers were the best hockey skates money could buy, and Charlie could not have been more enthusiastic. They drove his mom's favorite route: up across Underhill Road, past Ossining High School, and down to Main Street. As luck would have it, there was a parking space right outside of Bob's. Charlie would have to wait till Christmas morning to officially have the skates, but he didn't mind at all.

"This is much better than me buying the wrong thing. Plus, you stopped believing in Santa Claus years ago."

"No argument here, Mom!" said Charlie. They walked to the back of the store to the sporting goods department and found a pair of the skates on display. The only question was if they had Charlie's size in stock. Bob himself came over to greet them. He took Charlie's foot measurements and headed to the storage area behind the curtain. Moments later he came out with a single box.

"Last pair in your size, Charlie. Let's try these on to see how they fit." Charlie was thrilled to slip them on and happy to confirm that they felt perfect.

"Okay then. Will there be anything else?" asked Bob. "Need pucks or a stick? We have some new right-handed CCM and Koho's that just arrived. How about a hockey helmet? Kids and even some NHL players are beginning to wear them. I think it'll be mandatory before long."

"I think the skates are enough. Thanks though," said Charlie.

"Okay then, follow me to the cash register and I'll ring this up." Charlie felt euphoric. These were the same skates worn by all his favorite players on the Rangers. He could not wait until the day after Christmas to use them.

"Mom, thank you," he gushed. "I don't really know what to say. This is the best Christmas gift I've ever received."

"You're a good boy, Charlie, and we're very proud of you. I know you'll take good care of them."

On the way back, they made their way up Highland Avenue and turned right at Roosevelt Square for a quick stop at Books 'n Things in the Chilmark Shopping Center. Charlie needed some school supplies as well as some extra help with Shakespeare. Books 'n Things sold Monarch notes, which would help him to understand The Bard and his otherwise, to Charlie, indecipherable plays.

A popular destination, Books 'n Things also sold stationery products, jewelry, and other assorted odds and ends. Charlie was at that age when he was beginning to get into the gift-giving act and spotted something for his mom. She loved turquoise jewelry, and there was a beautiful pendant he knew she would like. While she was browsing, he quickly took it to the cash register and used some of the money he made from yard jobs to pay for it. Later that night, he'd find some wrapping paper and a bow, then put it under the tree. Just as the cashier was handing him a small bag, his mom returned.

"What do you have there, Charlie?"

"Oh…nothing," Charlie fiddled with a bowl of key chains next to the cash register.

"A gift for someone special?"

"You could say that." Charlie smiled as he managed to tell the truth without giving away the surprise.

"I wonder who that could be," she asked playfully, thinking it must be for Michelle.

"You can try to guess, but I won't tell ya!"

A lot of kids Charlie knew complained about their parents from time to time. But he had always felt fortunate for the mom and dad he had been blessed with. They headed out to the car as dusk began to set in.

"Thanks again, Mom. Love you and love Dad," he added.

"Thank you for saying that, Charlie. We love you right back."

CHAPTER 26

HOME FIRES

---

*Do nothing from rivalry or conceit, but in humility
count others as more significant than yourself.*
—Philippians 2:3

That Sunday, PBS aired their annual Christmas movie marathon. Mrs. Riverton liked to tune in as she wrote out the over 150 personalized Christmas cards they sent each year to family and friends. Not surprisingly, she had a highly organized system. First, Charlie's dad would set up a card table in front of the TV, along with a special chair and throw pillow to prop up her back. Then, left to right, she'd position her assembly line: overflowing address book, a jar of red and green pens, a stack of Christmas cards with envelopes, and a supply of postage stamps.

Fortified with an oversized mug of coffee in hand, she'd sit down, take a deep breath, crack a few knuckles, and dive right in. Each card received a personal note. Usually, she tried to offer a word of encouragement, some support, or congratulations for something specific each recipient had experienced that year.

Charlie was stationed to her right. His job was to stuff the envelopes, lick the flap, and stamp a return address on each envelope. He liked tamping the ink pad with the engraved rubber stamp, then applying a clean, crisp watermark.

Finally, Charlie's dad, while donning a Santa Claus hat, would meticulously place a postage stamp on the front of each envelope and a Christmas seal from the American Lung Association on the back.

Periodically, Charlie's mom would look up to make sure her helpers were doing a conscientious job, just like she watched over her students at Todd School. It was amazing how all three could stay focused on their individual tasks while not missing a scene from any of the movies playing just a few feet away. The movie marathon set the tone. There were musicals like *White Christmas* and *Holiday Inn* and others that had a valuable message such as *The Bishop's Wife* and *It's a Wonderful Life.*

Generally speaking, Charlie didn't care for black-and-white movies, but Christmas movies were in a whole different category as far as he was concerned. He loved them and the featured actors and actresses like Donna Reed and Jimmy Stewart, both of whom seemed to transcend their craft. *It's a Wonderful Life* was his favorite. Local legend had it that the setting for the fictional town of Bedford Falls was actually modeled after Katonah, New York, about fifteen minutes north of Briarcliff.

But that year, the movie resonated with Charlie in a whole new way. As he sat elbow-to-elbow with his parents, he was intrigued by the ways in which one life touches so many others. *True enough,* he thought. His dad often said that the most valuable currency we have is the affect we have on others.

"How many more to go, Mom?" Charlie asked, stretching out his fingers for a second.

"We're only on the L's Charlie."

"An entire movie just played, and we're only halfway through the alphabet?"

"Hey, these movies are being presented without commercial interruption, so they run a little faster than normal," his mom replied, reaching for a pile of cards.

"Well, can we take a break? I'm thirsty from licking all these envelopes, and my hand is tired from stamping."

"Maybe you should get Barnes and Noble lick the rest," quipped his dad.

"Okay, Charlie. I think we can stop for a bit," said his mom. "Let's head over to the kitchen to see what's in the fridge." Out came a bottle of ice-cold milk, which paired perfectly with the Christmas cookies sitting in a tin canister on the kitchen table.

"What's your favorite Christmas gift of all time, Mom?" asked Charlie.

"Gosh, Charlie, this will be my forty-fifth Christmas, so I've been blessed to open a lot of gifts over the years." She tilted her head and looked off into the dining room to give the question more thought.

"I remember getting a yo-yo when I was a little girl. All the kids had one, and we'd spend hours trying to learn new tricks with them. I also remember getting a Radio Flyer red wagon, which was fun because we used it for everything, including giving each other rides around the block." More memories came to her. "I also loved the Lionel electric train set I got when I was ten. Grandpa and I used to spend hours setting up a whole miniature village in the basement of our house, then we'd lay the train tracks all throughout it."

"Funny, none of those things lasted. Sooner or later, they broke or wore out. But there was another gift I received when I was little that I still use regularly. It's that pocket Bible right over here." She pulled a small, well-worn Bible from the cabinet where she kept her stationary. "This Bible belonged to my dad, who took it with him to Europe during World War I. He read from it whenever he could. He used to say that it helped keep him high and dry."

"That was Grandpapa's? Cool!" Charlie looked at it as if it was a family heirloom.

Charlie's dad added, "Then when I went to fight in Europe during World War II, Grandpapa gave it to me. I read from it each night too."

"Wow, it's in really good shape considering where it's been and how old it is," noted Charlie.

"Well, you have to take care of your important possessions, and during those tough times, this was the most important thing I had. Not my helmet, not my gun, not my canteen—God's Word."

Charlie rubbed his hands over the cover. It had such character and, now knowing its history, it had that much more meaning to him.

"So this Bible crossed the Atlantic four times?"

"Yep! Made it home safely after each tour of duty."

On the inside flap, there was a note referencing 2 Timothy 1:7. He turned to it to see what it was. *"For God gave us a spirit not of fear but of power and love."* Charlie was intrigued at how the Bible seemed to have verses and messages that were relevant for all of life's situations. The very verse that kept his father and grandfather calm and focused, while fighting in a foreign war, was also relevant to him and his current everyday life in Briarcliff.

"Tell ya what, Charlie, I think it's time we keep this tradition going. Here, this is for you," said his mom, handing the Bible to him.

"Mom, that's really awesome, but are you sure?"

"Absolutely! I know you'll put it to good use."

"This is special. Thank you, Mom!" His parents looked on smiling as Charlie carefully turned the pages of his new gift. "I'll keep it on the nightstand by my bed," he said.

"That's a great place for it, Charlie," said his dad. "That way, if you read from it before you go to bed, your mind can work on the verses all night as you sleep."

"That would be an improvement over some of the dreams I've had lately," said Charlie.

His mom looked at the clock which hung above the picture window by the kitchen sink and saw that a whole half hour had passed. "Okay, team. It's time to get back in the game," she announced, putting the lid back on the cookie tin.

"Let the games begin!" said Charlie's dad. And with that, they headed back to the den. The opening credits for *Miracle on 34th Street* had just finished—perfect timing for them to restart their card writing/envelope stuffing production line.

CHAPTER 27
TRIAL BY FIRE

As for you brothers and sisters, do not grow weary in doing good.
—2 Thessalonians 3:13

The week before Christmas had finally arrived! Everyone was filled with that special childlike anticipation that only seemed available between Thanksgiving and Christmas. Peace on earth and goodwill to all carried the day as people stopped to chat, embrace one another, and spread holiday cheer.

At school, Christmas break was set to commence that afternoon—right after the annual holiday concert, which was performed by the chorus, orchestra, and band. As two o'clock rolled around, the middle school student body began to file into the auditorium in the original 1928 wing of the building.

One of the highlights each year was the pageant scene starring all the teachers. The very popular and highly energetic Mrs. Dice accompanied on the piano and led the sing-alongs. In between songs, Mr. Kersting and Mrs. Oraby, dressed in full Dickens garb, read Victorian era Christmas poems. Even Dr. Angulo, the much beloved Spanish teacher, got into the act, coming out on stage to sing an exuberant "Feliz Navidad" in an oversized sombrero.

The concert was anchored by a rousing version of "Hanukkah, Oh Hanukkah," enthusiastically conducted by Dr. Polivnick and the Middle School Orchestra. Then, a group of children from Todd School came out on stage for the crowd-pleasing "Dreidel, Dreidel, Dreidel" song.

After the last sing-along, Principal Van Hoven made his closing remarks and wished everyone well on their school break. With a loud cheer, people began to exit the auditorium and milled around outside the school. It was a happy time with lots of laughs and hugs. After a while, Charlie and the guys headed home. They planned to go sledding after dinner that night at Briar Hall Country Club.

Sleigh riding at Briar Hall was somewhat of a rite of passage growing up in Briarcliff. One slope in particular provided a breakneck thrill. Known as "Heineken's Hideout" among the older kids in town, it started up near the clubhouse by the 17th tee box and went steeply downhill and across the 11th hole fairway.

The ride was vertical and intense and provided plenty of opportunities to get airborne, thanks to a smattering of bunkers along the way. It also required that everyone kept their wits about them; the short level-off at the bottom of the hill necessitated a well-timed bailout to avoid flying headlong into the woods—and riding an even steeper incline down toward the town center.

The night was cold, crisp, and crystal clear. The stars were brilliant and glistening in the deep night sky. The full moon cast such a bright glow that the leafless trees pitched exaggerated shadows across the sweeping hills and fairways. The boys were having a rollicking good time. Down the hill they went, one swashbuckling ride after another, trying to top one another in the daredevil department as boys their age were wont to do.

A fresh coating of snow had cast a still hush over the winter landscape, which allowed sound to travel much farther than normal. They could actually hear the klaxon of tug boats and barges out on the Hudson River, way over on the other side of town. The brittle air, the radiance of the moon, and the noiseless backdrop made for a 360-degree sensory experience.

The boys particularly welcomed the new, powdery snow because it helped absorb crashes and wipeouts. Invariably, as one was tearing down the slope, another was walking back up and would pelt the oncoming sledder with snowballs. Sometimes, a flat-out flying dive tackle was in order.

As the boys escalated the competition over who could be the most daring, DMarks, true to form, decided to ride the four-man toboggan standing upright, as though it was a surfboard.

"You're not seriously planning to go down like that, are you?" asked Charlie.

"You bet your sweet bippy I am!" replied DMarks.

"You're crazy, DMarks," warned George. "That would work on the hills over by Todd School, but this one is way too steep!"

"Stand back, ladies! And please, don't try this at home."

"Go ahead, but if you spend Christmas in the hospital, don't say we didn't warn you!" said George.

"Hey, it takes guts to try this," said DMarks.

"And a total lack of brains!" said BB. "Someone just call for the ambulance now!"

With that, DMarks inched forward and began his ride, yelling back to the others, "The lion sleeps tonight!" Almost immediately, he knew it was a risky mistake. He was going so fast already that all he could do was hold on for dear life—and scream at a pitch so high it would have been the envy of the girl sopranos in the Glee Club.

The boys doubled over in laughter. "Cowabunga, dude!" yelled George.

"Watch out for that tree!" shouted BB.

"Buckle your seatbelt!" added Charlie.

DMarks tried to control the direction the toboggan was going in. As it veered to the left, he braced himself knowing that was where most of the bunkers were; he hit one and went completely airborne. The toboggan flew out from under him as his feet shot up above his head. The boys watched wordlessly in awe. He was at least twelve feet in the air. Then, with an unforgettable thud, DMarks landed seat-first, tumbling head over heels the rest of the way down the slope.

The laughing stopped. This wipeout was as bad as the famous downhill skier featured on the opening sizzle reel for *Wide World of Sports*. The boys sprinted to where he lay in the snow—lifeless as a frozen hockey puck and seemingly unconscious. The boys dropped down on their knees for a closer look.

"We told him not to try that!" said BB.

"I think this is serious, you guys! He's not moving!" said George, giving DMarks a tentative poke.

"Quick, someone run over to the Zirmans' house to call for help," said Charlie.

"On it!" said George as he jumped to his feet. "I'll get my dad to come with the ambulance!" He took off running.

"Should we try to move him?" asked BB. "Maybe we could put him on the toboggan and tow him over to Pine Road while we wait for help."

"I don't think we should touch him," cautioned Charlie. "I saw a situation like this in an episode of ChiPs…and they didn't move the guy because it could paralyze him if he had a back injury."

"We can't just do nothing. He'll freeze lying there in the snow."

"Here, let's put our jackets over him to try to keep him warm." Charlie started to take off his parka. "I swear, if he survives this, I'm going to kill him!"

DMarks couldn't contain himself any longer and jumped up and let out the loudest, most obnoxious laugh he could. "Merry Christmas to all and to all a good night! Here, you can have your jackets back, they don't suit my taste in outerwear."

The boys were stunned at first. Then, they did the only thing they could at a moment like that. They dove on DMarks in a frenzied dog pile and gave out dead arms, kidney punches, and charlie horses at a frantic pace. But DMarks couldn't feel anything through all the winterwear. To the boys' further irritation, it only seemed to make him laugh harder.

"This is like a pillow fight with my younger sister!" he shouted through his guffaws.

"You're such a dweeb!" said Charlie. "We thought you were really hurt!"

"Awe, I didn't know you cared. Here, let me give you guys a big hug," said the taunting DMarks. As he reached out, BB shoved a handful of snow under his sweatshirt and down his back. It didn't even phase him. Having heard all the commotion, George came running back. One look at the smirk on D'Marks' face and he immediately dive-bombed him.

They continued to wrestle around in a scrum, when suddenly a harsh, jarring siren pierced the night air. It was coming from the firehouse just below them in the valley section of Briarcliff. Somehow though, this was different than the normal signal sent out when there was a fire or if an ambulance was needed; it was like whoever was sounding the alarm was in a complete state of panic. It kept wailing on and on well beyond the normal cycle.

The laughter and adrenaline-filled fun gave way to an eerie, disconcerting feeling among the boys. The shrill, earsplitting siren was harrowing and unsettling out there on the barren hillside in the evening darkness. Slowly, without a word, the boys untangled themselves and just stood there, shoulder-to-shoulder, looking out over the moonlit scene.

"You guys hear that? Once the siren cycles through four times, it's a general alarm. That means a house fire," explained George. "This is on the twelfth cycle, so it's really serious. It's like the switch is broken."

"This is alarming," cracked Derrick.

"Don't be a jerk, DMarks. I don't think this is something to joke about," said Charlie.

"Yeah, DMarks. Sometimes you don't know when to shut up," said George, shoving him away. "Something bad awful is happening. I bet this means they're calling for mutual aid from Ossining."

"Wait, I can hear the fire trucks starting to roll. It sounds like they're headed over toward North State Road," said BB.

"Yeah, like over by Squires, maybe?" said Charlie.

"Man, I could sure go for a Squires burger about now," DMarks exhaled.

"Everyone loves Squires burgers, but only you could think of food at a time like this" chided BB.

They were standing at one of the highest points in Briarcliff. During the winter months, when the trees were bare, they could look out over the entire valley area in town including the central business district dotted with shops and restaurants.

With a gasp, DMarks shouted, "You guys, over there!" He was pointing toward the northeast section of town. There in the distance was an absolutely ferocious fire, raging out of control. It seemed like the flames were reaching a hundred feet in the air or higher as they cast an ominous, orange sheen across the sky.

The boys didn't really know what to make of it. Nothing they had ever seen could compare, save for *The Towering Inferno*, which they all regretted going to the prior week. In their short lives, none of them had encountered any kind of tragedy, but they could plainly see that this was a ruinous thing.

Even though it was happening in the distance, it made their stomachs churn. They knew they were witnessing a cruel catastrophe unfold. As they lingered in a confused state, no words were spoken. They just stood there and stared at the sickening, awful spectacle. None of them had any desire to keep sledding. Quietly, they just turned and started heading home, dragging their sleds and toboggans behind them. No one spoke a word.

That night, the most heartbreaking disaster in the history of Briarcliff Manor was taking place. The fire started in one of the wash houses over on North State Road. Since they were built so close to each other, it was only a matter of minutes before they were all fully engulfed. The late-December wind only helped fuel the flames as they spread from house to house. The fire was so fierce that it reached all the way down to Gilmore's Garage and across to The Huddle, where half the volunteer fire department had been hanging out enjoying a few beers.

Because of frozen snowbanks around the hydrant, the fire-fighters had a hard time getting access to water. They were literally chopping away at the ice and snow with axes. Meanwhile, Sky sped down from the college in his pickup truck. He jumped out and went straight to the hydrant. With each stride he took, the snow and ice began to miraculously melt away. It was as though his feet were radiating heat like a blast furnace. Then, he reached down and opened the hydrant cap with his bare hands.

He called out to the volunteer firefighters, who were staring in complete amazement. "C'mon, boys! Let's hook up those hoses!"

"Did you see what I just saw?" asked one.

"No way he could have just done that," said another. "And how'd all that snow and ice just disappear?"

"How much *did* we have to drink at The Huddle?"

"Not enough!"

The chief interrupted, "Let's talk about it later! Get those hoses over there!"

They were in business now that they had water, but it was too late. Everything burned to the ground. All was lost. The students up at The King's College could see the tragedy unfold from up on Lodge Road. As they came out of their dormitories, they locked arms while Dr. Cook led a candlelight prayer vigil.

A few people were taken to Phelps Hospital for treatment of minor burns and smoke inhalation. But amazingly, no one was seriously hurt. In the end, twenty-five families were out in the cold. They had nothing except the clothes on their backs and their frightened, aching hearts. It was a scene of total despair and destruction. Some people stared blankly as though life itself had been cruelly ripped right out of them. Others stood nearby, quietly weeping. There was no consolation, no solace to be had—just shock and a dreadful sense of hopelessness.

Huddled together, Rafael Ortiz and his family looked on at where their home had been standing just an hour ago. He tried to be strong, but it was too much as he choked back tears.

"How could this happen?" asked his wife. "Where is God in this?"

"I no understand either, but God, he always there and willing to hear our prayers," said Rafael. He and his family could not bring themselves to leave. The other families were also wandering near the site with similar looks of despair. No one could quite fathom what had happened nor could anyone seem to think clearly. The shock of it all was hard to swallow and all but impossible to comprehend. It was a life-shattering event. Where would they go? Where would they live? How would they pick up the pieces? As the heat from the fire subsided, the frigid December air began to take over, chilling the stranded families.

Just then, the beginning signs of God's involvement began to manifest, as if in response to Mrs. Ortiz's question. Even though it was well into the evening hours, the Briarcliff community mobilized in ways that would have made Mr. Law himself proud. Sky drove back up to King's to gather blankets, which the students took right off their own beds. He personally wrapped them around the victims, looking each of them in the eye and imparting a solemn measure of reassurance.

The Beickes were on their way home from The Briar's when they encountered the scene. They went straight home and right away started a phone tree. They also opened the Parish Hall at the Briarcliff Congregational Church to provide shelter and temporary living space for these unfortunate families. Dozens of people came in response to the phone calls with food, clothing, and financial donations. Sky ferried people over to the Parish Hall, as did so many others who had vans and station wagons.

Parker Jones was as actively involved as anyone, setting up a makeshift campsite and triage station for the volunteer ambulance crew. He was also able to pull his Volkswagen bus up-close so people could climb inside for some warmth. Mr. Weldon rushed over to his deli and began making sandwiches, while Mr. and Mrs. Pete opened their store to fill coffee urns.

When Charlie got home, he told his parents what they had witnessed. "We know, son, we got a call about it just a short time ago. We're going over to the Parish Hall to see if we can help. Would you like to come with us?"

"I definitely do." When they got there, it was a muddled scene: people weeping and families trying to stake out a small spot on the floor of the main hall as they sorted through what little they were able to salvage as they fled their homes. Charlie spotted Sky trying to help organize things.

"Sky! I knew you'd be here helping out," said Charlie.

"Hi, Charlie. Rough night."

"I know! We were sledding up at Briar Hall, and we could see the fire raging from up there…all the way across town. It was terrible to see."

"Yes, we could see it from up at King's too."

"I feel horrible for these families. They lost everything."

"I've been around a long time, Charlie, but I have to agree, this one's hard to take."

"I can't understand it. How does God allow things like this?" Sky knew Charlie would be asking the tough questions.

"John 16:33," Sky replied. *"In this world, you will have tribulation. But take heart, I have overcome the world."*

Charlie tried to absorb what Sky said, but it wasn't the easiest thing to grasp. Sky paused, then tried to elaborate. "Charlie, we don't always have a perfect understanding of everything that happens in this life. No one ever has. When innocent people suffer, it's especially hard to figure out."

"Yeah, but why does God let it happen, especially at Christmas!" asked Charlie.

"We'll never have a complete answer to that question in this life. But we do know that God shares in our sorrows and struggles and, in a way, that's what the Christmas season is all about—God coming to be with us in human form."

"Okay, I'm grateful for that. Mary, Joseph, angels, shepherds, the birth of Jesus. I get it. But why does God allow tragedies like this?"

"Is it God who allows this sort of thing? I'm not sure that's the right context to try to understand this."

"Yeah, but where was he during the fire when these families lost everything they had?" asked Charlie.

"I'd say he was right there with them," responded Sky. "I think he was there mobilizing people to open the Parish Hall at the

Congregational Church. He was there...leading Mr. Weldon and Mr. and Mrs. Pete with sandwiches and coffee. He was there...gathering blankets from the students up at King's. And how about the ways Parker got involved?"

Charlie reflected on Sky's words. "But still, if God's in control of everything, I don't understand how this could have happened."

"Charlie, when God created this world and everything in it, he gave humans the gift of freewill. That means we get to live our lives however we want. But it also means we're responsible for our decisions and actions. Who knows how that fire started? Did someone maybe leave a candle burning too long? Did someone fail to extinguish a cigarette? Did someone overfill a kerosene heater? Who knows? Whatever caused the fire, we can't blame it on God. Sometimes we make mistakes, and sometimes those mistakes result in tragedy."

Sky continued on, looking straight at Charlie. "Through it all, God promises to never leave us or forsake us. Right now, we need to pray hard and focus on how we can help to make things better for these families," Sky added.

Charlie scratched his head and looked down. This was hard for him to grasp.

"Life is full of highs and lows, Charlie. It's all part of living in this world."

"I think I get it, Sky. I'll be praying that God will bring something good out of this whole situation."

"Tell ya what, Charlie, I believe there's a major blessing in the offing here. Mark my words." Sky put his arm around his shoulder, and they headed off to help families settle in.

CHAPTER 28

IN WITH THE NEW

In Him we have redemption through His blood, the forgiveness
of our trespasses, according to the riches of His grace.
—Ephesians 1:7

Something had been working on Winthrop Smythe. He'd been experiencing unusual emotions and sentiments that he couldn't quite understand or define. It was akin to a faint but insistent tapping at the door of his heart.

As he came downstairs for breakfast, he folded over the lapel of his Hickey Freeman tweed blazer and went out in the chill of the morning air to get the newspaper. His usual irritable mood was made worse by the fact that the paper boy had managed to toss his *Citizen Register* under his car. He grumbled and griped, then grabbed a rake from the garage to retrieve it. *There goes his Christmas tip!* he thought.

After dusting off his pressed chinos, he put the rake away and headed back toward the house. As he walked, he took the rubber band off the paper so he could scan the headlines. Instantly, he was brought to a halt at the sight of the bold print headline blasting the front-page news: WASH HOUSES WIPED OUT IN TERRIBLE BLAZE.

It hit him like a depth charge from a naval warship. The dizzying shock to his system was completely overpowering, and it took a few minutes for him to regain his orientation. He hurried inside to his study and locked the door behind him. No sooner did he reach his desk when he collapsed in a cloudburst of tears.

In a matter of seconds, a lifetime of caged, raw emotion came heaving from the depths of his soul. He tried to suppress the torrent of feelings but was helpless to stop the deluge. This was completely foreign territory to him. The only rational thought he could muster was to stay right where he was, where no one could see or hear him.

After sobbing at his desk with his head in his hands, he began to pace back and forth trying to figure out what uncontrollable thing was happening inside of him. He stopped at his desk to pound his fist repeatedly, as though it might help him to contain the turmoil. For someone who was always in control and utterly insensitive to emotional feelings, he felt shaken and confused, time and again reaching for his handkerchief. The fact that he couldn't understand this "thing" or bend it to his will troubled him all the more.

Tired from pacing, he sat back down and just gave in to it all. One minute he'd be hunched over whimpering quietly; the next, he'd bolt upright wailing loudly. His core began to ache from the gut-wrenching onslaught, and his face grew numb from continuous, twisted grimaces.

He was totally unaware of time and all alone in a deep, dark emotional labyrinth with no clear way to advance or get out. He felt desperate and hopeless. Panic alternated with dread, followed by anguish as he strived unsuccessfully to compose himself. It was like spinning his wheels in a snowbank—the harder he tried, the deeper his troubled state became.

Then, ever so faintly, came a ray of light. Very gradually he began to regain some semblance of equilibrium. The storm clouds in his head and heart cleared away little by little, and he actually started to feel buoyant, even joyful. As his spirit took flight, his tears of anguish were replaced by tears of wonder and delight. Once again, the weeping began, but this time, it came with a cleansing kind of joy, purification, and release. His mind raced trying to understand the cathartic rollercoaster he was riding.

He swung around in his studded leather desk chair, rose to his feet, and went to the wall of floor-to-ceiling windows. Stretching out before him was the most coveted, panoramic view of the Hudson

River to be found anywhere. The sun was now directly overhead, and he realized he must have quarantined himself for the entire morning.

He looked out at the magnificent Palisades across the river to the extreme western horizon. There was no interruption in the vast sightlines of the northwest hills of New Jersey and beyond. He had looked out on this view countless times before, but it was never so beautiful to him. The river was as majestic and grand as ever. The sky was clear and brilliant, punctuated only by a few passing, puffy clouds. Seagulls few reconnaissance missions for daily sustenance as the currents eddied around the tip of Croton Point and across to Haverstraw Bay.

To God be the glory, he thought, as he looked out at the vista. *Yes, indeed. God is present, and all the earth testifies of his majesty.* He dropped to his knees in ardent prayer, something he hadn't done in fifty years, but he poured his heart out nonetheless. It felt so good doing it, and he was sure that God was listening and receiving his prayers like a parent embracing a long-lost child.

As his mind cleared, he resolved to do something to help with the disaster at the wash houses. Those poor people needed a safe place to live and opportunities to rebuild their lives. His heart was filled with sympathy and compassion for them, and he greeted these benevolent feelings with authenticity and a sense of urgency. He mentally scrolled through his various options, then lit upon something that he could take action on right away.

He picked up the phone to call Sleepy Hollow Country Club where he was a longtime member and current president of the board of trustees. When the receptionist answered the phone, he thanked her and complimented her on the job she was doing—even inquired about her family. Heretofore, it would have been a gruff "This is Smythe, put me through to the club manager."

The clubhouse was a former Vanderbilt mansion overlooking the Hudson River with twenty-five guest rooms throughout the second and third floors. He asked if any were available and was delighted to discover that all of them were. He reserved them on the spot under his member number until further notice. It was a bold step, but he knew in his heart that he had to make sure those families would have a safe, comfortable place to live while they put their lives back together again. He also instructed catering to stock the rooms with snacks, beverages, and candy for the children. His only instruction was to "please spare no expense" to make sure these families had anything and everything they needed.

He then called the Briarcliff Police to see where the families were being sheltered. After a brief conversation, he opened the door to his study and called out to his wife, suggesting that she should dress down and get ready to drive over to the Congregational Church. "But we attend St. Theresa's," Mrs. Smythe said a bit confused.

"My dear, something awful happened in Briarcliff last night. The wash houses all burned to the ground. The Parish Hall at the Congregational Church is serving as a temporary shelter for the families, but we have to do more for them. Much more! I reserved each of the guest rooms at the club, and the sooner we move them over there, the better it will be. Let's move quickly, dear, time is of the essence."

Mrs. Smythe was completely gobsmacked by her husband's sudden, inexplicable sympathy, warmth, and compassion, to say nothing of the inviting tone of his voice. She didn't know whether to change her clothes or lie down from the sudden dizziness it was causing her.

"You haven't called me 'dear' since our honeymoon," she said softly, putting her hand over heart.

"I know. And I'll be eternally sorry. Beginning right now, I plan to devote myself to making up for lost time." She managed a bemused smile, wondering what on earth had come over him, but was certainly receptive to whatever it might be.

A few minutes later when she came downstairs, he was standing in the front foyer holding the door for her. As she stepped outside, he then raced around in front of her to open the car door as well. He had already gone out to start the car so it would be warm when she got in. As she sat down, Mrs. Smythe noticed a smattering of feathers on the ground. *Feathers? At this time of year?* she wondered.

Smythe glanced at her as they got situated in their seats. "You look lovely today," he said, then touched her face tenderly looking deeply into her eyes. Mrs. Smythe was now completely thrown. She had only ever known him to be all business, with a shot of impatience. She didn't quite know how to respond but loved the growing sense of hope that this change in behavior was something real.

As they drove, he found a radio station playing Christmas songs and actually began to hum and whistle along. "Something's come over you, my dear," she said, reaching for his hand.

"I know." He squeezed her fingers gently. "And I know it's genuine!" he said. "I feel as though I'm an entirely new person—as if God himself took a giant sponge and soaked my old self right out of me! I can see and feel a wide-open horizon in my heart and mind and soul!"

"How…when…where did it come from?" she asked.

"Where else? Our Father who art in heaven! In fact, I was looking for answers this morning when these feelings first began to wash over me. I was rudderless and locked in my study. Then, I dusted off my Bible and was able to find a few verses I recalled from my childhood."

"*You* turned to the Bible?" asked Mrs. Smythe, completely stupefied.

"It surprises me too. But there it was in Ezekiel, chapter 11, verse 19: *'I will give you a new heart, and a new spirit I will put within you. And I will remove your heart of stone and give you a heart of flesh.'*"

"Well, he sure did!" said Mrs. Smythe as they both broke out in happy laughter. It occurred to her that laughter was another thing she had barely heard from him since their honeymoon.

"As terrible as it sounds, I feel like God might have used the awful thing that happened last night to recondition me," said Smythe somewhat tentatively. "I'm a changed person. My heart has changed, and I'm going to see to it that something good can come from this. Mark my words!"

"But why would the fire at the wash houses have touched you in such a way?"

"Dear, my mother was born in one of the wash houses and lived there when she was a child. She was a distant niece of Walter Law. He brought her mother, who had been living in poverty in England, to America and gave her a home and a job running the laundry station for Briarcliff Lodge," he explained.

Mrs. Smythe was bowled over. "You never told me any of this!"

"It never seemed important. In fact, I was always a bit embarrassed by their lower station in life," he said, ashamed of himself. "She was a common laborer, working for a day's wage. If anything, it inspired me to want something better."

He continued, "I never wanted to visit or even drive by my mother's birthplace, yet somehow, its destruction had a purging effect on me."

"That humble home on North State Road was a tangible connection between you and the person who brought you into this world, and you never really appreciated it until now," she said. "I think I can understand why you'd be so upset."

"Yes, dear, that's right. I was a blind fool most of my life, but now I see clearly what a cold, hard man I was toward my family, my heritage—even my own mother. But from now on, I will set my eyes on the horizon and I promise to chart a new course."

He parked the car by the Parish Hall and paused for a moment realizing he was totally out of his element. He felt humble, meek, and chastened as though brought down a peg by his God-delivered transformation.

He stepped out of his car and ran around to open the passenger side door for his wife. They clasped hands and strode together through the front door. What they saw broke their hearts into a thousand pieces: rows of cots with sleeping bags everywhere, parents warming cans of soup on hot plates, entire families living in confined, open spaces with little if anything tangible left from the fire. It looked like a refugee camp, not unlike what was seen in Vietnam on the nightly news with Walter Cronkite.

The young innocents were able to maintain their childlike spirit, but the forlorn looks on the faces of the adults told the whole story. Smythe fought hard to keep his tears at bay as he walked among them asking how they were and if they needed anything.

Meanwhile, the outpouring of help from local residents had ramped up. Doris from the A&P brought boxes of Carnation Instant Breakfast. Mr. Olson came down through his backyard to invite people to take hot showers at his house. Even DMarks delivered a box of old toys for the kids who were there. One boy reached immediately for the Batman utility belt, two brothers set up the Rock 'em Sock 'em Robots game, and a little freckle-faced girl shyly put the Mattel View-Master to her face. The sight of these things lifted Smythe's spirits. *God truly is amongst us in the midst of our troubles,* he thought.

Mr. Anthony, who barely got out of his house alive, approached Smythe. He used to provide him with car service to the airport. As they embraced, Smythe seemed to extend the hug as though wanting to actually impart something of meaningful substance.

"John, I'm truly sorry," said Smythe in a subdued voice. "Is there anything you need? Anything at all?"

Mr. Anthony's eyes welled up as he gave a two-word answer. "My home," he replied.

"We'll rebuild," Smythe boldly declared. "I promise you that. And we'll do it soon. Your home will be better than ever. You can hold me to that!"

Mr. Anthony was overcome. He appreciated this reassuring talk, but he still had to deal with the harsh realities of being without a place to call home. A father of four growing boys, he had a hard time responding to Smythe with words. Instead, he thanked him with his tear-filled eyes.

Smythe eventually found Reverend Higgins and told him that the guest rooms at Sleepy Hollow Country Club were reserved and ready to be used by the families. For perhaps the first time in his life, Reverend Higgins was rendered speechless. He just looked at Smythe for a long time and then reached out to administer one of his trademark bear hugs.

"All we have to do, Reverend, is arrange for transportation to the club. Can I leave that in your hands?"

"Well, that won't be a problem at all, even if I have to drive them over one family at a time all by myself!"

"Good. Great! While you're organizing that, I'd like to get over to the club to make sure everything is in order for when the families begin to arrive."

"You go right ahead. I'll mobilize the troops on this end!" The reverend gave him a mock salute.

With that, Smythe turned to leave and bumped right into Rafael Ortiz who was passing by with a tray full of coffee, some of which spilled and landed on Smythe's shoes. Rafael froze with genuine fear. "Mr. Smythe. I sorry. Very sorry. It was an accident. My fault. I clean this up. Please forgive me."

Smythe's heart all but caved in. "Oh, Rafael, please don't you worry. These shoes can be replaced. There's no need to apologize!" Rafael was confused. What was this peacemaking tone coming from the most scorned man in town?

Smythe moved closer to him and looked him straight in the eyes. "Rafael, I'm truly sorry for the ways I've treated you and even more sorry for what happened last night. But you'll be back, stronger than ever. I'll personally see to it. I solemnly promise that to you and your beautiful family!" Then, of all things, he reached out to give Rafael a hug. Being a man of God, Rafael warmly received the embrace and smiled, but the look on his face caused Reverend Higgins to burst out in laughter. There was nothing like the sight of a person to whom God had brought a mighty work.

Mrs. Smythe, who was happy to have witnessed all this, beamed with delight. At that point, she was officially convinced that her husband was indeed a changed man. She happily walked hand-in-hand with him out the door and to their car. She was so proud of what he was doing and eager to be actively involved in supporting these families.

Smythe knew there was only one thing that could explain this complete transformation. "Praise God from whom all blessings flow," he whispered, smiling to himself.

CHAPTER 29
CHRISTMAS SPIRIT ABOUNDING

For unto us a child is born, to us a son is given
and the government shall be upon his shoulder
and his name shall be called Wonderful Counselor,
Mighty God, Everlasting Father, Prince of Peace.
— Isaiah 9:6

All around town, in spite of the tragedy, or perhaps in part because of it, spirits were running high. It didn't hurt that the morning sky, a crystal clear turquoise made all the more vibrant by invigorating rays of sunshine, bolstered the heartening scene. Tragic events can sometimes bring out the best in others and draw people closer together. In this case, it was like the heart of the village grew stronger and more tender.

In the aftermath of the fire, Charlie's cause was picking up even more momentum. People were darting from place to place with last-minute holiday shopping and all the way, seeking to lend a helping hand in any way they could.

Over at Manor Esso, Tony Marsala, an otherwise reserved man who preferred to exist quietly in the background, made a huge, extravagant banner. It read: "Make Your House a Home this Christmas." He hung it across the portico of his service station, completely covering the massive "PUT A TIGER IN YOUR TANK" sign.

Mr. Weldon, sweeping out in front of his shop, saw what Tony was up to and shouted from across the street. "Hey, Marsala, did you make that banner yourself?"

"Banner? What banner?" replied Tony, as they both enjoyed a good morning laugh.

Over at the A&P, Doris talked up the cause with everyone who came through her checkout lane, even if they were from one of the neighboring towns. Inspired by Charlie's idea, she petitioned the store manager to give away cans of Ocean Spray cranberry sauce to anyone who was planning to bring someone to their home for Christmas dinner. Doris had already invited Mr. and Mrs. Pete to join her and her family over in Ossining.

Herbie, who owned the Camelot five and dime, hooked up a speaker on the outside of his store so that he could fill the whole village with Christmas songs from the likes of Nat King Cole, Frank Sinatra, Elvis Presley, and The Beach Boys. For shoppers going from store to store, the familiar standards along with the fresh renditions playing in the open air were magical.

Inside the Manor Barber Shop, John, Nick, Nat, and Joe were spinning Christmas favorites popular in Italy. They donned Santa Claus hats and set out two punch bowls: one marked "Con," the other "Senza," with and without. John held court telling everyone about the traditional Christmas Eve dinner in Italy, known as La Vigilia. He told the adults in great detail how to get the sauce just right—heavy on the basil, light on the oregano. And he loved hearing the younger boys howl as he pointed out that the meal was made up of two things they least enjoyed: fish and vegetables.

The Wappinger Indians, who long ago occupied the Briarcliff region, had a wise saying: "The smile you send out, comes back to you." That was very much the case around town—smiles, handshakes, and hugs prevailed on every street and corner. There was an all-in feeling, even among those who didn't celebrate the Savior's birth. They too were caught up in the feel-good wave washing over the village.

But the biggest, most sincere smile around town was on the face of Charlie Riverton. As he saw it, God was stirring in their midst. For one wonderful day, loneliness would be purged. His cousin Lore, who was an animal lover and foster parent to numerous dogs and cats, organized an effort to go to the local ASPCA on Christmas Day to walk the dogs who were kenneled there and waiting for adoption. Not even our four-legged friends would be left out.

Down at the Briarcliff Police Department, Officer DiLoreto and the rest of the staff got into the act, decorating their squad cars with a Christmas wreath, reindeer antlers, ornaments, and other seasonal trimmings. Eddie also loved to sing, which he did with great gusto while handling the crosswalk in the middle of town.

A big draw was the annual, live manger scene down at the Post Office, complete with sheep, a few ducks, a goat, and a donkey. One day, the donkey, whose name was "Bear," somehow got out of the corral and wandered uptown, stopping traffic in both directions. Luckily, it was Mr. Weldon who came out with some carrot sticks and got Bear to follow him back to the Post Office.

Word of Charlie's campaign even reached Governor Rockefeller, who lived just down the street at the Kykuit estate in Pocantico Hills. One afternoon, he freed up his schedule so that he could make the short drive over to Briarcliff to see firsthand what was happening there. He personally called the village offices, and the clerk transferred his call to Henry in the Rec Department.

"Henry, this is Governor Rockefeller. I'm told you might be able to help me track down young Charlie Riverton. I'd like to pay him a visit."

The governor needed no introduction; that gravelly voice was unmistakable. "Yes sir, Mr. Rockefeller. Unless he has some kind of emergency somewhere, you'll be able to find him playing hockey in Law Park."

"Splendid. Would it be okay if I show up around four o'clock?"

"I don't see why not! I'll be there all afternoon, and so will our seasonal skating supervisor, Skylar Northbridge."

"Excellent. I'll look forward to meeting you both this afternoon."

Later on, as the governor was being driven to Law Park, it struck him as such an obvious thing to gather with others at Christmas, even if some weren't immediate family—and especially if they would otherwise be all alone. Yet no one else had thought of it in the context Charlie had. It was very impressive, and he looked forward to an opportunity to personally shake his hand.

His driver parked near the library at Law Park and "Rocky," as he was affectionately known, walked across the common to Gooseneck Pond. He arrived in the middle of a hotly contested hockey game. He was a tall, handsome man and well-appointed. After enthusiastically greeting Henry, he tossed out compliments on how well everything was running at the park. Looking out at the hockey game being played just a few yards away, he wondered if Charlie might be one of the boys speeding about.

"Did you see the one who just scored on that slick backhander?" asked Henry. "That's Charlie!"

"You know I used to play hockey all the time on Swan Lake over in the Pocantico Hills. This brings back memories of fond times with my brothers." He motioned toward the ice. "I was hoping to personally say hello to Charlie. Do you think it would be a good time to interrupt the game?"

"Sir, you can interrupt any time you want," said Henry, blowing his whistle to call a timeout.

"What?" yelled DMarks. "What's with the whistle? We're in the middle of a game, and now we're playing catch-up because our goalie, who looks more like a giant slice of Swiss cheese, couldn't stop that shot by Mr. Wonderful over there."

Henry cut him right off. "Derrrrrrick! Stop! Boys, please come on over for a minute. I'd like to introduce you to Governor Rockefeller."

"Governor Schmovenor! This is hockey time. Tell him to come back at dark when the pond closes," complained DMarks.

"Yo, Marks, you better clam up fast," urged George. "That's the Gov!"

"Yeah, I think he might, like, own everything in New York or something," added BB.

"This is your last warning, Marks," said Henry. Clueless as usual, DMarks continued to run his mouth, "Yeah? What are you going to do? Sick the Clifton brothers on me again? My parents are taxpayers in this village. I'll sue!"

To his credit, the governor was gamely amused. "Brash young fellow," he whispered toward Henry. Henry nodded to Tommy and Robbie Clifton and asked if they might help DMarks to quiet down a bit.

"Our pleasure," they responded in unison, skating over to DMarks and swiftly putting their arms under his to lift him up off the ice and deliver him to the other side of the pond. After tossing him into a snowbank, they stuffed a portion of his own hockey glove into his mouth. As he sat there in the snow, they held his hands and arms behind his back. The other boys, now all leaning on their sticks, took great pleasure in this scene.

"Charlie, can you come on over for a second?" Henry asked.

"On my way, Henry." Charlie didn't really know why he was being singled out and was a bit concerned trying to figure out if he was in trouble for something. The governor was sporting his famously warm, toothy grin, but still, this was something out of the ordinary.

"Hi, Charlie. My name's Nelson. Nelson Rockefeller. I'm so impressed with the project you initiated here in town and wanted to tell you so in person."

"Thank you, sir, but I'm pretty sure that I don't really deserve much credit."

"Charlie, you'll never make a good politician with that kind of talk!" said the governor. "While humility is the highest virtue, I think you're being too modest, young man."

"Thank you again, sir, but it's not like I was thinking or acting alone."

"Well, from my perspective, you saw a problem in plain sight that none of us adults noticed and then you had the gumption to do something about it."

"The truth is, I had this really strange and upsetting dream a few weeks ago, and afterward, I heard a voice. Everything just kind of flowed from there…like it was God's plan or something," he said. "Oh, and Sky too. He's been as involved as me right from the beginning."

"Ah yes, and you must be Sky," said the governor. He reached out for Sky's hand who was standing in the background.

"How did you know it was him?" deadpanned Henry.

"I heard he kind of stands out in a crowd!"

"You heard right!" said Henry.

"I appreciate it, Governor," said Sky, shaking his hand. "But Charlie's right. No question, this had to be of God. However, Charlie's the one who put in the time, thought, and effort to make it happen, and he deserves all the accolades."

"I couldn't agree more!" said Governor Rockefeller. "Say, Charlie, do you think you and your family might like to join us at Kykuit on Christmas night for desserts?"

"Wow, sir! I mean, yes! That would be fun!" said Charlie. "Um, would it be okay if Sky, Parker Jones, Mr. Olson and Reverend and Mrs. Higgins came with us? They're coming over for dinner that day."

"Why Charlie, that would be fine. Just fine. No one should be left out on Christmas Day," said Governor Rockefeller, giving him a big wink. He then wished the boys well, thanked Henry, and headed back to his car. As he bent down to get into the back seat, he saw a large white feather on the ground. *Well, I'll be,* he thought, picking it up and examining it in the car. He was an avid outdoorsman and prided himself on knowing the features of each of the over 130 bird species that nested in the area, but this feather was not characteristic of any of them.

As soon as the governor's car pulled out of the parking lot, the Clifton brothers removed the glove from DMarks' mouth. Without missing a beat, he started up again. "And another thing...his car was illegally parked! You can't block the crosswalk like that even if you're the governor! He should get a ticket. Where's a police officer when you need one?" And just as fast, Tommy and Robbie nodded at each other and stuffed the glove right back in place. Only this time, they took hockey tape, always hanging from their belts while working the pond, and wrapped it across his mouth and around his head to make sure they wouldn't have to hear any more of his petulant carping. For good measure, they took out a magic marker and drew a mustache over the tape covering his upper lip.

A visit by the governor of the State of New York was quite an honor. Yet for the boys, it was like water off their backs as they quickly resumed their game. Henry and Sky looked on, admiring their innocence. The youthful exuberance on display was delicious to see. "Boys will be boys," said Henry, and they headed over together to help unwrap DMarks.

CHAPTER 30
CHRISTMAS CLUES

*For unto you is born this day in the city of David
a Savior, who is Christ the Lord.*
—Luke 2:11

Christmas Eve, the holiest day of the year, had arrived. And in that mystifying way that happens sometimes at the holidays, the cold and clear conditions mirrored those described in the Bible when Joseph and Mary arrived in Bethlehem, almost two thousand years prior.

Charlie's mom was in the kitchen baking up an incredibly delicious-smelling storm. As she worked, she sang and swayed along with her favorite Christmas records. She had more than a few stacked up on the record player, ready to drop and play in succession on the turntable. Charlie and his dad looked on in amazement. When she got focused on baking, nothing could distract her. Much like her Christmas cards routine, she had a whole system in play: there was one batch in the oven, another batch placed evenly on a cookie sheet ready to bake, a measured quantity of cookie dough to be cut and formed, and a bowl full of batter waiting to be mixed.

She had all kinds of family recipes that had been handed down through generations: Gingersnaps, Butter Spritz, Pizzelles, Snickerdoodles, and the list went on. Some were, of course, meant for dessert after Christmas dinner. However, she had become locally famous in the cookie exchanges around town. She also was a popular contributor to the "Sweets & Treats" deliveries made to shut-ins by the Women's Society at church.

Charlie kept making up excuses to visit the kitchen so that he could lick the mixing spoon after each batch was stirred and blended. There was nothing better than raw cookie dough—except *baked* cookie dough.

"Are you going to have that for lunch?" his mom asked, wiping her hands on her red-and-green apron covered in Christmas trees

"Can I?" Charlie kidded.

"I think you've reached your limit, mister."

"I'm just getting started!" He grinned and took another lick of the wooden spoon.

"I think not! Now you get out of here before you get sick and miss all the fun tonight!" She reached over and snatched the spoon from his hand.

"Okay, okay. I think I'll take Barnes and Noble down to Jackson Road Park for a while. They like to walk through the swamp when the ground is frozen over," said Charlie.

"Okay, son. You three have fun, but be safe."

Charlie bundled up and headed out the front door with his two wildly enthusiastic Boxers tugging him along. Nothing got them more excited than getting outside, except when the Rivertons had company over. As they walked through the swampy area behind the park, they headed on a southward path along the Pocantico River. Eventually, they came to the locally well-known "God Answers Prayers" sign. It had been placed there by the Woyden family a generation ago, outside their property along the adjacent 9A roadside. As the story goes, Mrs. Woyden had become gravely ill and the doctors didn't think she would survive. But in response to a prayer chain her husband started, miraculous things began to happen. She rallied and went on to live a full life and, in gratitude, Mr. Woyden placed the sign in that spot.

Charlie stopped to reflect on the meaning of the message. *God answers prayers...how incredible!* he thought. The creator, sustainer, and orchestrator of all things in the universe wanted to hear about our daily needs, hopes, and fears. And through the blessed Christmas event, we could have a family-style relationship with him, just like we do with our earthly parents.

Inspired by the sign, he offered up a silent prayer: *Dear God, most of us are overjoyed at Christmas and are blessed to be with family and friends. Others find it to be a difficult time because they don't have anyone to be with. Please, don't let anyone suffer for being alone tomorrow.*

Charlie, Barnes, and Noble decided to keep walking. Across 9A they went, up and over the old Putnam Line railroad bed and onto South State Road. From there, they strode up the hill toward Briarcliff College. Eventually, they made it to the south end of the college grounds. The normally bustling campus was deserted and closed for semester break. This allowed Charlie to let the dogs off-leash.

As they wandered along, they ended up in front of Dow Hall, a beautiful and stately, red-brick building that held so much history— once Mrs. Dow's Finishing School for Girls, it was now part of the College, which was an elite, all-female academy. He liked how still everything was. Not another soul in sight. It seemed to center his very being as he picked up ambient sounds he wasn't normally able to hear. It was complete solitude.

Suddenly, he heard Sky's voice. "You're building up treasures in heaven, Charlie." This time, nothing could have convinced him that Sky wasn't there right behind him.

"Sky! Merry Christmas!" He spun around with great anticipation. "Are you coming to midnight services?" he asked, voice dropping off. The only sight in front of him was the open grassy area and then the Schutte house across Tuttle Road. Barnes and Noble cocked their heads, wondering if he was talking to them.

Charlie stopped in his tracks. He was absolutely convinced that he wasn't hearing things. And that phrase—he was sure that he had heard Sky use it before, perhaps the night when they had pizza at Vinny's in Pleasantville.

Then, just as before, he felt the uniquely warm and tender embrace, which had also accompanied the other instances when he heard Sky's voice. He was getting used to it by now, but this time, it filled him with a profound sense of strength and conviction. As he stood in the middle of campus all by himself—and with that special grounding presence all around him—he felt steadfast as the North Star.

Then he began to think more about it. The hugs he got from his mom and dad were wonderful. The hugs he got from Barnes and Noble were great. The prolonged hug he got from Michelle after the skating party—well, that was truly awesome. But this was unlike anything he had ever experienced; he felt blessedly singled out for these special encounters.

He remained in place trying to simply relish the experience. Instead of trying to figure it out, he just let go so he could absorb it. It was a transcendent moment for Charlie. In time, he put the dogs back on-leash and they headed home. He carried with him an uncontrollable urge to smile. These experiences were better than anything else. *Was this what Reverend Higgins and his Sunday school teachers meant whenever they referred to the joy of the Lord?* he wondered.

On their way home Charlie passed by Law Park. It was deserted. Everyone was home wrapping gifts, prepping a special Christmas Eve dinner, and perhaps, even resting. After all, it wasn't easy to stay up for midnight services even with all the excitement and anticipation of the day to come. The trio continued on, and soon they were home. Charlie gave the dogs some fresh water and headed to the kitchen to see what was available for lunch. His mom was still baking away, oblivious to his dad who was sitting at the kitchen table reading the *Citizen Register* and having lunch.

"Hi, Mom. How's Keebler's number one elf?" he asked. Completely unaware of him, she didn't even look up from her two-handed cookie conveyor belt to answer.

"She's in a zone, buddy. Don't take it personally," said his dad. "Pull up a chair and have some lunch with your old man." Charlie shrugged his shoulders and poked around in the fridge for something to eat. Cold pizza! He forgot about leftovers from the other night. He poured a glass of ice-cold milk and added some Bosco. Glancing at his mom between bites of pizza, he started to laugh thinking she looked like a robot.

"Dad, what do you think would happen if we made a loud noise or something?"

"Well, it might not even register with her considering the state she's in. On the other hand, it could shock her back to reality. Let's try not to disturb her, though. Better if she reenters on her own time."

"How far has she gotten?" asked Charlie.

"Good question, son. I think I just saw the Ginger Snaps come out of the oven, and now she has the waffle iron plugged in. So I guess she's up to the Pizzelles," observed his dad.

"That makes sense. She's got powdered sugar on her nose and chin," noticed Charlie. "Should we tell her?"

"Actually, I think it's kind of loveable as is. What do you think?"

"Now that you mention it, yeah, I see what you mean."

"If she hasn't noticed by the time we head to church later, we'll clue her in." His dad pushed his lunch plate away. "So you took the boys on a good long walk? How was it? Did you see any of your friends?" Charlie hesitated, then decided to give a completely honest answer. He'd been wanting to talk with someone about these unique visits and voices anyway.

"I didn't actually see anyone, Dad, but I had this experience where, out of nowhere, it feels like someone's giving me this incredibly big hug. And it also feels like it's coming from a really large person because I get totally wrapped up in the warmth of it all."

"Wow, Charlie, that's unusual. You're all alone when this happens—and yet you feel someone else's presence?"

"Well, I'm not always all alone, but either way, I know it's not in my imagination. And there's something else. It's hard to explain, but part of it reminds me of what it's like whenever I'm around Sky. You know, like everything is so calm and under control. And like everything is going to work out fine."

"I believe you, son, and honestly, I don't doubt what you're saying in the least." Then it was his dad's turn to pause before continuing with a completely honest response.

"You know, angels are real. In fact, God sometimes sends angels to intercede in some way in our lives. Maybe these hugs are an example of that."

"But why me?"

"Well, it's just a thought, but maybe God wanted people to have a home for the holidays and decided to dispatch a heavenly messenger to help you advance his plan." This was a lot for Charlie to absorb. He looked down toward his plate of food as he listened closely to his dad.

"Sometimes the greatest gift you can give another person is companionship. And that would certainly be a great way to honor God at Christmas. You were born with the gift of compassion, Charlie, just the kind of person God would want to work with on something like this."

Charlie struggled to take all this in. "As for Sky, he does seem to have a certain kind of quality that sets him apart. He's won over everyone in town, your mother and I included! It's a curious thing. On the one hand, I feel like we've come to know him really well. On the other hand, we don't actually know a single thing about where he came from or who he really is. Strange how he can make everyone feel like family and yet be so hard to figure out."

Now Charlie was really absorbed. His mind went back to the conversation he had with Ms. Miller at the library. "Dad, getting back to what you said before, do you really think God knows us individually like that? Cares about our personal needs? Wants to hear our prayers? I mean, there's a lot of people in this world!"

"I do, he does, and you betcha! The Bible says God knows us by the hairs on our head. So really, he knows us better than we know ourselves!"

Charlie was simultaneously happy and a bit anxious over hearing that. Then, in the midst of their conversation, his mom turned around and looked at them. "How long have you two been sitting there? You don't even say hello?" she asked, powdered nose and all. Charlie and his dad just smiled back at her.

"What's wrong with you guys?" she asked, then shrugged her shoulders and returned to her baking.

After lunch, Charlie headed upstairs to stretch out on his bed, while his dad retreated to his reclining chair in the den. This was a rare afternoon of downtime, and they both wanted to take advantage of it.

The afternoon hours passed uneventfully until dinnertime. Each year on Christmas Eve, Charlie's mom made homemade clam chowder for dinner. It was a tradition she got from the Cape Cod branch of her family tree and a time-honored ritual that had been going on for over a century.

They all cleaned up the kitchen together, then read and reflected in the glow of the lights of their Christmas tree. Before leaving for church, there was one more Riverton family tradition to take care of, as the three of them gathered by the crèche. Charlie carefully unwrapped the statuette of an infant Jesus and placed it in the middle of the manger scene. It was a meaningful ritual symbolizing the crowning moment of all recorded history. All three of them paused to think about the reality of God's grace and mercy embodied by the child born in Bethlehem. No words were exchanged. None were needed.

A short time later, they bundled up, got into their car, and headed to church. As they arrived, the greetings were even more joyful than normal and each pew was filled to overflowing. Beautifully lit by candles, the sanctuary could not have been more gloriously decorated, with evergreens, wreathes, garlands, and poinsettias placed throughout.

The whole congregation sang along with the choir to all the favorite Christmas hymns: "Hark! The Herald Angels Sing," "O Come, All Ye Faithful," "Angels We Have Heard on High," and more. In between the well-known carols, Reverend Higgins held forth in the pulpit, delivering the entire birth narrative in the braid Scots as had become his personal tradition. He felt the primal Scottish accent might help accentuate the stirring passages.

When it came time to light the Christ candle in the Advent wreath, Annie Peterson and her five adult grandchildren came forward to do the honors.

"Tonight, we light the fifth candle—the Christ candle, representing light and purity," she said. "This candle signifies the heart of the season, God providing light to the world. The candle is located in the center of the wreath, just as Christ is meant to be at the center of our lives."

Next, the grandchildren read from the gospel according to Luke:

And there were shepherds abiding in the fields nearby, keeping watch over their flocks at night. And lo, an angel of the Lord came upon them and the glory of the Lord shone round about them and they were sore afraid. But the angel said to them, "Fear not, for behold, I bring you good tidings of great joy which shall be to all the people. For unto you is born this day in the city of David a Savior which is Christ the Lord. And this shall be a sign unto you: ye shall find a baby wrapped in swaddling clothes lying in a manger." Suddenly, there was with the angel the heavenly host praising God and saying: "Glory to God in the highest, and on earth peace, goodwill to all."

After a brief homily followed by closing prayers, the young acolytes in their white robes processed up the center aisle to the Christ candle, from which they lit their tapers. Then, they slowly walked back, stopping to light the handheld candles each parishioner had been given when they arrived that night. The ushers turned out all the lights so that the sanctuary glowed with sublime candlelight. After a brief pause for everyone to gather themselves in the moment, the organist began the familiar introduction to "Silent Night," which everyone gently sang while holding their candles high.

After the final chorus, the deacons, who were gathered in the back of the sanctuary, rang the church bell to signal it was midnight. Christmas had officially arrived! The chimes pealed through the thin night air, and an abiding sense of joy filled the hearts of all the faithful believers in attendance.

"Joyous Christmas to you, Charlie," said Sky wholeheartedly. Charlie swung around in his pew thinking he might be hearing voices again, but this time, Sky was there, beaming with a smile so bright it seemed incandescent. He reached out his burly arms and gave Charlie an extended bear hug. For Charlie, Sky's raise-your-spirits embrace felt exactly like the ones he had been receiving at those key moments when he also thought he had heard Sky's voice. It was unmistakable at this point.

In that moment, Charlie made the connection. It was now recognizable and discernable for him. He drew back, and he and Sky looked at each other. No words were spoken, but definite, non-verbal confirmation was exchanged. Sky knew the embrace might be a giveaway for Charlie. But it was time to bring things to light as Sky's assignment in Briarcliff would not be lasting much longer.

"Bless you, Charlie," said Sky, looking down at him as both a loving big brother and a proud mentor. "In all my years—and trust me, there have been a lot—I can't recall enjoying a new friendship quite like I've enjoyed ours. There are a few things I've been wanting to talk with you about. I'm sure we'll get a chance tomorrow at your house." Charlie just stood quietly, absorbing every word.

"You're a very special person, Charlie. A long time ago, I had an acquaintance named David. The Bible says he was a 'man after God's own heart.' I think you fit that description pretty well yourself. I'm proud of you, buddy." They shared a big grin. Although they were surrounded by tons of people, it was as though time froze and the whole church fell silent, leaving just the two of them in a transcendent moment.

Then, Charlie's parents turned to greet Sky. "Merry Christmas, Sky!" said Charlie's mom. "Thanks ever so much for being such a good friend to Charlie."

"Thank *you*, Mr. and Mrs. Riverton! As far as I'm concerned, it's been a divinely appointed friendship!" Sky gave them both a hug.

"I don't need any convincing!" Charlie's dad chimed in, giving Sky a telltale look.

As they continued to chat, Charlie noticed more spontaneous hugs were breaking out all around the sanctuary. Parker Jones was in the rear, patting Mr. Olson on the back wholeheartedly. To the side, near the stained-glass window depicting the prodigal son, Mr. and Mrs. Smythe were both beaming and greeting others devotedly. It was their third service that day. They had been to the 3:00 p.m. at Union Church in Pocantico Hills and also attended the 7:00 p.m. at St. Theresa's.

To Charlie's delight, Michelle and her family came over to give a special Christmas greeting to the Rivertons. She gave Charlie a hug, then handed him an envelope.

"What's this?"

"Don't ask, just open it silly!" Charlie excitedly tore open the envelope. Inside was a five-dollar bill. "As you sow, so shall you reap! Merry Christmas, Charlie!"

He was confused at first. "Wait, is this somehow connected to that time in Central Park during the New York Amble?"

"Yep. When I told my parents what you did, they were so impressed that they gave me the money and told me to find a good time to pass it back to you."

"Wow. I don't really know what to say."

"Say you'll take me to the Penny Candy store with it!" said Michelle playfully.

Midnight services on Christmas Eve were always wondrous and singular, but this one was unusually so. As the Rivertons headed out the large double doors in the vestibule, Charlie was having the best feel-good experience of his young life. At the same time, he was still somewhat spellbound by the confirmation Sky had given him about the hunches, hints, and clues he'd been grappling with. He needed more time to comprehend a few things, but he was sure that he'd be able to talk it over with Sky in a day or two. For now, he was beyond grateful for all he had to think about—and more special it could not be.

CHAPTER 31
THE CHRISTMAS CLUB

Behold, the virgin shall conceive and bear a son and they shall call his name Immanuel, which means God with us.
—Matthew 1:23

On Christmas Day at Sleepy Hollow Country Club, Winthrop Smythe was relishing his new outlook on life. He bounced around in perpetual motion, joyfully seeing to it that everyone had enough of whatever they might need. It seemed like he was everywhere all at once, giving out hugs and words of encouragement.

The club itself was gloriously decorated for Christmas. Wreaths were hung on all the doors and above each fireplace, with flowing, red velvet ribbons positioned at five o'clock as per the impeccable taste of long-time member, Carrie Garrison. A massive Douglas Fir, adorned with oversized glass ornaments, was placed in the foyer and lit with what seemed like a thousand and one lights. Fresh-cut garland was strung all the way down the great hallway, leaving the invigorating scent of evergreens in its wake.

Just being able to live for a while in a place like Sleepy Hollow Country Club was a unique blessing for the visiting families. That, coupled with the festive decor, helped encourage the childlike faith in them all.

Earlier in the week, Smythe had gone to the Briar Rose to shop for Christmas gifts for all the mothers and fathers who had lost everything in the fire and were now living at the club. He wanted to be sure that there was a wrapped gift for everyone under the giant Christmas tree.

"Here's what I need, Mr. Bethke," he addressed the gentlemanly owner of the shop. "If I may, I'd like to rely on you and your flawless taste to select twenty-five items for the wives and twenty-five for the husbands. Hopefully, the items you pick will be useful but also of great beauty, so as to help take their minds off all they lost in the fire. Please charge everything to my store account. Oh, and by the way, I thank you for your help on this." He put a folded one-hundred-dollar bill in Mr. Bethke's right hand and then covered his hand with both of his and gave it a firm shake.

For the kids, he stopped at Camelot in town and asked Herbie to pick out the most popular toys and games in the store, then wrap and mark them for a girl or a boy. Herbie did his best to hide his surprise but could barely speak in full sentences. He was astonished to have the otherwise unsociable, unapproachable Mr. Smythe in his store.

"Spare no expense, Herbie! And here's a blank check...fill in whatever amount is needed. Oh, and please add an additional 35 percent for your extra effort for all this."

"For real, Mr. Smythe?" Herbie looked slowly around thinking he might just be on *Candid Camera*.

"Oh yes, my friend. And I'll be watching for the cashed check to make sure you didn't short-change yourself!"

He had something special in mind for Rafael Ortiz too. On Christmas morning, he presented him with his best Brooks Brothers suit, recently dry-cleaned, so that he'd have some fine apparel of his own. Never mind that he also hid one-hundred-dollar bills in each pocket—of which there were six! The thought of Rafael discovering them at random times later on gave him great joy.

Soon, the other members at the club saw what was happening and offered their time and hands-on help as well. Some gathered the children around to hear Christmas stories, several donned festive aprons and milled about serving refreshments, and a few, who were members of the Scarborough Singers, organized whoever was available to stand on the grand staircase for sing-alongs of all the great Christmas carol favorites.

Smythe generously tipped the club chef and worked with him to prepare a Christmas dinner that this special group of guests would never forget. He happily put on an apron, rolled up his sleeves, peeled potatoes, and diced vegetables for the stuffing. He insisted that the wait staff serve everything buffet-style so they too could sit down and enjoy Christmas dinner with the larger group.

After all the gifts had been opened and dinner was finishing up, Smythe stood and tapped the side of his glass to get everyone's attention.

"If I may, I'd like to say once again how deeply, deeply sorry I am for what happened to your homes." His voice tapered off as he choked up. Clearing his throat, he continued, "But I personally and publicly pledge to donate a tract of land farther up North State Road for development of affordable housing for each family here today. I've instructed my lawyers to draw up contracts, and architectural plans are being designed right now and due to be completed by December 31."

People didn't really know how to respond. It was too good to be true. Some thought they were imagining things. Over the din of their excited vices, he added, "I've also been in contact with the best construction company in the area to commence clearing and preparing the site for building as soon as possible and no later than January 2!" Euphoria broke out along with handkerchiefs at each table.

In the past, people would have taken a we'll-believe-it-when-we-see-it attitude toward what they had just heard. But, in this case, they knew Smythe would make good on his word. Everything he had done and planned to do made all the difference to them and helped turn many a hopeful eye toward an expectant future.

"Who wants to help me light the fireplaces?" Smythe called out to the children. "Okay, I need a few of you to grab some kindling. You three follow me with those newspapers, and I need a few dads to lug some logs for me." He knew he was acting like a big kid, but at that moment, his considerable personal wealth meant nothing to him. Being with others and being helpful at the same time was beyond the best business deal he had ever struck.

"I used to love building fires when I was your age," he said to a few of the younger boys. "Let me show you how it's done. First, you crumple up some newspapers and create a base for the fire. Next, you pile on some kindling. Then, position the logs in a way that will allow air to get between them, like so." As the fire began to glow, he stood up to absorb the warmth—of both the flames and the children's attention.

From there, they migrated to each of the other five fireplaces on the main floor and repeated the process. As they went, families curled up in blankets near the glowing hearths and reflected on their blessings. A more peaceful setting was not to be found anywhere.

"You're being so wonderful, dear. I'm truly touched by your generosity," said Mrs. Smythe.

"How I wish I could turn back the clock to make up for lost time."

"Dear, it seems to me, the best is yet to be." She reached for his hand.

"Oh, yes...yes indeed. I will make sure of that. I give you my solemn word. The bitterest of tears are shed for words left unsaid and deeds left undone. I've shed those tears and don't ever want that experience again! From now on, I will never, ever miss an opportunity to honor God in whatever time I have left on this earth."

For the first time in his life, Smythe smiled from the inside out. His personal transformation was complete, and he knew he would never be the same. As he leaned down to throw some more logs on the fire, he noticed a few feathers scattered around the hearth. He was about to sweep them up, then decided to just leave them be.

A few of the children walked over, picked up the feathers, and brought them to him. "Mrs. Smythe just told us," one of them began in a sweet little voice, "that if you find a feather in your path, it means you were visited by an angel." Smythe wanted to respond verbally, but he was too choked up to talk. The simple gesture and the beautiful sentiment behind it pummeled him emotionally. With watery eyes, he got down on one knee to hug the child and to thank her. Then, he gave whole-hearted hugs to the others.

A few minutes later, he took his wife by the hand and suggested that they bundle up and walk out on the expansive back lawn overlooking the Hudson River. It was a beautiful, clear night, and the moon cast a golden shimmer across the river all the way to the shores of Haverstraw Bay. As they snuggled into each other, a star shined brightly above Sleepy Hollow Country Club.

"Thank you for being the wonderful person you've always been," he said.

"Thank you for being the wonderful man you've become." She smiled up at him and pulled him closer. Smythe gently held her like she was the most precious, delicate treasure in the entire world.

Eventually, the night's festivities wound down and most people turned in for a glorious Christmas night's sleep. Some, including Smythe, just didn't want the night to end, and they all retired to the couches by the fireplace in the Library Room, where they spent the night like college kids home on Christmas break.

CHAPTER 32
LET IT BE

Glory to God in the highest and on earth peace
among those with whom He is well pleased.
—Luke 2:14

The Christmas gathering at the Rivertons' house glowed with a joyful, gracious warmth. Sky was there, spreading his customary charm. So was Parker Jones, clean-shaven and wearing his formal Army Service uniform. Reverend and Mrs. Higgins had stopped to pick up Mr. Olson and arrived full of good cheer.

"Merriest of Christmases to the Riverton clan!" bellowed Reverend Higgins as he knocked twice then bounded through the front door.

"And merriest of Christmases to our favorite pastor and his wonderful wife!" replied Charlie's dad, gathering coats and hats.

"Glad to know I'm your favorite pastor! Wait a minute, I'm your only pastor!"

"And we hope that will continue for a long time to come!

On into the living room everyone went, and it was heartfelt greetings and hugs all around. "Well now, I'd say that the joy of the Lord is present right here in your lovely home!" said Reverend Higgins, detecting something different about the tone and tenor of the gathering.

"Where two or more are gathered in his name," replied Charlie's dad.

"Right you are! And God never makes promises he doesn't keep!"

After saying hello to everyone, Mrs. Higgins headed toward the kitchen to see if she could lend a hand to Mrs. Riverton. Reverend Higgins and Mr. Olson made a beeline toward the eggnog and a spot near the fireplace.

Charlie's mom had been hard at work preparing a beautiful table overflowing with scrumptious food: roast turkey with stuffing, cranberry sauce, and her special homemade gravy. True to her reputation for always cooking for an army, a spiral ham with honey glaze and sliced pineapple rounded out the offering. The centerpiece of the table was a beautiful cut glass vase Parker Jones picked out at the Briar Rose gift shop. In return for unloading a few pallets of goods, Mr. Bethke let him choose something from the store to bring to the Rivertons'.

Everyone mingled by the crackling fireplace, sipping seasonal beverages and reflecting on the blessed and providential events of the last several weeks.

"Say, Parker, that's a good-looking uniform you've got there," said Mr. Riverton.

When dressing earlier, Parker humbly but proudly donned his Bronze Star from Vietnam, which he received for valor and meritorious achievement on the battlefield. Tonight was the first time he had actually worn it. In fact, it wasn't too long ago that he was standing at the water's edge in Scarborough Park and almost threw the medal in the Hudson River because of the contemptuous ways he had come to feel about the war.

On the lapel of his blue blazer, Mr. Olson wore his Distinguished Service Cross from World War I. Given for extreme gallantry in risking one's life in combat, he was heartened to see that he and Parker had something special in common. Both wore their medals to pay tribute to the fallen comrades they had served with.

As honorably discharged officers in the US Army, Parker and Mr. Olson quietly approached each other, stood at attention, then saluted as is military custom. Regardless of their different wartime experience, the duty, honor, country credo was still sacrosanct to them.

After a while, Mrs. Riverton and Mrs. Higgins brought all the dishes to the table and it was time for Christmas dinner. Mr. Riverton normally said grace at dinner time, but he was planning to cede the responsibility to Reverend Higgins. Then, to everyone's surprise, Charlie spoke up, asking if Parker would do the honor. Through a wellspring of joyful tears, Parker bowed his head and began to pray out loud.

"Dear Lord God, thank you for the birth of your Son, our Savior. You've blessed us with your presence, your grace, and your love—and we are grateful. Thank you for this amazing feast and for the amazing hands that prepared it. We ask your blessings on us and our absent loved ones. In Jesus's name, amen. AMEN. "

He then held his glass aloft to offer a toast. "To Charlie Riverton, who has done more for our village in the past month than anyone since Walter Law himself!"

"Here, Here!" said Reverend Higgins, raising his glass. "That's quite a lesson in friendship you gave us, Charlie!"

Sky sat back and smiled that broad, megawatt smile—this time allowing himself a tad bit of gratification. As he looked around the table, he was grateful for the outcome of his latest God-given assignment.

The Rivertons deeply appreciated the ways in which Charlie had sparked this promising new tradition. And, in fact, the family later agreed that it was the best, warmest, most wonderful Christmas they had ever experienced.

After dinner, everyone gathered again around the fireplace with their choice of pie and other tasty desserts to enjoy the last vestiges of the season fast coming to a close. Mr. Olson asked Parker if he might like to team up with him to host Christmas next year.

"Yes, sir. I'd like that very much, sir!" he replied in military style, saluting.

"Okay, soldier. We're on K-P duty 365 days hence! Taylor will handle clean-up!"

Sky walked over to Charlie, smiled, and patted him on the back. "One month ago, Charlie, Mr. Olson was faltering and all alone," said Sky. "And Parker was angry and isolated from the world. Now they know that they're loved and not alone. It's given them new outlooks on life. What you did to foster that is a really good example of what the Bible means when it talks about building up treasures in heaven."

That last phrase stunned Charlie. His mind went right back to that moment the day before standing on the campus of Briarcliff College with Barnes and Noble. He had never heard that phrase before, now he had heard it twice within twenty-four hours. The parallel was instantly recognizable. He looked back at Sky searching once again for confirmation in his face, anything that would eliminate any last doubts about these unique experiences with his heavenly friend. He was about to press Sky further, when the clock struck 6:00 p.m. and Mr. Riverton reminded everyone that they had a date with the Rockefellers.

"The governor is expecting you, Charlie," said his dad.

With that, Parker and Mr. Olson got into the Rivertons' Caprice Classic and Charlie rode with Sky in his pickup truck. The Higgins' followed right behind them. Down South State Road they went, across Route 117, and over to Pocantico Hills. As they made the short drive, Charlie tried to reengage Sky.

"Sky, I'm really glad we got to spend so much time together over the last month. I think you're the greatest, and I'm so glad you came to Briarcliff. But there's something different that's been going on, and I can't completely figure it out."

"What do you mean, Charlie?"

"Well, as real as you are, you're like, different. It's hard to describe, but...I mean...it's almost like you're not a completely normal human being or something."

"Gosh, Charlie, should I take that as a compliment?" Sky laughed.

"Sorry, I didn't mean that the way it sounded. It's just that you have these ways about you that are so different from anyone else I know. It's peculiar…I can't really explain it."

"Charlie, you might not realize this, but I think you're kind of special too. In fact, I'd say that you too are put together a little differently compared to most kids your age. When I look back on all that has happened since the day after Thanksgiving, it's my belief that God set you apart for a special purpose."

"Why do you think that?" Charlie looked down at his hands. "I don't feel special in any way at all."

"The fact that you don't feel special is part of what *makes* you special! Colossians 3:12 tells us, *'Put on as God's chosen ones, holy and beloved, compassionate hearts, kindness, humility, meekness and patience.'* I think you naturally fit that description pretty well, Charlie."

As they drove along, Charlie decided that he still needed more confirmation. Who was Sky really? Where did he come from? Could it be that he really was some kind of a guardian angel or something? If so, should he feel comfortable or scared? Could he actually be in the presence of a higher being? This last thought was at least slightly frightening to him. *Forget it,* he thought. He was just going to come right out with it point-blank.

"Sky, there's something I've wanted to ask you."

"Fire away, Charlie." Just then, they arrived at the gatehouse entrance to the Rockefeller estate. "Hold on a minute," said Sky, rolling down his window to speak with the security guard.

"Merry Christmas! You must be the Riverton party," said the guard, clipboard in hand.

"Yes, we are!" said Sky.

"Excellent. If you'd be kind enough to park your truck over to your right, we'll have you brought right up to the governor's residence."

"Thanks. Will do!" Sky and Charlie parked the truck, then hopped out. Charlie would have to wait to ask his question another time. The governor had arranged for horse-drawn sleighs to bring the visitors up the winding hillside from the gatehouse to the Kykuit mansion.

"This is awesome!" shouted Charlie as they all piled in and got under heavy fleece blankets.

"Now we know how Santa must have felt last night!" said Reverend Higgins. Everyone laughed and sat back to enjoy the charm of being towed along to the sound of sleigh bells affixed to the dressage on the magnificent Rockefeller horses.

As they arrived at the mansion house, they were greeted as guests of honor by Governor Rockefeller himself, who personally tended to Charlie and his family and friends. After checking their coats, they were all immediately impressed by the exquisite holiday decorations throughout the main floor. A ten-piece chamber orchestra played Christmas music for all to enjoy; and a friendly wait staff, clad in black tuxedos, white gloves, and Santa Claus hats, passed back and forth with platters of delicacies and desserts.

As carolers dressed in red and green came to stand behind him, the governor clinked his glass to get the attention of everyone present. "Good evening, everyone. I'd like to introduce you to my young friend, Charlie Riverton, and his friends and family. I've lived long enough to know that sometimes, life lessons are best learned from our children—and this year, Charlie gave us all a master class on how to honor Christmas!"

Everyone politely applauded and began to introduce themselves to Charlie. The guest list was impressive indeed. John Cheever, the acclaimed writer who lived in Ossining, was there with his wife, Mary. Senator Goodell and his family drove up from Bronxville along with their friends, the Blairs. Marc Chagall was present, having just completed installation of his famous stained-glass windows at the Union Church in Pocantico Hills. He was staying with Reverend and Mrs. Smith who came with their beautiful daughter.

The singer-entertainer Cab Calloway, who lived over in Greenburgh near the Gibbes property, was particularly excited to meet Charlie. Doris, who worked at the A&P, was his cousin, and she told him all about what was happening around Briarcliff. Other celebrities included Peter Falk, who had come east to be with family at his childhood home over in Ossining. New York City's Mayor Lindsay also came after an early dinner at Gracie Mansion. Charlie wasn't really old enough to know the significance of most of these people, but he had a great time meeting "Columbo," of television fame, in person.

"A toast," said Governor Rockefeller. "There was no room at the inn for Mary and Joseph in Bethlehem all those years ago…but young Charlie Riverton and his friend Sky made sure there was room for everyone this Christmas!"

What followed was the warmest, most memorable night of Christmas fellowship and caroling anyone present had ever experienced. It was almost midnight before the final guests took their sleigh ride back to the gatehouse. The Rivertons thanked the governor and his wife, as did the rest of their companions.

Turning to Charlie, the governor said, "I'd love to have you look in on us up in Albany sometime. I'll give you a personal tour of the state capital."

"I'd like that. Thank you, sir!" said Charlie.

"Splendid! Let's shake hands on it," said the governor.

"It's a deal!" said Charlie.

The group got back into their sleigh, which glided easily down the hill to the security gate. Everyone hugged and bid a heartfelt farewell as the morning of December 26 was fast approaching. Charlie returned home in his parents' car, and Parker rode with Sky and Mr. Olson. The level of contentment and joy could not have been any higher. While no one wanted the evening to end, most were looking forward to what surely would be a peaceful night's sleep.

CHAPTER 33
GOODBYE, SKY

===

*Trust in the Lord with all your heart and do not lean on
your own understanding. In all your ways acknowledge
Him and He will make straight your paths.*
—Proverbs 3:5–6

The day after Christmas was filled with plentiful sunshine and seasonal temperatures. Charlie woke up in high spirits and feeling blessed. He covered his normal routine: washing his face, brushing his teeth, taking care of the dogs, then hitting the kitchen for breakfast.

"Hi, Mom, Dad," said Charlie as he breezed into the kitchen. "Merry day-after-Christmas!"

"Good morning, son," said his parents in unison as they rose to give him a hug dressed in their bathrobes and pajamas. "And Merry day-after-Christmas to you!"

Charlie headed straight to the fridge full of leftovers and helped himself to a sizeable slice from each of the pies from the day before. Pouring himself a big glass of milk, he took a seat at the table. Raising her eyebrows over this choice of breakfast, his mom tilted her head down, looking over her glasses, "Excuse me, young man?"

"Oh, let him go, honey. It's the day after Christmas," said Charlie's dad. "In fact, I think I'll join him!" With that, he grabbed a plate and paid a quick visit to the fridge himself. Charlie just smiled at them both, alternating between forks-full of pie and gulps of milk.

There were so many thoughts running through his head that morning, but mostly, he was bonfired-up to hang out with Sky at

Law Park. After taking his plate and glass to the kitchen sink, he grabbed his brand new Bauer Black Panther skates and headed out the front door, walking energetically to Gooseneck Pond. Normally, he'd wait for the rest of the gang, but he was too eager to be with Sky and bask in the afterglow of what had been a wondrous Christmas season. Charlie picked up his pace as he got closer, but when he got to the pond he found Henry tending to the fire pit himself.

"Hi, Henry. Hope you had a nice Christmas," said Charlie.

"Sure did, Charlie. We had a few elderly neighbors over, and they told stories of their childhood Christmases to my kids. It was fun and heartwarming. How was yours?"

"It was so much fun! Parker Jones and Mr. Olson wore their medals from when they served in the Army and Sky ate enough for three people!"

"He's a big man. I'm sure he has an appetite to match. Did you take Governor Rockefeller up on his invitation for desserts at his house?"

"Sure did! I got to meet Columbo!"

"You mean…Peter Falk?"

"Yeah, Columbo, that nutty detective…but he wasn't wearing his trench coat!"

"Well, good for you, Charlie. It's always nice to see someone get their just recognition when they've done good."

"Thanks, Henry. Hey, by the way, where's Sky?"

Henry knew Charlie would be asking. Now he had to be the one to break the news. He stopped what he was doing and stood up so he could look Charlie straight in the eye.

"I don't know exactly how to tell you this, Charlie, but Sky phoned early this morning. Apparently, he got a call late last night. Seems he's needed elsewhere right away and had to leave town bright and early."

Charlie was stunned. His knees buckled, and his heart raced with this news. Totally bewildered, all he could muster were a few half-questions. "He's gone? Wait, what? When did he? Hold on. Say again?"

"I'm afraid it's true, Charlie."

"But he didn't even say goodbye!"

"I'm sure he would have if he could have."

"Did he say where he was going?"

"Actually, no."

"Did he leave a phone number where he could be reached?"

"Sorry, son. No."

"Did he say what he'd be doing?"

"Strike three. I'm sorry, Charlie, no." Charlie was about as dejected as was humanly possible. He felt like crying and being angry all at once. Did God summon his friend to be a blessing in some other place? What did it matter? Charlie was completely let down.

Then, right on schedule, a wonderful sense of calm gently washed over him. No voices this time, just the warm hug that he now knew was patented Sky. He knew he was receiving a special message; it was almost as good as if Sky was physically present. Charlie's spirit began to regain altitude.

Henry felt for Charlie, reaching out to pat him on the shoulder. "But, Charlie, he did mention that he left something for you up in the pavilion." Charlie took off, practically sprinting up the hillside to see what it could be. On a picnic table in the middle of the pavilion was a wooden box with Charlie's name carved on it. He picked it up and held it in both hands, admiring it top to bottom. It seemed antique, and it had the smoky scent of burning wood, which Charlie had come to associate with Sky around the fire pit.

A thousand thoughts rushed through his mind. Would he ever see Sky again? Why did he have to go so suddenly? Why did he have to go at all? Would he ever come back to Briarcliff? Would he ever know for sure where Sky came from? There had to be a way for them to keep in touch. Maybe Dr. Cook would know how to find him. Finally, he put the box down and opened it. Inside was Sky's cross with the crown of thorns pendant: the very same one Charlie admired the first time they met. There was also a note from Sky:

Dear Charlie,

It's been an eventful few weeks! Thank you for your friendship and for the godly example you set for us all. Getting to know you was this year's high-water mark for me. You're a wonderful young man, and I'm certain that all you did for others caused God to smile on Christmas Day.

Everything happens for a reason, Charlie— and I believe that God intended for you and me to cross paths. I wish that I could have stayed in Briarcliff for a while more, but the person I answer to has a new project for me...so I'm off to my next chapter.

They say that Jesus is the reason for the season. True enough, after all, it's his birth that we cele- brate. However, if Jesus is the reason for the season, that would mean he came into this world for him- self. You and I know nothing could be further from the truth.

He came to demonstrate God's love for human- kind and to establish a path to salvation for any and all who might want to follow. That means you, Charlie, are the reason for the season, and the Smythes, Mr. Olson, Parker, your parents, Reverend Higgins, Dr. Cook, Coach Cadman, everyone else in Briarcliff, and beyond. Please always remember that. No matter what, God knows you, loves you, and cares about you!

When all's said and done, God's law is love. I'm sure that the Christmas tradition you began this year will take root and that the "Home for the Holiday" initiative will continue on.

I'll think of you whenever I hear the sound of hockey skates slicing and gliding across a frozen pond—and I'll do my best, wherever I am, to make sure that no one is without a friend around the holidays.

I hope to see you again someday, if not in this world then in the next. Until then, Charlie, continue to do what you can to make glad the hearts of others on this journey with you.

Blessings to you and your family,
Sky

It wasn't easy for Charlie to read Sky's letter. He was upset that Sky had to leave but glad and grateful they were able to forge such a unique bond of friendship.

Charlie glanced down in the box and saw a large, single feather. Strange, but he hadn't noticed it just a moment before. He picked it up, looked at it closely, then paused and looked heavenward. In his mind's eye, it matched the one he had found in his bedroom after that memorable dream about a month ago. It was crystal clear to him now.

He carefully slipped the pendant over his head and put the feather and Sky's letter back in the box. Tucking it under his arm, he slowly walked home with a heavy heart—though at the same time, he felt fortified by all he had experienced with his heavenly friend.

Although Sky was no longer there in person, Charlie was certain that the two of them had begun a special relationship that would continue on forever. He had a lot to think about and even more to be grateful for as he walked along. By the time he reached the Tree Streets, he began to feel a smile coming on. It started deep within his heart and soon was lighting up his whole face.

There would be no hockey that day.

EPILOGUE

In the days following that Christmas, there was a new spirit of community in Briarcliff Manor. It was apparent to all. People seemed to care more genuinely about one another, and it turned out to be enduringly true. Something fundamental had changed. The landscape inside people's hearts and minds had softened. Love and mercy were in bloom, and there was an abiding sense of alignment with a higher code.

Although Sky was gone, his spirit remained. The story of his intriguing arrival and brief stay in Briarcliff was told time and again over the years, especially during Thanksgiving and Christmas gatherings.

Charlie went right on living a normal kid's life around town: playing sports, going to school, doing his homework, and hanging around with his friends. However, he did begin to spend more and more time with Michelle, to the griping lament of DMarks, George, and BB.

Smythe was true to his word, and construction began on January 2. He started each day attending 6:00 a.m. mass at St. Theresa's, and he even helped serve morning communion from time to time. From there, he'd head over to the construction site to give encouragement to everyone involved and to make sure the project stayed on schedule.

Parker Jones, who had been an outstanding student in his younger days, began a tutoring service, which kept him very busy and provided a handsome source of income. He also became head coach of the Briarcliff Bears varsity basketball team, taking over when Doc Prewitt retired. His scarred memories of Vietnam were still there, but somehow, they were no longer hurtful or destructive. This, no doubt, was helped by the fact that he and Suzie Berkshire began dating.

Mr. Olson threw himself into the Seniors Program run by the Briarcliff Rec Department. There he found fellowship with other veterans and retirees. Each year, when the World War I curriculum was being taught at the middle school, Mr. Hunt would ask him to come in for open discussion with his students so they could hear firsthand about his experiences at war in Europe. He also managed to get Taylor certified as a therapy dog, and weekly the two of them were a welcome sight for patients at Phelps Memorial Hospital.

Dr. Cook continued on as the affable president of The King's College. From time to time, he featured lessons learned from Sky and Charlie in his popular "Walk with the King" radio broadcasts.

Reverend Higgins kept right on "preachin' and teachin,'" as he liked to say, and the Congregational Church Parish Hall became the go-to spot whenever the community or school district had a temporary need for extra facilities.

The ever-popular Coach Cadman continued to make his happy presence felt at Todd School and on the coaching sidelines.

Mr. and Mrs. Riverton carried on in their devotion to Charlie and to each other. They also remained dedicated to their church and community. With endless enthusiasm, Barnes and Noble lavished their rescue dog love on family and friends throughout the Tree Streets and beyond.

The blood-brothers relationship between DMarks, BB, George and Charlie continued to solidify with all the same adolescent horseplay, escapades, and their special brand of boy banter. They had a unique bond—and it was destined to stay that way, even as time marched on.

Charlie often thought about Sky and wondered if they would ever see each other again. Although he continued to be a bit upset that Sky had to leave so abruptly, he also felt a certain kind of peace about it all. Instead of dwelling on how badly he missed his special friend, he allowed the rich memories to resonate in his head and in his heart.

In that way, Charlie carefully nurtured an abiding sense that Sky was still very much with him. From time to time, he had imaginary conversations with him, which was an easy thing to do. After all, he knew what Sky's voice sounded like and what he would likely say in response to any given topic or situation. Plus, Charlie had grown used to hearing from Sky when he wasn't physically present anyway. Deep down, he had full faith that their sacred friendship would last forever.

> *Praise the Lord!*
> *Oh give thanks to the Lord,*
> *for He is good,*
> *for His steadfast love endures forever! (Psalm 106:1)*
>
> *The purpose of life is not to be happy.*
> *It is to be useful, to be honorable, to be compassionate,*
> *to have it make some difference that you have lived and lived*
> *well. (Ralph Waldo Emerson)*

The End

ABOUT THE AUTHOR

Photo by Doug Leihbacher

Tom Leihbacher grew up in Briarcliff Manor and has lived there for most of his life. After graduating from Briarcliff High School and then The University of Florida, he returned home, began a career in media ad sales, married and became a father. He and his family enjoy a rich life filled with church and community involvements and great friendships. After 35+ years in the corporate world, this is his first novel. A summer sequel is nearing completion – visit us at www.tomleihbacher.com.